Resounding praise for

TO THE BONE

"*To the Bone* is a tautly written mystery embedded with characters as real as the surprises are many."
Michael Connelly, author of *Chasing the Dime*

"Vividly written with a satisfying twist to the end—the perfect prescription for those who enjoy an original, well-crafted story about the lengths to which some people will go to preserve the illusion of youth."
Orlando Sentinel

"A deftly crafted tale with engaging characters, blending gripping action, high suspense, and medical intrigue."
Kathy Reichs, author of *Bare Bones*

"Exhilarating . . . crackles with suspense and narrative tension throughout."
Publishers Weekly (*Starred Review*)

"Entertaining . . . *To the Bone* is recommended . . . McMahon always makes it work."
Fort Lauderdale Sun-Sentinel

Books by Neil McMahon

REVOLUTION NO. 9
TO THE BONE
BLOOD DOUBLE
TWICE DYING

TO THE
BONE

NEIL
McMAHON

HarperTorch
An Imprint of HarperCollinsPublishers

HARPERTORCH
An Imprint of HarperCollins*Publishers*
10 East 53rd Street
New York, New York 10022-5299

Copyright © 2003 by Neil McMahon
Excerpt from *Revolution No. 9* copyright © 2005 by Neil McMahon
ISBN: 0-06-052917-2

First HarperTorch paperback printing: January 2005
First HarperCollins hardcover printing: September 2003

HarperCollins®, HarperTorch™, and ❦™ are trademarks of Harper-Collins Publishers Inc.

Printed in the United States of America

Visit HarperTorch on the World Wide Web at www.harpercollins.com

10 9 8 7 6 5 4 3 2 1

For Drs. Barbara and Dan McMahon

Heart empowers mind
Mind informs heart

Acknowledgments

The author is deeply indebted to many people who helped in the making of this book. Special thanks to:

Kim Anderson; Carl Clatterbuck; Dan Conaway; Drs. Barbara and Dan McMahon; Dr. Dick Merriman; Mary Pender; Linda Ross; Jill Schwartzman; Nikola Scott; Xanthe Tabor; Jennifer Rudolph Walsh . . . and to many good and dedicated folks at HarperCollins, both behind and in front of the scenes.

.

She was not old, nor young, nor at the years
Which certain people call a "certain age,"
Which yet the most uncertain age appears.

—*Lord Byron*

TO THE BONE

Prologue

A feverish tormenting dream of fire, spreading through her, forced her awake. She was in bed, knees drawn up to her chest, hands clenched tightly. The apartment was dark and still. The overhead fan whispered, cooling the air, but the sheets were soaked with sweat. Her blurred eyes could just make out the glowing red numbers on the alarm clock: 3:18 A.M.

The fire stayed behind in the dream, but the pain was real. She twisted with nausea, moaning.

"Ray?" she whispered. Her throat was parched, her voice hoarse. "Is anyone here?"

Nothing stirred in the darkened rooms. Her mind was foggy from drugs, but she remembered that the boyfriend who was supposed to stay with her had gone out for cigarettes. Someone else had stopped by after that—someone kind, feeding her soup and more painkillers, that had eased her into sleep.

But that was hours ago. The pain had been only in her breasts then, but now it was everywhere—fierce cramping and burning that worsened in quick stages, like the tightening of a vise.

She focused her teary vision on the phone, on her bedside table. It was out of reach, and the thought of moving was intolerable. But the pain pierced like shards of glass. Sobbing, still curled up tight, she inched across the endless expanse of bedsheet. As she groped for the phone, an image flitted through her brain, a memory or dream as she had drifted into sleep, of hands disconnecting and lifting away her answering machine.

Her fingers found the receiver and pressed the lighted numbers 911.

"Please help me," she managed, to the operator's crisp answer. "I need an ambulance." She gasped out the syllables of her address.

Then she dropped the phone, distantly aware of the concerned voice saying, "Ma'am? *Ma'am?* Are you there?"

She tightened back into herself, hugging her knees with all her strength as if she could compress her body into a point so tiny, the agony would have no place to remain.

It remained.

But then, inside her mind, she glimpsed a hazy image, like a window opening up. Someone was on the other side—a taffy-haired teenaged girl, dancing alone in front of a full-length mirror. She was bold, saucy, her movements graceful and provocative. The girl was herself, she realized, ten years ago, already showing the earthy beauty that she would grow into.

When the chance had come to make that beauty perfect—to turn herself into a different person, a better one—she had taken it.

Who wouldn't have? she silently asked her younger self. Why should that have led to this?

The girl ignored her, continuing to prance, absorbed in her own reflected promise.

The window was getting brighter and closer, with thousands more images springing up, a swirling videotape of her life fast-forwarded into a few instants, and yet all perfectly clear. She knew that she could step through, into it—that that would free her from this nightmare. But if she did, there would be no coming back.

In the distance, she heard a siren.

1

"Mercy ER, this is Medic Twelve with Code Three traffic."

The voice, choppy with static and backed by a wailing siren, came over Mercy Hospital's paramedic radio, from an ambulance out on the San Francisco streets. Code Three meant that it was racing toward the hospital as fast as the night allowed.

The Mobile Intensive Care nurse monitoring the radio leaned closer and pressed the talk button on the handset.

"Medic Twelve, this is Mercy ER," she said. "Go ahead."

Carroll Monks walked across the Emergency Room and stood beside her, listening.

"Mercy ER, we're bringing you a young white female, age approximately twenty-five. She's unconscious, with almost no blood pressure. She does have a very weak femoral pulse, but no radial pulses. Ah, hold on a second, Mercy."

Monks heard the driver yell something to his partner in the ambulance's rear. His words and the reply were lost in noise.

The driver's voice came back on. "We haven't been able to start an IV. We can't find any veins. Repeat, she does *not* have an IV running. She has respiratory depression and we are oxygenating her."

The nurse said, "Medic Twelve, do you have any history on her?"

"Negative, Mercy, not much. She was in an apartment, alone. Looks like she's had a recent surgery, probably her breasts. We found some Valium, but we don't think it's an overdose."

"Who called her in?"

"She managed to call 911. We got sent by City Triage."

Monks took the microphone from the nurse, and said, "Any signs of massive bleeding?"

"There's some vomit with blood in it," the driver rasped through the static. "But not massive."

"Nothing from the surgery? Other external wounds? Blood around the apartment, or in the bathroom?"

"Negative, Mercy," the driver said again.

Monks's mind started tracking a flow chart of

probabilities, for a young woman who was bleeding badly, with the blood staying inside her. None of them were good.

The nurse watched him questioningly, a look asking if he wanted any more information. He shook his head, giving her instructions as he handed her the microphone.

"Take her directly to the trauma room, Medic Twelve," she said.

"Roger, Mercy. ETA is six minutes."

Monks turned back to the ER and the next pressing task—organizing who was going to need to be where, during the next half hour. Screws had been tightening in his head all night, and this had the feel of being the most severe one yet.

It was 3:51, an early Friday morning in July. San Francisco was going through a heat wave, with temperatures that had hovered in the nineties for the past several days. The usual cooling sea breezes and evening fog were gone, driven off the coast by hot winds that swept through the Central Valley like blasts from a furnace. Inland, the thermometer had been topping 110.

But inland, they were used to it. Here, the leaden air and damp armpits and gummy asphalt underfoot were like a sudden sneaky enemy, one that worked just below the level of consciousness. Monks could sense it in faces—tension, friction, as if a layer of social lubrication had been eroded by the heat. People were rubbing too close together, and the ER had been simmering hotter as the hours passed. It was amazing how many human beings were up, about, and in need of medical help, all through the night.

He had just left the bedside of a seventeen-year-old girl who was giving birth to her third baby, a process she had started some twenty minutes earlier in her boyfriend's car. Staff were trying to get her sent to OB, but OB was busy, and the on-call obstetrician was not yet available. It looked like the youngster was going to appear in the ER any minute now.

In the next bed, a fat middle-aged man was doing his best to die of a heart attack. They had shot him full of clot-busting drugs and shocked him back to life three times, but the monitor kept quavering in the danger zone. This was tying up two nurses and the other ER physician on duty. A cardiologist was supposed to be on the way to take him to the Cath Lab, but cardiology was busy, too.

The knife wound in Bed Five was coming around without complications, but during the past minutes, his voice had risen from querulous to strident and he was becoming combative. The SFPD cops who had brought him were gone, back on the streets to deal with their own hot night. Hospital Security would probably have to be called to put him in restraints, but Security had their hands full right now in the lobby. One uniformed officer was moving uneasily among the crowd of at least twenty, while another flanked the desk where the triage nurse worked to separate out the most gravely ill and injured. Many were in pain, most had been waiting a long time, and there was a volatile racial mix of young black and Hispanic males, with girlfriends or wives who looked at least as tough as the men. Monks had been peripherally aware of a lot of restless movement on the other side of the lobby's glass doors—bobbing heads and strutting bodies, a dizzying collage that made him think of a huge, many-limbed beast about to fall into a frenzy and tear itself apart.

And now an ambulance was on its way, bringing a woman in critical condition. At least, Monks thought, this would bring more uniforms. It might help stabilize the tense crowd.

He stepped to the main desk. "Call City Dispatch Center," he said. "Tell them we're going on diversion."

Leah Horvitz, the charge nurse, nodded and reached for the phone. Leah was a fiercely competent veteran, uncowed by any situation Monks had ever seen. But even she looked relieved. The ER would now be temporarily closed to any more ambulances bearing the victims of shootings and stabbings, wrecks and rapes, overdoses and organ failure and madness. The staff were already overwhelmed—they could barely handle what they had, and to take on anything more could be dangerous to patients. But it was something Monks had only done rarely, and it left an unpleasant taste. There was the unavoidable sense of letting down the team.

He caught the eye of a magenta-uniformed nurse named Jackie Lukas and motioned her to meet him at the Trauma Room. She was slim, ponytailed, athletically attractive. He knew from experience that he could count on her to stay cool.

"We've got an ambulance coming in five minutes," he said. "A woman with no blood pressure, and they can't get an IV in her arm. I'm going to put a big tube in her ankle vein."

"Fourteen-gauge catheter?"

"Make it IV tubing. Sterile unopened package. And a cutdown tray."

Jackie immediately turned to her work. Monks stepped into the cubicle that housed Bed Seven and the heart attack victim. Vernon Dickhaut, the other ER physician, was at the bedside, looking impatient at being stuck there.

"How is he?" Monks said.

"About the same. The cardiologist's on his way."

"That's good, Vernon, because I'm going to be out of it for a while. There's a critical coming by ambulance. The ER's all yours." Vernon was a North Dakota farmboy with lank straw-colored hair, cornflower blue eyes, and an IQ off the charts. He had been bound for a career in surgery, until a residency rotation with Monks had given him a taste for the ER's adrenaline and action. Monks took a certain pride in having corrupted him, and it had paid. A couple of years ago, Vernon would have come close to panicking at taking full charge, but now it was a challenge he savored.

"Don't let anybody die, huh?" Monks said.

Vernon saluted with mock trepidation.

Later, many times, Monks would remember his own words.

Monks heard Medic Twelve's siren coming from blocks away. After more than two decades in the ER, that sound still touched him with anticipation tinged with fear, like what a journeyman fighter must feel on hearing the first-round bell. Then it was gone, leaving him heightened and ready.

The siren died, giving way to the rumbling vibration of a large motor, and red lights flashing outside the ER's ambulance entrance. Monks dropped his white coat onto a chair at the nurses' station and walked quickly into Trauma One, a cubicle with operating-room surgical lights overhead and glass-fronted cabinets on both side walls. Jackie Lukas and two other nurses were present. One pulled back the curtain that separated the cubicle from Trauma Two, converting the area to one large space with two empty beds. The other nurse had hung two IV bottles on floor stands and was connecting them to plastic tubing.

Jackie pulled a tray from a cabinet and stripped off the sealed plastic covering. She placed it on a Mayo stand, careful not to touch anything sterile, and gave Monks a packet of rubber gloves, size 7½. Monks tore it open and gloved his hands with automatic precision. Then he started selecting and arranging equipment from the cutdown tray. He scissored the end off a three-foot plastic IV tube, angling the cut, then snipping off its sharp point. Jackie took the other end and attached it to an IV bottle.

"Get lab down here right away," he told the other nurses. "I want a full trauma panel on this woman. I need the hematocrit stat, and we'll want blood. Tell X Ray to bring their portable machine."

The paramedics were coming in fast, wheeling their stretcher.

"We kept trying to get fluid into her, Doc," one said. "We couldn't get a vein."

The woman was still unconscious, covered by a blanket and strapped down, eyes closed and head lolling to one side. Her hair was tawny and disheveled. What Monks could see of her face around the oxygen mask might have been pretty, except that it was ghostly white and drawn with pain. She was slim and shapely, wearing a filmy black bed wrap and panties, an expensive matching outfit. But she also had on a heavy surgical bra, the kind worn by women after breast surgery.

They lifted her quickly onto the trauma bed. Monks pulled open the blanket, fingers going to her throat to try for a pulse. It was near zero, and her breathing was shallow and rapid.

The nurses were already stripping off the wrap and bra. Both of her armpits had bandages taped into place, and there were purple bruises down to the waist on both sides. Her surgery had been very recent—probably a breast enhancement via saline bag, with the bandages covering incisions where an endoscope had been inserted. Everything else Monks saw at first glance was in line with what the paramedics had reported. There were no signs of bleeding from the bandages, or anyplace else external.

"Prep her ankle," he said, putting on a new pair of sterile gloves.

Jackie poured an iodine solution on the patient's lower leg, from the ankle upward several inches, and scrubbed it with gauze pads. She lifted it while Monks slipped a sterile towel underneath. Then an eye sheet, a drape with a hole in it, went on top of the area. He chose a number-ten scalpel and felt for landmarks—one inch above the ankle bone, and a little toward the front—and cut a one-inch slit completely through the skin. He traded the scalpel for a clamp and inserted its closed end into the fatty tissue, opening the clamp's tip to spread the tissue apart.

The saphenous vein, the size of a thin pencil, was white against white—like her skin, the cut, and the tissue around the vein, bloodless.

A lab tech had come in and was trying to draw blood from a vein in her arm. Monks glanced up at him and said, "You're not going to get anything there, Lab. I'll do a femoral puncture as soon as I'm done with this."

He quickly isolated the vein, lifting it gently on the clamp to separate it from the surrounding tissue. With a new number-eleven blade, he opened the vein and eased in another clamp two inches toward the knee, stretching the vein enough to accept the beveled end of the IV tube.

"We're in," he said. "Open it wide." Just over three minutes had passed since her arrival.

Monks tied the tube in place, took two quick skin stitches to close the incision, and stepped out of the way for Jackie to dress the wound and tape the exposed tube to the leg.

"Pour the fluids to her, ladies, warm saline," he said to the nurses. "Start her on Narcan, one milliliter, IV. And get a Foley catheter into her bladder. Let's see if she's making urine."

He moved to her groin and placed his fingers by her pubic bone, feeling for the femoral artery. There was a faint pulse. He wiped the area with an alcohol swab, accepted a syringe, and slid the needle into the artery's pulse. Blood filled the syringe slowly. He gave it to the lab tech.

"Give me an immediate tox screen, plus a trauma panel," he said. "And give me four units of type-specific or O-negative red cells." The tech scurried away. Giving blood that had not been checked against the patient's own type was risky, but there was no time for a complete cross-match. This woman needed blood, now.

"How are we doing?" he asked Jackie.

"Blood pressure's sixty over zip. It's not coming up yet. She's gotten almost a full liter of saline. We'll start the red cells as soon as we get them."

With the urgent business of the IV and fluids under way, Monks started concentrating on a diagnosis. He put his stethoscope to her chest. Hemorrhaging from the surgery, into the chest cavity, was one of the first possibilities he had considered. But while her breathing was slow, it did not sound like chest cavity or lungs were filled with the missing blood.

Her GI tract was a more likely possibility. Her bed wrap was stained with vomit, dark and granular, the classic "coffee-grounds" vomit of stomach bleeding. There was no obvious link to her breast surgery, but that was something to worry about later. Monks moved his stethoscope to her abdomen.

"Very active bowel sounds," he said. His guess was getting stronger that the blood was in her abdomen, causing irritation. "I need to do a rectal." A nurse gave him an exam glove, while Jackie pulled the woman's knees up and her panties down. Monks noted a tattoo of a bright red apple, with a slyly winking green snake coiled around it, on the left side of her rump. He accepted a dab of lubricant on his fingertip and gently pushed into her. It came out covered with black bloody matter.

"That's it," he said. "She's bleeding into her gut. Get a nasogastric tube into her stomach. Let's see if it's there or lower down. X Ray, film her abdomen, please."

The X-ray tech was a trim energetic Filipino man, poised with his machine. "Right now, sir," he said. He positioned machine and film cassette, then called "X ray!" Monks and the nurses stepped back. The machine buzzed and clunked. The tech pulled the machine back out of the way and left with the cassette.

Monks put his hand on the patient again. The presenting scenario had pretty well arranged itself in his mind by now. She had probably taken Valium for pain from the surgery. Sedated, she had not realized how sick she was getting. At some point, she had started hemorrhaging. She had regained consciousness long enough to call 911.

But by then she was in serious trouble, and she was not getting better. Her blood pressure wasn't rising and her oxygen saturation level was very low, 89 percent out of 100, even though she was on pure oxygen. That was largely because there wasn't enough blood circulating to carry the oxygen to cells. But it was *still* damned low.

And she had too many bruises—in her armpits, down to her waist, around her breasts, even on her arms and buttocks. Much more than a plastic surgery like that should leave.

Monks ran through a quick differential diagnosis in his head. GI bleeding in the upper intestinal tract or stomach was usually caused by ulcers. She was young, but it was possible. He dismissed liver failure from alcoholism, at least for now; she didn't have that look. A diverticulum, an outpouching on the colon, was another possibility, especially if the bleeding was lower GI, in the intestines.

Then there was the surgery she had just undergone. It was hard not to speculate that there might be a connection.

Monks stepped to the door and caught Leah Horvitz's eye. She hurried over.

"Any ID on her?" he asked.

"The paramedics found her purse," Leah said, in staccato, no-nonsense syllables that matched the rest of her. "Her name's Eden Hale. A Los Angeles address on her driver's license. Home phone's here in San Francisco, but nobody answers."

"See if you can get hold of a family member. Find out if there's any history of ulcers or other GI bleeding."

"She had a discharge form from a plastic surgeon's office," Leah said. "Dr. D'Anton. The Valium's from him, too."

"D'Anton, huh?" Monks said, surprised. Dr. D. Welles D'Anton was San Francisco's premier plastic surgeon, with a clientele of the rich and beautiful. Monks knew him only by reputation. D'Anton was considered to be arrogant, but extremely competent—not the kind of surgeon who might have botched a relatively simple procedure.

"I already called his office," Leah said. "The nurse is looking up Eden's records, and she'll call back if there's anything that might be related. She didn't want to wake Dr. D'Anton."

Monks nodded. He did not expect that D'Anton would be taking phone calls at four A.M.

Monks went back to help the nurses keep working at replacing the body's fluids, the first and by far most critical step to stabilization for any of the blood-loss scenarios. Her veins were filling and her blood pressure rising a little, but she was still unconscious—still not responding in any way he could sense.

His concern was turning to worry.

A small eternity later, eight minutes by the clock, the second unit of blood was going in through the IV. Monks was more and more unhappy. The nasogastric tube showed bleeding, but not that much, and it looked like it was upper *and* lower. That did not make sense. And there was all that goddamned bruising.

Something was swimming under the surface of his consciousness, but refusing to come to light.

He considered wild shots, like typhoid fever. He had seen a few cases in Asia, and recalled that there might be rose-colored spotting on the skin, along with the severe abdominal distress. But the resemblance of those spots to these was superficial, and typhoid was virtually unknown in this environment.

He kept touching her, probing, looking, listening. Then he realized that some of the bruises were new—they had appeared since she had entered the ER. There were several on her arms and legs, about the size of a nickel, where his own and the nurses' fingers had touched. She was bruising as they watched, on the spot.

Then the nagging thought in his unconscious broke through.

"DIC," he said, in astonishment.

The recording nurse at his elbow, Mary Helfert, was writing down times and procedures. "Say that again, please?"

"DIC. Disseminated intravascular coagulation."

She looked uncertain—she had probably never encountered the term, except maybe for mention in a nursing school textbook, years ago—but this was no time to explain. Monks flipped the sheet away from the rest of Eden's body. Fresh blood trickled steadily from the needle punctures in her groin and from the cutdown incision at her ankle. Her nose oozed blood from where the NG tube had been inserted. There were new bruises on her hip.

DIC was what it looked like, all right. Her small blood vessels were clotting off, using up the clotting factors in her blood. Without those, she was bleeding everywhere else.

"What the hell is going on?" he said. His rising voice made the nurses glance nervously at each other. "Ulcers don't cause DIC. Diverticulitis doesn't cause DIC. Is she septic?"

Monks turned away from the bed and forced himself to another place in his mind, a place he hated and feared. It was a court of last resort, where he had to make an instantaneous decision with too little time and information, and a life at stake. He stood stock-still, eyes closed, weighing the facts he was sure of against his deductions and intuitions, the known against the inferred, the risks of what he was considering against the near-certain consequences of playing it safe.

He turned back and said, "Tell the lab to run blood cultures and a pregnancy test. Get me six platelet packs, two units of fresh frozen plasma, and ten bags of cryoprecipitate. We're going to treat her for severe DIC. Get an IV in her arm. Jackie—"

He could see that she was surprised, but ready.

"Give her ten thousand units of heparin IV, and hang a drip at a thousand units per hour."

Mary, the recording nurse, lowered her clipboard and stared at him. "You're going to give her a blood thinner? When she's already bleeding?"

"She's bleeding because she's *clotting*," Monks said. "If we don't break that cycle, she's dead."

"Are you sure it's DIC, Doctor?"

Monks's temper jumped another notch toward the snapping point. "I'm not sure of *anything,* except that we've got minutes. Everybody get moving, *please*."

Jackie, stable, competent, and obedient, was already taking out a vial of the clear heparin and drawing it up. But she looked worried, too.

She had a right to be. It was a very long shot. If Monks was correct about the DIC, Eden Hale was probably going to die anyway.

If he was wrong, the heparin might kill her.

Monks pushed down hard with the heels of his hands on Eden Hale's sternum, five times, at one-second intervals. Then he leaned close to her face, his head turned to the side and his ear to her lips, listening for a sound of life. He straightened up and stared at the monitors, willing a miracle. He had been doing this for fifteen minutes. CPR was like running a race, a desperate physical effort to stay ahead of the enemy, death.

Finally, he admitted that he had lost. He stepped back, shoulders sagging with fatigue.

"All right," he said. "We'll stop now."

In fact, it had been all over for at least the last five minutes. The nurses knew it, and were quietly tidying up. Their body language said it all.

"What time are you pronouncing her, Doctor?" Mary Helfert said. She was stiff, all business, holding her clipboard like a shield. Her body language was unmistakable, too. She did not approve of his decision to use heparin.

Monks looked at his watch. "Four forty-three A.M.," he said. "I can't sign a death certificate. The DIC killed her, but I don't know what caused that."

"Will this be a medical examiner's case?"

He nodded. The death fit several criteria that automatically put it in the city's jurisdiction for autopsy. It was unexpected, and she was young and healthy.

"Keep trying to find the family, and have them notified," Monks said. This was usually done by contacting local police or sheriffs and having them send an officer to the house. It was considered more humane than a phone call from a hospital. "And call Dr. D'Anton's clinic as soon as it opens." Any history that D'Anton might have been able to give them was academic now, and probably would not have helped anyway. But he might know how to contact the family, and he should be informed.

The recent surgery was one more criterion that made Eden Hale a city ME's case. The possibility remained that the DIC had been caused by surgical infection.

Monks walked out of the cubicle, washed, and went to the ER physicians' room.

They had come close to saving her. The heparin had started to dissolve the clotting, and her circulation had started flowing properly again—but by then it was just too late. Weakened by the long lack of blood and God knew what else, her heart had stopped. The coroner's report would help them fill in the blanks.

Monks hated to lose a patient, and hated like hell to lose one who was essentially healthy—hated the helpless anger at not being certain what was wrong. It was like being sniped at by an enemy he could not see.

What had come in from Lab and X Ray so far had confirmed what he already knew or guessed. Her hemoglobin was very, very low, at 3.7 grams per deciliter. Normal ran at about 15. The platelet count was 2,880, with normal upwards of 150,000. The coagulation panel showed prolonged PT and PTT. All of which meant that she had almost no blood, and what she did have wasn't clotting. Her urine was dark orange, 4+ for blood, negative for white cells. That was a reasonably sure indication that she did not have a urinary tract infection as the source of the DIC. The X rays showed nothing unusual except the two whitish circles of the breast implants.

Monks looked again at the material the paramedics had found in her purse, from the clinic of Dr. D. Welles D'Anton—a discharge form from the surgery, and a glossy informational pamphlet. Its cover featured a stunningly beautiful woman, smiling in invitation to the world of glamour. Several pages of text, with drawings, briefly described available procedures. The back flap showed a photo of D'Anton himself. He had a handsome patrician head and a confident stare.

D'Anton—pronounced Dan-*ton,* and heaven help the fool who said it wrong in his presence—had spent some fifteen years developing a reputation as a miracle worker for models, actresses, and socialites. They came from all over the globe to his luxury San Francisco clinic, to be transformed by him.

And D'Anton had graced Mercy Hospital by making it his venue of choice for more extensive procedures. He contributed generously to the hospital and had helped to fit out a top-flight reconstructive surgery unit that brought in a lot of money and prestige.

Apparently, Eden Hale had been one of his devotees.

Monks lingered in the physicians' room a minute longer, wishing to Christ he could pack it up and go home. But his shift was not over until seven A.M. He walked back out to the triage desk to take the next case in line, acutely aware of the closed curtain of the trauma cubicle where Eden's body would lie until the morgue attendants came to get her.

2

Just after seven A.M., Dr. D. Welles D'Anton looked over notes for his first consultation of the day. The patient's name was Lucia Canter. She was new to the clinic. She was forty-three and recently divorced from a husband who had left her for a young trophy wife. Lucia had been born rich and had come out of her marriage richer still. Her children were almost grown. Now she wanted a new life.

D'Anton stepped briskly into the procedure room where Lucia was waiting. She was standing in a corner, wearing only a loose, open-backed examination gown. Stripped of clothes and makeup, she was nervous, even a little frightened. But her eyes were trusting. D'Anton had long since realized that the more naked and vulnerable women felt beneath his hands, the more they adored him. It was strange but exhilarating, and he used that power confidently.

"Good morning, my dear," he said, and gestured at the padded table in the center of the room. "Please sit."

She did, fingers fidgeting at the hem of her short robe, but then leaving it alone. She wanted to please him.

"Look straight ahead, Lucia," D'Anton said. She obeyed like a schoolgirl, folding her hands in her lap. He pulled up a chair and leaned close to her, studying her face, his manicured fingers tracing its contours. She was attractive, her skin and figure good. She had had the time and money to take care of herself through the years. But her face was on the gaunt side—a little horsey, in fact, and lined by stress.

D'Anton's words were more tactful. "You're lucky; you have good bones," he murmured. "Yes, we can do you a world of help. The Miriam Elena look, do you think?"

Her nervous smile widened, almost into a giggle, at the mention of the supermodel's name.

"I'm afraid nothing could make me look like her," she said.

"Don't be so sure, Lucia," D'Anton said archly. "After all, I gave her *her* face." He pulled the skin gently tighter at the corners of her eyes. "A browlift. A bit of AlloDerm here and there. And cheek implants. They'll soften these grooves beside your nose."

He sat back. "I'll take some facial measurements, then computer-image projections. You'll have several options. Now, you wanted to consider a breast augmentation?"

She lowered her eyes and nodded. "When I had the children—you know."

"Of course," he said soothingly. "Let's have a look."

She reached behind to untie the gown, then lowered it shyly, her eyes still downcast, like a woman unveiling herself for a first-time lover.

D'Anton studied the pendulous breasts for a moment, quickly deciding on implant type and size. He lifted the nearer one, gauging the condition of the tissue, and felt her shiver slightly. Her lips were parted; her breath quickened, her eyes half closed. He almost smiled. It was a moment he always savored.

"Very good, Lucia," he said, clasping her hands in both of his. "I'm betting we can make your daughter jealous. Why don't you go ahead and get dressed, and I'll have my staff set you up a schedule."

D'Anton stepped out into the hall. Then his body jerked slightly, at the abrupt realization that one of his nurses, Phyllis Quires, was waiting for him. She was a squarely built, stolid woman, but she moved with amazing stealth; often he would turn around and find her simply there. He demanded deference, but sometimes she set his teeth on edge.

"Yes?" he said, in the clipped, brusque tone he used with employees.

Phyllis did not usually show emotion, but now her face looked pale.

"Doctor, Mercy Hospital just called," she said. "A woman who had breast surgery yesterday, Eden Hale? She died early this morning in their Emergency Room."

D'Anton's mouth opened as comprehension took hold. His right knee buckled a few inches suddenly, as if he had taken a hard punch to the jaw. His hand fluttered from his side, groping for a wall to brace himself against.

Phyllis stepped to him quickly and took his other arm.

"I'm so sorry, Doctor," she said. "It's not fair that something like this should come along and bother you."

3

You know this as soon as you wake, hours before
dawn: that tonight you will find the one who
calls you. Stride through the city like a lion, your
coat radiant, your teeth swords, your lungs filling
with the scent of her sweet perfume, and blood.

In the closet where you keep your secret things
are souvenirs from earlier times, pieces of jewelry
that glow in the darkness with the light of the
women who wore them. You can feel it in your fingers as you rub them—a little trace left over from
that warmth they gave to you. Each piece has a
voice, replaying her last words and sounds, music to
accompany the film in your head. You like to listen
to them one at a time, but sometimes you hold them

all together and close your eyes and crouch there in the dark, until they blend into one murmuring song, like wavelets into surf.

You knew long ago, when you first began, that all women want beauty—but it comes at a cost. Changing their flesh is a start. But getting to the real, deep perfection they secretly crave is something only you can do.

The first hint of daylight starts to enter the room.

It's important to make this day look like any other, so you get ready for work. But first, you check to make sure of the other things you're going to need. Scrubs and gown. Latex gloves. Plastic bedding. Plenty of towels.

A sterile surgical tray, with a selection of scalpels.

4

Immediately after his shift ended at seven A.M., Monks walked downstairs to the hospital's basement and through the long corridor to the morgue. This was a different world than the floors above, which had their elements of grimness, to be sure—they were filled with sickness and pain—but were devoted to healing.

This world below belonged to the dead: here, hope had been abandoned. The hall was deserted and sepulchral, like a subway tunnel, with none of the bustle of upstairs. Footsteps gave off faintly sinister echoes. The faded paint on the walls and the chipped floor tiles, intended to be complementary shades of off-white, had merged over the years into

a monotone the color of yellowed teeth that no
amount of cleansing or repainting could freshen for
long.

But research on the dead provided much of the
knowledge that healed the living.

Monks pushed open one of the morgue's double
doors, gray steel except for small squares of glass at
eye level, and stepped inside. The room was barren
concrete, with drains in the floor and, along one
wall, what looked like a row of giant filing cabinets.
Eden Hale was inside one of them.

The pathologist's glassed-in office occupied one
corner. Other furnishings included several racks of
surgical equipment, sinks, and two stainless-steel
tables. On one of these, a pair of bare feet, toes up,
faced Monks. A slender man wearing wire-rimmed
glasses and surgical barrier gear was bent over the
body. He was wielding the implement known as the
bread knife, a sixteen-inch blade sharp as any samu-
rai sword, which could literally cut a cadaver in half.
This was Dr. Roman Kasmarek, Mercy Hospital's
chief pathologist. Roman was usually in the lab
before six A.M., examining tissue samples from the
day's first surgeries, then starting autopsies as time
allowed.

Monks did a quick inventory. The procedure was
nearing its end. A scale was weighted with a hanging organ, and a brain was trussed with string and
suspended inside a jar of formalin until it was
"fixed"—the soft tissue hardened, to keep it from

being damaged by handling. There was a slick of blood and fluids around. Roman was neater than most pathologists Monks had known, but it was still messy business.

His longtime assistant, an ageless gray-haired black man, was rinsing the intestines in a sink, preparatory to opening them. His name was Clifford, but he was known in the hospital as Igor, a reference to his hunched shuffle. He was crafty and wise, and for some reason seemed to like Monks. He flashed a sidelong grin that suggested some illicit secret between the two of them.

Roman, absorbed in his dissection, had not yet looked up. Igor moved to tap him on the shoulder but prudently waited until Roman set down the bread knife before getting that close. Monks recalled a legendary nineteenth-century British surgeon who had made his reputation via lightning-quick amputations, with the limb typically hitting the floor in as little as ninety seconds. Since these were performed without anesthesia, the shortening of the patients' agony was a blessing. The downside was, they usually died of sepsis or shock, and the doctor's scalpel tactics were so aggressive that he was prone to severing testicles along with legs. On one stellar occasion, his flashing blade gutted his assistant, and an observer was so horrified that *he* keeled over with a heart attack. When the patient succumbed, shortly afterward, the mortality rate reached a whopping 300 percent.

Back at the sink, Igor was wielding his own knife. The first smell of sliced intestines, an experience never to be forgotten, reached Monks's nostrils. He stepped into the hall. Roman joined him a minute later. Dabs of Vicks glistened under his nose. It was probably not easy to look sympathetic while dissecting a cadaver, but he managed.

"Is this about the young woman who died?" Roman said.

Monks nodded.

"I'm sorry, Carroll. I know it's tough on you to lose somebody."

"Somebody young and healthy. What happened doesn't make any sense."

"I only know that she was brought in. Not the details."

"She had DIC, Roman."

Roman's eyebrows rose. "Really." DIC was unusual in itself; the designation "young and healthy" made it extremely so.

"I'm sure of it. But I don't have a clue what caused it. Goddammit, the circulatory system of a vital twenty-five-year-old does not just shut *down*."

"I'm not disagreeing, Carroll," Roman said soothingly. "Any history on her?"

"It's not available yet. She was in good enough condition to have a breast augmentation yesterday."

"Could it have been an infection from that?"

"That was my first thought, and it's possible," Monks said. "But there was nothing apparent."

"Maybe pregnant? Retained dead fetus?"

"Also possible. I ordered up a test. But—" Monks shook his head. "It just didn't have that feel."

"Carcinoma," Roman said. "Bad transfusion reaction. Trauma. Those are the major DIC causes that come to mind. Doesn't seem likely that she'd have had a surgery if there was anything like that going on. Who performed it?"

"D'Anton," Monks said.

"Well, he has a reputation, but not for being sloppy."

"Anything else come to mind?"

"There are fifty or a hundred idiopathic causes for DIC."

Monks grimaced. *Idiopathic* was medical jargon for *unknown/could be anything*.

"She's a city ME's case," Monks said. "Would you have time to look her over before they come get her? Check tox screen and lab?"

"I'll do it as soon as we get this one cleaned up."

Monks thanked him and left. Roman would not be able to open the body or take tissue samples—a big hindrance to a thorough investigation. But he had performed thousands of autopsies over twenty years, in San Francisco and adjacent counties. There was not much he had not encountered, and he was very clear-eyed. It was just possible he would spot something that pointed to the DIC's cause.

If not, Monks would have to wait for the medical examiner's findings—a minimum of six weeks,

probably more like months—with the possibility
that, even then, nothing new would turn up.

He walked back upstairs to the Records library,
poured himself a cup of bad urn-brewed coffee, and
sat down to do his charts. He was a firm believer in
getting the information on paper while it was still
fresh in his head, and in noting extensive details. He
had worked as an investigator for a malpractice
insurance company for more than a decade, reviewing cases where other physicians were being sued
and advising the company as to whether to fight it in
court or settle out. Time after time, he had encountered situations where another sentence or two on a
chart might have made the difference in justifying
what a physician had done and why.

But his concentration kept returning to Eden
Hale. He gave up on the other charts, went to the
hospital's main library, and started looking for
information on DIC and heparin. An hour later, he
had tapped several sources, but he was not much
wiser.

The major causes of DIC were what Roman had
named—sepsis, malignancy, trauma, reaction to
transfusion, complications of pregnancy, with many
other idiopathic possibilities. DIC had a mortality
rate of 85 percent. Some findings indicated that
heparin might help in small-scale DIC. It had not
been shown to help in large-scale DIC. But then,
nothing had.

Eden's onset had been massive and fast. It might

have gone differently if he had gotten her a few hours earlier.

He was staring at her chart, pondering, when he realized that the name being called on the hospital paging system was his:

"Dr. Monks, please call 5100 immediately."

5100 was a direct line to the office of Mercy's chief administrator, Baird Necker. A summons like this was rare.

Monks went to a house phone and spoke to Baird's secretary, who told him that Baird would like to see him. The word *immediately* was used again.

Monks packed his charts into his daypack and took the elevator to the sixth floor. It was just after eight A.M.

Baird Necker's secretary greeted Monks cautiously. Necker and Monks respected and even liked each other, with a common interest in keeping the hospital at top performance. But circumstances sometimes made them adversaries, and when Monks showed up here, it was usually because there was trouble.

The secretary picked up her phone, spoke to Baird briefly, and nodded. Monks walked through to the inner office. It was spare and orderly, decorated only with a photo of Baird's wife and children, and several framed certificates hanging on the walls—diplomas, professional affiliations, and an honorable discharge from the Marine Corps.

Baird, bullnecked and crew-cut, was sitting at the desk, reading the schedule of today's meetings and events. A foot-long Tabacalero cigar was laid out with military precision in the desk's left front corner, square to both edges, with a brass dovetail cigar cutter resting beside it. When Baird finished lining out his day, he would go up onto the hospital's roof and light up, then return there many times to relight for a few minutes, until the cigar ended up a soggy stump that he would abandon, with great regret, at quitting time.

"So I walk into my office, and first thing, I get a call from Welles D'Anton," Baird said. "Hot enough to fuck twice. Yelling that we killed a patient of his."

Monks felt his hands tightening—a sign that he was getting seriously annoyed.

"Not only that, we even had the nerve to try to interrupt his beauty sleep," Monks said. "In case he had information that might have helped keep her alive."

"Calm down, Carroll. D'Anton's touchy."

"My nurses and I were frantic trying to save that girl, and I'm supposed to worry about *him* being touchy?"

"You want to tell me what happened?"

"She came in comatose," Monks said. "No clear reason. Within a few minutes, I recognized a condition called DIC. Widespread clotting that was blocking her circulation. Breaking that up was the only hope of getting fluids in. I tried, but her heart failed—she was just too weak. What caused the DIC, I still don't know."

Baird picked up the cigar, held it for a few seconds, then put it back down, straightening it carefully.

"I also got a call from Paul Winner," Baird said.

"Winner? What the hell does he have to do with this?" Winner was a sixtyish internist, an old-schooler who did not care for ER docs in general, or for Monks in particular. When Winner was starting out, ER medicine as a specialty did not exist; internists and GPs were on call to handle emergency duties. This did not necessarily make for a high level of competence—certainly not by current standards—but he still considered himself highly qualified.

"He heard about the case—heard you treated the girl with heparin," Baird said. "He wanted me to know he thought it was insane, administering a blood thinner to someone who was bleeding out."

Monks remembered that the recording nurse had objected, too—wondered if she knew Winner and had put this bug in his ear.

"Paul Winner wasn't *there*," Monks said. "And he doesn't deal with situations where somebody's life's on the line. You're right, he'd have done it by the book—never in a million years would he have taken that chance."

"The bottom line is, the chance didn't work, Carroll. Sorry to put it like that."

"But it might have, Baird. It came close. What would you rather, that she didn't even have that?"

"I'd rather not have the situation I'm facing."

Monks put the heels of his hands against his eyes and pressed hard. It felt good and gave the illusion of helping to clear his head.

"Look," Monks said. "There had to be another factor at work, something that was assaulting her overall system."

"But you don't know what?"

"Not yet."

"Any hard evidence of it?"

"No," Monks admitted.

"Will it turn up in the autopsy?"

"I don't know."

Baird slapped a heavy forearm down on the desk, glaring. "What am I supposed to do with that?"

"Remember that I've been doing this a long time. If I don't go by Paul Winner's book, I've got a reason."

"If you'd recognized that mystery cause and treated it," Baird said, "would it have turned out different?"

"I don't think anything could have brought her back from that DIC."

"But it sure would look better, Carroll."

Baird got up, walked to a west-facing window, and stood staring out with hands shoved into his slacks pockets, sport coat hiked up over his wrists. The hospital was located in San Francisco's south-west quadrant, less than a mile from the Pacific shore. Monks could see that there was not a trace of fog; sky and ocean were both pale blue, the horizon indistinguishable. It was going to be another hot day.

"I'm not saying you were wrong," Baird said. "I'm telling you what it could look like to an outsider. Like you followed your hunch, instead of standard procedure."

"She wasn't *responding* to standard procedure," Monks said. "And it wasn't a hunch. It's what the literature says. And it's what I know in my bones from twenty-five years of practice."

"You know I trust your judgment."

The implication was clear. Not everybody would.

Baird turned back to him with a gaze that was softened, even sympathetic. This disturbed Monks.

"How many shifts did you work this week?" Baird asked.

"Three. Why?"

"Busy as hell, weren't they?"

"They usually are." Monks was puzzled, frustrated by fatigue, unable to grasp where this was going.

Then he got it. Anger rose with a rush of blood to his face.

"You can't be serious, Baird."

"Take it easy. I'm trying to think like a lawyer. If somebody decides to cause trouble about this, we stand to get stomped. Lots of money, bad publicity. On top of everything else, it turns out she was an actress. Not big-time, but the papers are still going to eat it up."

"What happened to that trust in my judgment?"

Baird ignored the question. "Her parents have been notified. They're on their way here from Sacramento."

"I'll be available to talk to them."

"I don't know if that's a good idea or not. But her fiancé's here now, waiting in one of the conference rooms. *He* wants to talk to you. With a hard-on, in case you're wondering."

"Thanks for the warning."

"Go home and get some sleep."

"I doubt it," Monks said. "I'll have my cell phone. Give me a call if you want to meet." He paused at the doorway. "She did not die because of anything that did or didn't happen in the ER, Baird. She was dying when she came in, and we couldn't reverse it. There's a big difference."

Monks was sure of that, as sure as it was possible for him to be. But he admitted that he would feel a hell of a lot better if he knew what had caused the DIC—knew beyond question that there was no other pathway he could have taken that might have headed off its attack and saved her life.

Passing through the outer office, Monks said to Baird's secretary: "There's someone waiting to see me?"

"Conference room three, Doctor."

He stepped into the hall, trying to brace himself for the encounter. But there was no time. A man was waiting right there, pacing. He was in his early thirties, good-looking, with a deep suntan and dark moussed hair, wearing baggy slacks and a Hawaiian shirt. He seemed ill at ease, carrying himself with a sort of aggressive slouch. His eyes were angry, and it struck Monks that his refusal to wait in the conference room was a statement of defiance. But there was petulance in them, too.

Monks cleared his throat. "Are you here about Eden Hale?"

His gaze snapped swiftly to Monks. "Yeah."

"I'm Dr. Monks."

"Can you tell me—what—the hell—*happened*?" The words were spaced apart and emphasized.

Monks's hands tightened again. He made them relax.

"She was in very bad shape when she came in. Mister—"

He hesitated, as if his name was information he was not sure he should release. "Dreyer. Ray."

"I'm very sorry," Monks said. "We did everything we could."

"I leave her home, perfectly fine, then boom, she's dead?"

"You were with her last night?" Monks asked, his interest sharpened.

Dreyer's eyes narrowed warily. It seemed that he

did not like answering questions, period. Perhaps with good reason.

"Yeah."

"When did you leave her?"

"I don't know, about seven. I had business."

Eden Hale had been alone when the ambulance got her, at about three-thirty A.M. Dreyer's business had kept him out all night.

"She was all right then?" Monks asked.

"Well, her tits were sore. But yeah. She took some Valium and went to sleep."

"Did you talk to her after that?"

"No. I came back to her apartment this morning. She was gone. The building super told me the ambulance was there. Hey, is this important?"

"It would help if we could pinpoint when the sickness started," Monks said.

"Help how?" Dreyer said, abruptly assertive, as if he was trying to gain back what he had given away. "You done asking questions? Because you still haven't answered mine. What happened to her?"

"The short answer is, I don't know," Monks said wearily. "Maybe the coroner's report will tell us."

"If you'd *known* what it was, could you have saved her?"

"That's impossible to answer."

"Is it something you *should* have known?" Dreyer's voice was rising, his chin thrusting forward. "That another doctor would have?"

Monks shook his head. "I'm very sorry," he said again, and turned to go.

"I put *years* into her career," Dreyer yelled after him. "She was just taking off, and now she's fucking *dead.*"

Monks stopped walking, turned back, and almost gave in to the urge to drop his daypack and punch Dreyer in the face.

Instead, he said, "I hope that business that kept you out all night was important, Ray. Because if she'd gotten to the ER a few hours earlier, she'd have made it."

Dreyer's belligerent stare shifted away—just for a second, but it was enough.

This time, Monks took the stairs, walking the six flights down to ground level with even, unhurried steps—an absurd attempt to regain control of a situation that was rapidly slipping out of hand.

5

Monks was not surprised to find the offices and clinic of Dr. D. Welles D'Anton located in a premium area of the city, on the eastern edge of St. Francis Wood. The building looked like it had once been a gracious residence—three stories of post-Victorian architecture, with a sandstone exterior, red-tiled roof, and a large private yard that included a eucalyptus grove and a flowing fountain. The maintenance was pristine. There was no sign, and no indication that the place was a medical facility.

The freshly asphalted parking lot held a dozen vehicles, most of them luxury class: BMW, Mercedes, Lexus, and—in a space separated from the rest, like a stall for a prized stallion—one burnished gold Jaguar XJS, with a personalized license plate that read: RODIN. That would be D'Anton's.

His nurse had never called the hospital back about Eden Hale's records. Presumably, everything was fine. But Monks wanted to check for himself.

He parked his poor-relation '74 Ford Bronco and walked up the stone steps. He was wearing an open-necked shirt and jeans, his usual ER outfit. He pushed open the heavy oak door and stepped inside.

Most of the original architecture was intact here, too. The fifteen-foot ceiling was ornate plaster, supported by groined pilasters, and the many-paned windows reached from the floor almost to the room's full height. There was a huge chandelier, although the actual lighting was concealed and had a pinkish cast, flattering to complexions. The carpet was thick enough to give his feet the feel of sinking in. Monks guessed that there had once been a cere-monious curved staircase with a balustrade, and probably a grand piano. Now the room's central fea-ture was a large admissions desk that looked to be of genuine polished ebony. There was no one behind it at the moment.

The room had another striking addition that would not have been found in its century-old ele-gance—an eye-level collage of photographs along one wall, stretching roughly twenty feet. Monks walked closer and studied the images with his hands clasped behind his back, as if he were at a museum. They were all of beautiful women, and all of top professional quality. Some were close-ups of faces. Others were full-body, with the models artfully draped in diaphanous costumes or nude.

He had seen some of those faces; they belonged to well-known actresses and models. Presumably, all of them had been patients of D'Anton. The display was a brilliant tactic, a fabulous advertisement to the women who came here craving beauty. *Look!* it shouted. *This is what you can become.*

But Monks got the impression that it was more than that. It was a shrine, lavished with devotional images of the lovely sylphs who were sculpted to perfection by their medical Pygmalion. D'Anton considered himself an artist—the RODIN license plate said it all—who made attractive women beautiful and beautiful women sublime. He curved noses, lifted faces, injected Botox, rejuvenated skin, and shaped breasts that begged to be cupped by adoring hands. But he did not do tummy tucks or major liposuction. If you were fat, you went to somebody else.

Monks started to realize that he was not alone after all. Several private cubicles at this end of the room were divided off by tasteful, Japanese-style screens. He caught glimpses of well-dressed women sitting inside them, waiting for treatment or for conferences with D'Anton. A couple of them were watching him over the tops of their magazines. He nodded uncomfortably, toward no one in particular, and moved back toward the desk. He had begun to notice that the air had a faintly cloying scent, from fresheners or perhaps a years-old accumulation of perfumes.

After another minute or so, a door at the rear of the room opened. Monks got a glimpse of an area that looked more like an actual office, with two clerks working at smaller desks.

Then another woman stepped into the doorway. She was wearing a tight short skirt and sleeveless top, with her dark hair pulled back into a chignon. Monks got the instant certainty of genuine, world-class beauty. She was in profile, with something cupped in the palm of one hand, held close to her face. A makeup compact mirror, Monks thought. Her other hand rose, forefinger lightly smoothing her lipstick at one corner of her mouth.

She snapped the compact closed and turned. The sight of Monks apparently startled her so much that she dropped it. He moved forward to pick it up, but she waved him away and stooped to get it herself, long calves flexing with taut grace.

When she stood again, she stalked to the desk, ignoring him until she had assumed her position of authority behind its center. Then she folded her arms and smiled briskly. She was tall, at least five foot ten, and about forty, with age beginning to slacken her perfection just a bit. A gold-etched placard on the desk gave her name: GWEN BRICKNELL.

By now, Monks had recognized her as the woman

beckoning on the cover of D'Anton's informational pamphlet.

"And what can I do for you?" she said.

Monks handed her a business card—a real one, not one of the phonies he sometimes used for investigation work—identifying him as an M.D. and Fellow of the American College of Emergency Physicians.

"I'd like to see Dr. D'Anton," he said. "It won't take long."

"Do you have an appointment?"

"No."

Her smile brightened fiercely. "I'm afraid it's impossible. If you'd like to fill out an application, we'll try to schedule you. But I have to warn you, our waiting list is over a year long."

Monks said, "I'm not here as a patient. I think you and I should have a word in private."

"Really?" she said skeptically.

He nodded toward the women in the waiting room, whose ears were almost visibly perked up. "Really."

Gwen Bricknell's head tilted in cool consideration. Then she stalked, with that same imperious stride, to the front entrance and out onto the stone porch. Monks followed.

"This is about one of your patients, a young woman named Eden Hale," he said. "Your office has been informed of her death."

Her face changed swiftly, eyes going wary, mouth opening a little.

"Yes?" she said.

"I work at the Emergency Room at Mercy Hospital. I attended her when she died."

"That was *you*?"

"That was me," Monks said.

Her gaze had turned accusing, but Monks held it. Then her head moved with a sudden little tremor, and her eyes lowered.

"It's terrible," she murmured. "How—did she die?"

"Unpleasantly," Monks said. "Her circulatory system shut down, and she bled to death."

"What on earth could have caused that?"

"I'd like to find out, Ms. Bricknell." She looked up again sharply, perhaps at his use of her name. "She had a breast surgery yesterday."

One of Gwen's hands rose to her heart, or perhaps in an unconscious gesture to protect her own breasts.

"Yes, I remember Eden," she said. "Because of her name, mainly, it's so unusual. But she was fine when she left here."

"I'm sure she was. But the death was bizarre, and it's standard procedure to check out any recent surgery. I'd like to get her history, to see if that sheds any light on it. And to talk to Dr. D'Anton."

A car came pulling into the drive, a gunmetal gray Mercedes with smoked windows. Monks could just make out the driver's chauffeur cap. Gwen glanced at the vehicle, her mouth twisting quickly.

"I'll be frank with you, Doctor," she said. "He's very upset about this. He's canceled all his afternoon appointments. I'm not sure he'd want to talk to you."

"Ms. Bricknell, he called Mercy Hospital this morning, accusing the Emergency Room of being responsible for Eden Hale's death. He doesn't know a damned thing about what actually happened. And for the record, there's a chance that she came out of the surgery with an infection that *did* kill her. Tell him that, will you?"

The chauffeur was opening the Mercedes' rear door. A graceful woman wearing a wide-brimmed straw hat, scarf, and large sunglasses stepped out—another incognito actress or model or trophy wife.

"Someone didn't get the message," Gwen said with quiet annoyance. "Would you excuse me just a moment?" She hurried down the stone steps and met the approaching woman. Monks watched her explain that the appointment was canceled. Her body language, solicitous yet firm, made it subtly clear that the patient was all-important but that Gwen Bricknell ran this show. Sunlight and shadow played on her finely muscled golden-skinned arms as she gestured, and accentuated the hollows beneath her cheekbones as she talked and smiled. He wondered if her brittle energy was drug-induced.

The woman with the straw hat got back into the

Mercedes. Gwen returned to Monks. Her eyes were cool again. Whatever control might have faltered for a moment, she had regained.

"I'll go tell him," she said. "I can't promise he'll see you." He followed her back inside. She disappeared into the rear office, closing the door behind her.

Monks walked over to the photo collage again. There was no doubt about it—several of the shots, both facial and nudes, were of a younger Gwen Bricknell, displaying her perfection in poses that walked the edge between art and erotica.

He turned back toward the desk and stopped abruptly, startled. A nurse was standing right behind him, close enough to touch. He had not heard her make a sound approaching—had had no idea that she was there. Her name tag said PHYLLIS QUIRES, RN. She was sturdily built, with a Dutchboy haircut and not much expression, except for an accusing element in her gaze. He realized that she had caught him red-handed, leering at the photos. He was a voyeur, defiling a sanctuary that was not for men.

"I'm waiting for Ms. Bricknell," he said.

She looked dissatisfied with his explanation, but said, "I'm sure you'll be more comfortable in here, then." She ushered him to one of the screened-off cubicles.

The space contained two leather-upholstered office chairs and a glossy black lacquered table, with a large oval mirror and several photo albums arranged in a tasteful spread. Monks flipped through them. They were filled with before and after photos, not artful like the collage on the wall outside, but a more down-to-earth look at what clients might expect—reshaped noses, vanished wrinkles, enhanced and desagged breasts, tightened buttocks, bee-stung lips. It was another powerful advertisement for cosmetic surgery. The results were remarkable.

Out in the parking lot, a car door slammed. Monks glanced through a window and saw a woman getting out of a white SUV. She hurried toward the clinic's door, then across the reception room. She looked distraught. He assumed she was another patient who had not received a cancellation notice, perhaps agitated because she was late. But he saw with surprise that she went straight to the rear office door and pushed it open.

He could not hear exactly what she said, but he caught the name "Eden." Her voice was urgent, shaking.

Gwen Bricknell appeared in the doorway, reaching out to grip the newcomer's shoulder. It was not a comforting gesture—more like a shake. She made a harsh *shh* sound.

Then she looked over at Monks and said, in a louder, formal voice, "Dr. Monks? He'll see you now."

Monks walked to them, deciding to push it.

"I couldn't help overhearing," he said to the second woman. "I tended Eden Hale in the Emergency Room. Did you know her?"

Her mouth opened in surprise, or even shock. But whatever she might have said was cut off by Gwen's quick words.

"Like I told you, Doctor, Eden was just another patient. I'm sorry, I didn't mean that to sound harsh, but it's true. Julia's concerned because this might reflect on Dr. D'Anton. She's his wife."

Monks sharpened his appraisal of Julia D'Anton. She was in her mid-forties, with a bohemian look— her long thick red-brown hair was pulled back in a careless braid, and she was wearing baggy pants and a blue work shirt with rolled-up sleeves, as if she had been gardening. But she had the same indefinable air of superiority as the other women he had seen here, and her huge diamond wedding and engagement rings stood out from across the room. She was handsome rather than beautiful, with a big-boned frame, large strong hands, and a face that D'Anton had obviously not reshaped. Right now, it looked very unhappy.

"There's no reflection on Dr. D'Anton," Monks said, and thought, *at least yet.* "I just came to straighten out a misunderstanding."

Gwen's smile looked brittle to the breaking point. She touched Julia's shoulder again, easing her away from the door.

"We don't want to keep Dr. Monks," she said. "He must be very busy."

Gwen led him down a hallway that had several doors opening into procedure rooms. They passed a maintenance man, with dozens of keys on a belt ring and a box of tools on the floor beside him, taking the cover off a thermostat.

"Todd, you do know we're closing early," Gwen said.

"Yes, ma'am," he said cheerfully. "That'll give me a chance to check out the air-conditioning."

The door at the hallway's end led into the clinic proper—the sanctum sanctorum, domain of the high priest. Most plastic surgeons worked in partnerships, but D'Anton worked alone. Gwen pointed to the door with exaggerated politeness, then turned on her heel and walked away.

Monks stepped inside. Here, the walls were sterile white, lined with cabinets of medical supplies. A container of clear liquid, kept on ice, sat on one table, with a box of sterile-wrapped syringes beside it—Botox, probably.

D'Anton was waiting. He was in his late forties, of medium height, trim, and very dapper. His hands were perfectly manicured, but they were surprisingly heavy and thick-knuckled—working-class hands. His left wrist was encircled by a gold Rolex with a cerulean blue face. He wore a tailored white lab coat and expensive wool slacks with knife-edge creases, cuffs breaking perfectly over tasseled leather shoes. He looked pale, but his manner was precise, assured, and impatient. He did not offer a handshake. That was fine with Monks.

"You ought to have some facts in hand before you go slinging accusations, Doctor," Monks said.

"Eden Hale left here in perfect health," D'Anton said, in a tone bordering on outrage. "Less than twenty-four hours later, in your care, she was dead."

"And she came into my care too far gone to have a chance. She died of DIC. Are you familiar with it?"

D'Anton hesitated. "An abnormality in blood clotting, isn't it? I don't remember the details."

"It causes severe circulatory depression, and bleeding everywhere. It takes hours to develop. Whatever started it happened to her beforehand. Were you aware of anything that could have contributed? Low blood count? Carcinoma? Complications?"

"None of those." The sharpness was back in D'Anton's voice. "Of course I'd checked her history—she was pristine. The procedure was a simple one. I've done thousands of them. It went like clockwork and she came out in tiptop shape."

"Then let's talk about what might have happened in between."

"There was supposed to be someone with her for at least twenty-four hours," D'Anton said. "Her fiancé, I believe."

"I talked to him. He had other plans last night."

"He left her alone?" D'Anton said incredulously. Monks nodded.

"That's—criminal."

"We tried to call you, too."

"If I took night calls from every neurotic woman I treated, I'd never sleep. Besides, by that time she was 'too far gone,' isn't that what you're saying?"

This guy is Teflon, Monks thought. "Yes."

"Whereas her *fiancé* made a commitment to care for someone recovering from surgery."

"I've got a feeling that Mr. Dreyer's definition of 'making a commitment' is different from the medical community's," Monks said. "There's no help there now, anyway. What time was her procedure?"

"Late morning."

"That makes it roughly eighteen hours before I saw her. There are a couple of possibilities. Traumatic injury, but there was no obvious sign of it. Massive infection, as from the surgery—" Monks paused, watching with grim satisfaction as D'Anton's face flushed with indignation.

"Impossible." D'Anton almost spat the word.

"Or something unknown."

"You're groping for a diagnosis. That's pathetic."

"I'd appreciate a look at her records," Monks said.

"Certainly not, unless you're here in official capacity, Doctor—I'm sorry, your name's slipped my mind."

"Monks. No."

"What *are* you trying to do?"

"I'm trying to have a consultation with another

professional," Monks said. "For Christ's sake, you *knew* her. I'd think you'd want to help find out why she died." Monks shook his head and turned to go, angry at D'Anton, but at himself, too, for falling into this schoolboy exchange of finger-pointing.

"I'm distraught about it, of course," D'Anton said, stepping after him. "It's hard to believe. She was so vibrant."

The words had the feel of a clumsy attempt to cover his callousness, and Monks did not go for it.

"I guess I'm lucky there," Monks said. "I never saw her like that."

D'Anton bristled visibly. "I can't imagine how *you* must feel."

"In emergency medicine, people are going to die," Monks said. "It's not Rodeo Drive."

Julia D'Anton had left the reception room when Monks walked back through it. Gwen Bricknell was working busily at her desk. She did not look up.

So much for making a good impression, Monks thought.

Outside, the heat and bright sunlight hit him hard. He could already feel the day's grit on his skin beneath his clothes. Julia D'Anton's SUV was still parked in the lot, the only vehicle besides his own that did not fit here—a Toyota 4Runner, nondescript white, several years old, and a little down-at-heels. It seemed an odd choice in this glitzy world. The rear compartment was thick with dust and chips of stone. Monks remembered her work clothes and wondered if she was landscaping or redecorating.

He opened the Bronco's door and started to get in.

"That's yours, huh?" a man's voice said. "What is it, a seventy-five?" The tone was friendly—the first positive thing Monks had heard today. He turned. It was the maintenance man, Todd, walking toward D'Anton's Jaguar, carrying a towel and Windex.

"Seventy-four," Monks said.

"She's in great shape." Todd started polishing the Jag's glass, keeping his body carefully away, so that his belt buckle and keys would not scratch its finish. He was in his early thirties, good-looking, wearing tight jeans and a T-shirt that showed off a well-muscled torso. A floppy, dark blond haircut completed the look of a '60s-era Southern California surfer. But there was nothing laid-back about him. He exuded brisk competence.

"I know I should get something more sensible," Monks said. "She's like an old dog I can't bear to part with."

"Hey, I hear you. I had a seventy-five. I've been kicking myself ever since I sold it." He patted the Jaguar's hood. "Although I've got to admit, I wouldn't mind having one of these."

"It's a beautiful machine," Monks agreed.

"Only for the rich and famous. I try to take care of it for the doc. Especially, like now. He's pretty bummed out."

"So I've gathered."

"Yeah," Todd said, and this time Monks imagined accusation in his tone. He wondered if Todd had overheard his conversation with D'Anton, and—like everyone else—blamed Monks for troubling the great man; if his seeming friendliness had only been a setup to take a shot.

But then, Monks thought, he was imagining all kinds of things by now. He waved good-bye to Todd anyway.

Monks started the engine, sorting through his impressions. It seemed clear that Gwen Bricknell and Julia D'Anton knew each other well. Not many physicians' receptionists would feel comfortable shaking and scolding their boss's wife.

And it seemed that Eden Hale had been more than just another patient, whom Gwen remembered only because of her unusual name. The way that Julia had blurted it out, with Gwen picking up on it instantly and hushing her, suggested familiarity there, too. Monks had intended to lead the conversation in that direction, to see what he might uncover. But Gwen had headed that off.

Monks remembered the tattoo on Eden's rump, and Ray Dreyer's sleazy persona. These did not jibe with the elegant world of women like Gwen and Julia. He wondered what relationship they might have had with her.

Wondered why Gwen Bricknell had lied about it.

* * *

D'Anton stepped into an empty procedure room and slumped back against the wall with his face in his hands. It was the room where he had operated, yesterday, on Eden Hale. A few more sessions of sculpting her face, and the perfection within her would have shone forth.

He knew female flesh as very few people ever had—by sight, by scent, and, above all, by touch. He knew the strength and tone of the muscles under his fingertips, the suppleness of the skin. How best to enhance them, and how long that would last. Most of his patients were attractive, and many were beautiful.

But Eden was far beyond that.

To the uneducated eye, she had been nothing really special. But D'Anton had seen deeper the instant he first had noticed her. She had an ideal bone structure, a superb musculature, and a quality to her flesh that was the closest to perfection he had ever found—precisely the right combination of firmness and yielding, seeming to give off an energy of its own that spread through his hands and made touching her almost hypnotic.

He would never feel that warmth again.

He pushed away from the wall and strode to a conference room where Gwen Bricknell and his wife, Julia, were talking in low, urgent tones. At the sound of the opening door, both swiveled to look at him.

"That scum of a boyfriend left Eden alone last night," D'Anton said to Gwen. "Why the *hell* did you let her go with him?"

Gwen's eyes went fierce in return. "It's not up to me to make that judgment, Doctor. She chose him. He's a competent adult."

"He's neither of those things!"

"Then from now on, you can vet them yourself." She tossed her head defiantly.

"Blame yourself, Welles," Julia cut in. She was glaring, too, her earlier shock turning to rage, her voice trembling. "If you'd left Eden alone, none of this would have happened."

D'Anton stifled the urge to snap back at her. There were other pressing worries to be dealt with, and the most immediate one was Monks. D'Anton had gone through the charade of not remembering the name, but in fact he knew perfectly damned well who Monks was.

"Call that Dr. Monks," D'Anton said to Gwen. "Tell him I apologize for being rude. Stress, all that. He's welcome to look at Eden's records. We'll have them ready if he cares to drop by."

Gwen's eyebrows rose. "Mind if I ask why the sudden chumminess?"

"Because he's got a reputation for causing trouble. I want him to know I have nothing to hide. To leave me the hell alone." He looked at his watch. It was 9:47 A.M., a time when he would normally be brimming with energy, even excited, lost in the full swing of the morning's work. "How many more appointments?"

"Three."

"Send in the next one," he said. "Let's get this day over with."

Monks drove toward nowhere, heading west out of a vague wish to get near the ocean, as if that would ease the constriction he felt around him. He kept turning on unfamiliar streets, working his way farther from the city, until he topped the bluffs that crested the coastline to the south. He was not familiar with the area; it was somewhere in Pacifica.

He found a place to pull off the road and got out of the Bronco, leaning across the hood on his forearms. He watched the long white-capped breakers roll in, remembering some thirty years ago, when he had shipped out to tend the wounded in Vietnam, and come home with his own inglorious million-dollar wound, delivered by the tiny saber of an anopheles mosquito.

To the east, the traffic on Interstate 280 streamed nonstop down the long depression of the San Andreas Fault, an endless speeding line of hot little bumper cars darting in and out of clusters of eighteen-wheelers, sleek luxury European sedans, RVs towing boats or second vehicles. They all had one thing in common, the one thing that, right now, looked better than just about anything in the world. They were all on their way to someplace else.

There were plenty of things bothering him about Eden Hale's death, but now he pinned down an elusive one that had been growing underneath the others. Several different people had weighed in so far, all with their own very different perspectives. Most of their interests were self-oriented—Baird Necker's in protecting the hospital; Gwen Bricknell's, the plastic surgery clinic; D'Anton's, his reputation. Ray Dreyer seemed mainly concerned about the marketable commodity he had lost. And a lot of what was driving Monks himself, he admitted, was a desire to justify his own actions in the ER.

But in this shuffle, Eden had gotten lost. She was the seed that had started it all, but then she had been pushed aside, ignored, while the players squared off to pursue their own aims.

Monks got behind the Bronco's wheel and punched a number on his cell phone. While it rang, his gaze fixed on a welded patch on the opposite door panel, where on a rainy evening last fall, a 9-millimeter bullet had exited while he lay huddled on the floor, with one hand on the steering wheel and the other frantically jamming down on the accelerator, trying to escape the ambush he had driven into.

After four rings, he got the answering machine of Stover Larrabee, a private detective and Monks's partner in insurance investigations.

"I need a favor, Stover," Monks said. "There's a young actress named Eden Hale. It looks like she's going to figure into my life, so I'd like to know more about hers."

Monks paused. "Did I say 'There is'? I should have said 'was.'"

6

In Stover Larrabee's darkened office, a computer screen was showing a video. A pretty young woman, wearing a fiery red wig and nothing else, was down on all fours, mouthing the erection of a panting man with a weight lifter's torso. Another, similarly built, young stud mounted her from behind, pelvis slapping her rump with rabbitlike quickness. Her muscles were tensed, displaying their fine definition, and her breasts shimmied with each impact. Her eyes were closed, not with faked passion, but rapture that seemed real. All three players had tattoos in evidence, including one of a snake-wrapped apple on the woman's left buttock.

"That her?" Larrabee said.

"Yes." Monks had not been certain during the clip's opening moments. Eden Hale—starring as Eve Eden in the video—had obviously been a few years younger when she had made this, and she looked a lot better on-screen than she had last night in the ER. But when her tattoo came into view, that clinched it.

Monks saw now how striking she was physically. Her body was strong and yet graceful, waist and hips forming a perfect hourglass, legs long and tapering. Her not-yet-augmented breasts were pear-shaped, not large, and like most women's, a little uneven—lovely by his standards, but not the symmetrical jutting orbs that many men worshiped. But the bar to real beauty was the way her face looked from certain angles—nose somewhat thick at the bridge, and cheekbones protuberant, giving the impression of coarseness. It had probably not helped her acting career.

"Seen enough?"

Monks nodded. Larrabee clicked the video off and lifted the shades on his third-story windows. They were many-paned, old enough for the glass to have rippled from settling, and etched with grimy salt from the storms that blew in from the Bay they overlooked.

Neither man spoke for a moment. There was a sort of guilty weight in the room. Monks had no objection to seeing attractive women unclothed, nor to the occasional glimpse of pornography. But

watching someone who had just died in his hands
had a ghoulishness to it.

"She was a rising star, huh?" Larrabee said. He
was burly, forty-five, with a mustache and rooster-
like shock of dark hair.

"That's what her fiancé said."

"What was your take on him?"

"Some kind of small-time operator."

"Pimp?"

"On that edge."

Monks leaned his shoulder against a window
jamb and stared out toward the Bay. Larrabee's
immediate neighborhood was a holdover from
industrial days, when this part of the city had
belonged to factories and shipping. But a few blocks
south, gentrification had come in big-time, with
expensive high-rise apartment buildings and fancy
plazas. Sunlight flashed off the glass and metal of
the cars crowding the Embarcadero. Flocks of
pedestrians were drifting toward the afternoon
Giants game at Pac Bell Park, with the masts of the
China Basin yacht fleet spiking the skyline behind it.

"Lots of creepy people in that porn world,"
Larrabee said. "You remember Iris?"

"Sure." Iris had been a girlfriend of Larrabee's a
few years ago, a stripper at the North Beach clubs.
She had some things in common with Eden Hale,
Monks realized: physical beauty, breast surgery, and
a stage name—Secret.

"There were always guys after her to make porn

loops," Larrabee said. "They create a fan club. Seems that men get a lot more interested in watching a girl dance if they've seen her horizontal. She draws bigger crowds and higher pay."

Monks knew that Iris had left San Francisco, and Larrabee, for Las Vegas and a better career. He decided not to ask whether porn loops had figured in.

The Internet references Larrabee had found showed that Eden Hale had had several roles as a mainstream actress, bit parts in soaps and sitcoms. She had also made a few adult films. Someone had seized on the connection as a marketing ploy—the thrill of watching a legitimate actress, even a comparative unknown, having sex. A search of her name brought up several items along the lines of: WATCH EDEN HALE GET A FACIAL . . . A credit-card number and a few clicks of the mouse would then deliver action like they had just seen, with the star billed in the film credits as Eve Eden.

"This girl must have had money, huh?" Larrabee said. "Maybe her family?"

"I don't know. Why?"

"Because that guy D'Anton doesn't take on anybody who doesn't. But if she was rich, why would she do the porn? For kicks?"

Monks had not thought about that, obvious though it was. "I don't know anything more about her."

"I'm sure there's more to her story," Larrabee said. "I can keep looking, if you want."

"I don't think so, Stover. It's not like it matters. Just me being sappy."

"Well, let me know if there's anything else."

Monks said thanks and left. There *wasn't* anything else, but to wait—for Roman Kasmarek's appraisal, for the medical examiner's autopsy, and to find out if the beating Monks had taken over the past hours was going to continue.

7

Afternoon sunlight filtered through the tall windows of Julia D'Anton's studio, illuminating slowly drifting particles of limestone that settled onto the dusty old hardwood floor. Her strong fingers worked at the stone with a wooden mallet and the hand-forged iron chisels she had brought back from Tuscany more than twenty years ago.

The block was one-quarter life size. Julia had started by sketching a live model, then roughing out the sculpture in clay. Now the model was back, to lend living nuance to the flow of the stone. Her name was Anna somebody, a softly pretty and somewhat sulky girl in her late teens, full-bodied and large-breasted. In the past, Julia had preferred working with marble, and women with lean, well-defined musculatures, but now she did not want to look at either—maybe ever again.

She had been shaping the face with small tooth chisels, trying to render expression from the blank oval. It was not going well. Her hands were getting tired. When that happened, they started to tremble and lose control. Anna was posed nude, sitting up, with her legs curled beside her. Her face was turned in profile and down, as if she were contemplating a flower in the garden where the sculpture would probably end up. She looked like she was almost asleep.

Julia gave the chisel a delicate tap along the bridge of the nose. A hairline crack appeared, a tiny fault in the stone that she had not seen. She pressed a fingertip over it, but she knew already that it could not be repaired. She thrust the clawed chisel in and gouged out a chip the size of a small nailhead. It would mean a restructuring of the entire face. Hands shaking now with anger, she slammed down the tools on the workbench.

Anna's body jerked with the sound, her eyes flicking open.

"Is something wrong?" she said.

"It's *all* wrong. All this work I've gone to, and it's just getting worse. *You* are wrong. Your bones might be all right, but everything from there out is impossible."

The girl's mouth twisted in a little grimace of resentment.

"Is there anything I can do?"

"Try to look a little less bovine."

Anna's face turned suspicious. "I don't know what that means."

"Like a cow, darling."

Anna's mouth opened, then her eyes went teary. "You have—no right," she blurted out. She stood, grasping for her robe and flinging it around her shoulders, trying to look dignified but without the necessary presence.

"It's no use going knock-kneed trying to hide your bush," Julia said coldly. "It only makes your thighs look fatter."

Anna turned away with a flounce and started toward the studio's changing room.

"I didn't say the session was over," Julia said.

"You can't keep me if I don't want—"

"If you leave here without my permission, you will never come back. Do you understand?"

Their gazes met, but only for a second. This was no contest of wills. Slowly, Anna took her seat again.

"The robe," Julia said.

Eyes downcast, she shrugged it back off her shoulders and laid it aside.

Julia walked to stand behind her. She caressed Anna's neck lightly, feeling her shiver in response.

Julia's fingers moved on in slow exploration, feeling the lack of tone in the deltoid muscle, tracing the flaccid triceps down the back of the arm, then moving across the smooth padded rib cage and up, to cup one full soft breast. She squeezed the nipple gently, tugging it erect. The girl relaxed a little, settling back against Julia's thighs.

Then, suddenly, Julia pinched hard with her nails. Anna flinched and gasped, tried to rise, but Julia's other hand on her shoulder held her where she was. Julia could feel her panting. She held the pressure of her fingernails steady, just short of drawing blood.

"Did I say cow?" Julia said softly. "I meant *sow*." She released her grip and gave the breast a contemptuous slap. "Get out."

The girl hurried across the room, almost running, the robe left lying on the floor. Julia watched her, breathing hard with anger. But it was not really at Anna—she was only a place to put it.

Julia closed her eyes, remembering the alluring innocence of Eden's face, the restless energy in her finely shaped limbs. The dark fire that came into her eyes when she was caressed.

Julia had thought it would help, having another young woman here today. But after Eden, mere creatures like Anna were intolerable.

Outside, a car started and pulled away with a spray of gravel. Anna might never come back—or she might come back pleading. Either way, there were always others.

Julia walked through the studio, her gaze moving restlessly, looking for a project to interest her. But all her fine stone looked bleak and without promise now.

Then the door into the main house opened, and her husband stepped through. She was surprised, and not pleasantly. She could not remember the last time he had been in her studio—years ago, surely. It had been that long since they had shared much of anything.

"I was almost run over by a young woman driving out of here," D'Anton said. He was stiff, formal, still dressed in the business suit he had worn at the clinic this morning.

"She was modeling for me."

"Yes, I assumed so. She looked very upset. What happened?"

Julia shrugged. "She was unsatisfactory. Since when are you so interested in my work?"

"This isn't about your work. It's about your losing control of yourself."

"I have a temperament, Welles," she said haughtily. "It comes from having warm blood in my veins, instead of ice water."

D'Anton walked farther into the room, toward her. His face was concerned, understanding—the kind of look he used with his patients.

"I know you were in love with Eden," he said. "And that you're very, very angry."

"*Don't* you patronize me," she snapped back. D'Anton flinched a little. She began to step slowly around him, circling.

"Yes, I gave her love," Julia said. "But she went with you, because you promised her candy. You don't have any love to *give*."

"I didn't try to take her love from you. I saw what I could do with her."

"With her? Or to her? Your idea of beauty goes as deep as a magazine cover. You've never understood the first thing about real art. It *celebrates* flaws."

D'Anton grimaced impatiently. "Let's not forget who has the world-class reputation."

"Thanks to *my* family's influence. Your steel mill worker father didn't help much, did he?"

"What a shame your family's influence couldn't buy you any talent," D'Anton said, with cold pity. "All that schooling in Europe, and still the only people who'll buy your work are your friends."

"And you've never dared risk pushing for something more than nice tits and a pretty smile." She slapped her trembling palm down flat on a workbench.

D'Anton moved toward her again. His face had gone rigid, his eyes very intense.

"Julia," he said, speaking very quietly now. "Did you—interfere with Eden somehow? After the surgery?"

Her eyes widened in outrage. "What are you saying?"

"Out of jealousy? Revenge, because she left you?"

Her hand scuttled across the workbench and

tightened around an iron mallet. D'Anton stopped walking.

"I have ignored—certain things," he said, almost whispering. "But I can't continue. You'll destroy us both."

He turned abruptly and hurried out of the studio, fumbling to close the door behind him.

Julia stood with the mallet clenched in her shaking hand, aware of his fading footsteps, then the silence around her. A sudden spasm wracked her body, chattering her teeth and bending her over, with her muscles clenching in spastic contortions.

Panting, she walked swiftly to a large, canvas-draped marble in the studio's far corner. She yanked off the cover and raised the mallet, willing herself to smash it, to exorcise Eden Hale from her memory.

But her arm dropped to her side. This was all there was left of that passion.

She let the cover fall back into place and put down the mallet.

There would be others, she told herself again. There were always plenty of others.

8

Monks pulled the Bronco into his own driveway just after five P.M., sweaty and gritty. His place was in the coastal mountains of Marin County—a few acres of redwoods with a cabin that he had bought in the '70s and ended up with after his divorce. It was still rudimentary, with woodstove heat and plank floors. But it was quiet, private, and you could glimpse the Pacific on clear days.

He cut the Bronco's engine, got out, and walked to one of the giant redwoods. He squatted down with his back against it, then leaned his head back, too, and closed his eyes. It was something he had learned to do years ago, when he was feeling drained. Here, the afternoon sunlight was dappled through the thick foliage, a friendly warmth instead of a glaring blast. The tree's shaggy bark was sun-warm, too, and he imagined that a deeper healing force radiated from within its thick trunk. Monks basked in between, like a baby wrapped in a comforting blanket, until he heard the house's screen door open and close.

Martine Rostanov came out onto the deck. She was a slight woman with a mop of dark hair and a metal-braced left leg, the result of a childhood horse-riding accident, which she swung from the hip when she walked.

"You all right?" she called. Her forehead was creased with worry.

Monks nodded. He got to his feet and climbed the deck stairs into her embrace. Now her warmth flowed into him, strong and sweet.

"Did something happen?" she said.

"I lost a patient last night."

"Oh, hon. I'm so sorry." She pressed harder against him. "Can I get you a drink?"

"I'm going to work out for a few minutes," Monks said. "After that, I'd kill for one."

"I'll have it ready."

He changed quickly into sweats, assessing his physical condition for the first time in a long while. He had the coloration of the black Irish, green eyes and wiry black hair that was starting to gray, but was still mostly there. His face was craggy and pitted with old acne scars, his once aquiline nose getting thicker. Wild bushy eyebrows had earned him the nickname Rasp, for Rasputin, in the navy. Officially he stood six foot one, although he suspected that he was starting to shrink. But his wind was good, and his chest and gut were tight. After almost getting hamstrung by a psychopath with a grape-picker's knife, he had never let himself get badly out of shape again.

He walked to the old garage that he had outfitted as a gym. It was one of the original structures on the place, good-sized—intended for working on vehicles, not just housing them—with bare frame walls and roof. Monks had rebuilt the floor with pressure-treated two-by-ten joists and plywood. He had installed a Vitamax weight machine in one corner and hung a heavy bag in the room's center Most days, he spent fifteen minutes doing sit-ups and weights, then another twenty of hammering the bag. It was not a thorough workout, but it kept his body toned, and on a day like this it offered release.

The room was hot, with the faint good smell of the redwood it had been built from, back when that was cheap lumber. He went through a quick routine on the machine—fifty sit-ups with a ten-pound weight behind his head, sets of bench and military presses, butterflies, and pull-downs—then put on his bag gloves. Usually he started by standing still, throwing controlled left jabs at the bag to get his distance, then stepping in with right crosses and follow-up left hooks. Soon, his feet would start moving by themselves, and he would circle the bag, gathering speed and force.

But today, for no reason he was aware of, he unhooked the bag and set it aside. He started doing footwork, very slowly at first—the gliding step of the left moving forward with the jab, then the right catching up and planting itself to give power to the cross. The left foot stayed put but pivoted with the hook, the third punch in the classic combination, hip reversing at the moment of impact to give it extra snap. The importance of footwork could not be overestimated; placement of inches could make the difference. Rocky Marciano had been one of the all-time great punchers, but his trainers had to tie his ankles together with string to keep him from extending his left foot too far and losing power from his right.

Monks kept his hands at his sides, his gaze on the center of his invisible opponent's chest, concentrating just on his feet. A step forward with the left, quick catch-up with the right, left pivoting on the ball, hip swinging with it, then snapping back. Again, a little faster. Then again, and again. He shuffled his way around the room's perimeter as if it were a ring and the walls were the ropes.

But you could not always advance. The other man in the ring was going to punch you back. Retreating, with minimum damage to yourself, was the other half of footwork. Monks reversed his direction—not with the same steps, but more with side-to-side

dancing, as if he were jitterbugging or skating backward. Now he raised his hands defensively, fists protecting his face but just low enough to see over,
elbows close in to his ribs.

Monks started circling, combining advance and
retreat with unplanted pivots, either foot leaving the
floor to gain him a quarter or half turn. He concen-
trated on moving to his left, trying to herd his spec-
tral partner into a right cross. But the partner had
other ideas, and Monks swung the other way, spinning to his right, leaping clear of the swift straight
blows coming at him. He changed directions again
and again, ducking, weaving, his feet dancing across
the floor in a dizzying intricate pattern that could
only ever make sense during the few moments it
existed.

He slowed, like a toy with its battery running
down. He stopped, and let his hands fall to his waist.
He was panting and streaming with sweat. Outside,
a Steller's jay screeched, nervous from the commo-
tion, or maybe mocking him.

He pulled off the gloves and set them on the sill
of the garage's single crude window so they would
dry. He pulled off his sweatshirt, too, then kicked
off shoes and socks and stepped out of his sweatpants and jock. Barefoot, naked, he walked along
the hard dirt path back to the house, inside, and
down the hall to the shower.

Martine, standing in the kitchen, watched him
pass, without saying a word.

9

They're like deer on two legs, graceful creatures that prance not through the woods but along the sidewalks. They stream in and out of the Haight's little bar-cafés in tight jeans and short skirts, tossing their hair and smiling. Their earrings shimmer and you can see the ridges of cartilage in their throats, delicate as eggshell. Perspiration glistens on their skin. You walk among them, brush against them. They don't pay any attention. You look like one of their kind.

The street you're on is a blue-black tunnel of sky, slashed by car headlights. Music spills through the hot air, red electric and easy violet and the misty rose of an alto sax. It all blends together like voices, lifting the crowd's feet on an invisible cushion and moving them along. The shop windows are filled with bright tinsel. But the open doorways are like caves, with the glow of fires inside and figures eating and drinking and mating.

She's here somewhere, in one of those caves.

Her voice sings in your head, calling you. Sometimes it gets lost in the other noise, but if you close your eyes you can hear it clearly. It leads you into a doorway. There's a live band at the far end of the room, with a crowd dancing. Lots of tattoos and colored hair. Not really your kind of place.

But that could be her at the bar, sitting alone.

You take the empty seat next to her. She moves her purse over a little, to give you more room. The top of the wine list is a Mondavi Reserve cabernet at twenty-four dollars a glass. You order it, and listen hard to the voice inside.

"What kind of music do you call that?" you ask her.

She shrugs. "Mostly hip-hop, I guess," she says uncomfortably, and she turns to watch the dance floor. She's young, twenty-two or -three, and to her, you seem old.

You know by now that she's not the one.

The band quits. Another girl her age, who's been dancing, comes and sits on her other side. They start talking immediately, chattering like birds.

You pocket your change and slip away.

Outside, you find a quiet spot and lean against a

wall, close your eyes, and shut everything else out. The voice in your head is a blur of echoes hammering around.

But her song will start again sweet and clear, and lead you to her. It always has.

10

When Monks came out of the shower, Martine was waiting on the deck with an old-fashioned glass of cold clean Finlandia vodka, touched with fresh lemon. It hurt his teeth and brought a sharp pleasant ache to his throat.

"You're an angel of mercy," he said, and sank into a chair.

She sat beside him. "Tell me what happened."

He went through the story tersely—the ugly death of a pretty young woman, and the waves that had risen in its wake.

"Baird suggested, with his usual tact, that I'm getting old," he finished. He took another long drink. "Maybe he's right."

"That's ridiculous. You know it and so does he. He's just upset."

"He sure doesn't want any dust settling on Welles D'Anton's halo."

"I used to hear that name a lot," she said. "When I was working for those big-shot executives. Their wives were crazy about D'Anton. It was a status thing, like driving a Rolls. They'd pay a fortune for a Botox injection."

Monks recalled Larrabee's question about how a struggling actress like Eden Hale had been able to afford the surgeon to the rich and famous.

"He's got his own style, that's for sure," Monks said. "That clinic had the feel of a French whorehouse."

"Really?" she said archly. "You know that from experience?"

Only once, Monks thought, and it was true, the place hadn't been anything like D'Anton's clinic. He decided not to elaborate.

"Just a figure of speech," he said.

"He's supposed to have a magic touch," Martine said. "Fountain of youth, you know? But from what I could tell, his results were pretty much the same as any other decent plastic surgeon's. I think he's just managed to develop that mystique."

Monks drank again. "Why'd she have to get her breasts done anyway?" he growled, suddenly, unreasonably, angry about it. "They looked fine."

Martine shot a glance at him, swift and cool.

"You must have watched those movies very closely."

"Sorry," he said. "I mean—you know what I mean."

"Women are all wrapped up about beauty, Carroll. All the time and money we spend on hair, skin care, clothes. Look through a Victoria's Secret catalog some time. That's a zillion-dollar market, and those aren't even things that most other people *see*. It has everything to do with how we think of ourselves. Like me. After my accident, I knew I'd never be beautiful."

He slipped his arm around her waist, pulling her close. "You're a vision," he said.

"Not like what you think is beautiful when you're ten. *Baywatch* babes in bikinis, bouncing down the beach. It was something about myself I never trusted. I never believed any man would really want me." She shrugged. "Of course, women who *are* beautiful probably figure that's the *only* reason men want them."

Monks had never thought of it quite like that. Women were damned either way.

"There's an endless supply of pretty girls," he said. "They're being born every minute. Delectable fruit on the great tree of life. But youth and beauty fade away and pass on, even as the morning dew evaporateth in the sunlight."

She smiled wryly. "Sounds like you didn't get any sleep."

"What I'm trying to tell you is, you're not just a knockout. There's a lot more *to* you."

"I know a line when I hear one. You must be wiped out."

"Pretty much," he admitted.

"Did you eat, at least?"

"Coffee."

"Idiot. I bought steaks. Start the grill when you're ready."

He nodded, but went into the kitchen first and refilled his glass with vodka. He knew he had to be careful. Tomorrow was going to be bad enough in many ways, without the crippling burden of a hangover. One or two drinks would not hurt.

The problem was that one or two had never done him any good.

He got the grill going and the thick steaks cooking. He fed choice bits to the three cats who prowled like thugs demanding tribute—Felicity, the neurotic calico; Cesare Borgia, black, scarred, and streetwise; and Omar, the eighteen-pound blue Persian.

Cats were like creatures in dreams, operating with a logic that seemed to make perfect sense to them, although it was mostly impenetrable to humans. Monks was convinced that the real reason cats had become domesticated—or more probably, deigned to start hanging out with people—had nothing to do with anything so mundane as food or safety. It was because they had discovered the pleasures of hand and lap. The two males would stalk him, trying to trip him into sitting, then leap on him and pin him down by assuming a gravity of several times their actual weight. The calico would shamelessly offer her belly to be petted, then clasp his hand with her forepaws, licking it and drooling. He speculated that instinct told her it was the butting heads of the kittens she had never had.

He had brought several women to the house over the years since his divorce. The cats had treated them with a mixture of jealousy and contempt— with Felicity going so far as to burrow between the two humans in bed, trying to literally kick the intruding female out—and had outlasted them all. But they had loved Martine immediately. Now Monks was the one who felt their cold stares, particularly after he had been gone working for a night. He remembered that the first emotion he had felt about her was an urge to protect. Maybe it was the same with the cats.

Three or four drinks would be okay, he decided. But not five or six.

By the time the steaks were done, the knots in his brain were dissolving. He went into the kitchen to fill his glass one last time. Martine was putting together linguine with Parmesan and garlic.

"Tell me the truth," Monks said. "Are you getting bored with me?"

She looked surprised. "Don't be silly." Then she glanced at his glass. "How many of those have you had?"

This irritated Monks. "I'm doing fine," he said, careful to enunciate the words precisely.

"On an empty stomach, with no sleep?"

"If you want to play nurse, why don't you put on a uniform?"

She turned away stiffly. He had meant it as a joke, or at least he thought he had. He had been told that sometimes there was an edge to his voice that he himself did not hear. The edge tended to sharpen, and his hearing to dim, with alcohol.

"What makes you think I'm getting bored?" she said.

"The way you've been talking about getting back into practice."

"What's the matter with that? I spend half my life becoming a doctor, and I'm not supposed to practice?"

"Of course you are," he said. "I'm just wondering, you know, where. When. All that."

She turned to face him full on, holding a long wooden spoon like a fencing sword. "Why's this coming up now?"

"Well, it has to sooner or later. Don't you think I deserve to know?"

"Know *what*? I haven't decided anything yet."

"Know what you haven't decided, then."

"You're a little drunk, Carroll. This isn't funny."

"'Drunk' is a relative term, Martine. Strictly speaking, you have never seen me drunk. *Drunk* is a fifth or two of liquor in a day, and that's really only the beginning of drunk, because it can be sustained indefinitely."

"Do you turn into a different person?"

In his brain flared a dizzy, fragmented memory of a night when he had looped a black silk scarf around the slender neck of Alison Chapley—a sexual game, one that she had initiated—and barely caught himself before she had stopped breathing for good.

"In vino, veritas," he said.

"My lowbrow education didn't include Latin."

"'There is truth in wine.' Are you moving out?"

There was a longish hesitation before she answered. "I never really moved in."

Monks nodded. "It's been seeming more and more like that."

He walked back outside and leaned his forearms on the deck railing. The creek at the bottom of his sloping property was silent now, the last sluggish rivulets from the winter rains dried into a few scattered pools. They would be gone, too, soon. Evening came early up here in the woods, and jays flitted through the thick madrone foliage on their last errands, big birds that crashed around like vandals, flashes of iridescent blue that appeared with jarring swiftness at the corners of your vision and left again by the time you turned your head. They usually woke him at first light, seeming to take malicious pleasure in perching outside his window and screeching until he hauled himself to his feet.

Martine Rostanov had been with him for more

than a year—since the two of them had nearly been killed together. She had uncovered the fact that a giant software corporation, getting into the business of genetic manipulation, was using fetuses that were deliberately aborted for the purpose. Monks had gotten caught up with her in exposing this. When it was over, on a foggy March dawn, they had stumbled back to this house, singed, shocked, and exhausted, and made love right here on the deck.

They had moved into a tacit arrangement of living together, here, most of the time. But she had kept her house in Burlingame, south of San Francisco, and although Monks wasn't keeping count, he knew that he was alone more now. He stayed with her there sometimes, but he was rooted here, in his place, and he got restless when he was away for long. He loved solitude. The advantages of suburbia—shopping, movies, people—did not interest him. For her, the isolation of the country wore just as thin.

There were other practicalities that came into play. She was an internist and had spent several years as the in-house physician for that same computer corporation. She had come out of last year's emotional wrenching not ready to get back into the mainstream of medicine. But inactivity was wearing thin, too.

He heard the door open, felt her come to stand beside him.

"This isn't fair," she said. "You're making me the

bad guy. Kicking you when you're down." He noted that she had refilled her own glass, with a fine Carmenet sauvignon blanc, and she seemed a little unsteady.

"That's not what I'm doing," he said. "And it's not what you're doing. What's happening at the hospital and what's happening here, they're two different things."

"But that's *why* you're doing it. Isn't it."

The term that came into Monks's mind was one that Emil Zukich used—the legendary mechanic who lived up the road, and who had built and rebuilt the Bronco. *Metal on metal:* the point where bushings and bearings and all the other buffers had ground down to dust, and the machine crashed along tearing up its own bones. It was true that external circumstances might precipitate such a thing.

But between Martine and him, it had built on its own, unseen and unnoticed except in tiny increments—the unhappy expression in a passing glance, the slight reluctance to touch. The sense that there was something going on in the background that was never brought forth.

"You're changing the subject," he said.

"I don't want to be away from *you,* Carroll. I just don't think I can keep on making it here."

"I understand that, Martine. I really do."

But he knew in his guts, even if she did not, that that was not the entire truth.

"We can do it half and half," she said. "Your place and mine."

"You bet."

"I've talked to some people about work. That's all, just talking, feeling around. I think I could move into a practice without too much trouble."

"I'm sure you could," he said.

"I didn't tell you about it because—goddammit, quit giving me that stoic act."

"It's not an act."

"I know it's not," she said. "Fuck you."

They both drank.

"Let's take a walk," Monks said.

"The food will get cold."

"Just around the place."

"Okay," she said doubtfully.

He offered his hand. She took it. They walked down the deck's steps onto a hard red dirt path that skirted the perimeter of the property's three acres.

Thirty yards or so farther on, Monks paused, pointing at a tire-sized flat rock. "I killed a rattlesnake right there once."

Martine pulled her hand away and turned quickly in a circle, her gaze darting around the nearby earth, littered with twisted snakelike madrone twigs.

"Quit it," she said. "You're scaring me."

"I didn't want to. But the kids were still little. I couldn't take the chance."

"Did you face it hand-to-fang? Like those guys on TV?"

"Are you kidding? I snuck up behind it and whacked it with a garden hoe."

She shivered. "Are there a lot of them around? Rattlesnakes?"

"I only ever killed one other. I was getting firewood and it came out of the woodpile, between me and the door. Things got pretty tight for a minute there." Monks pointed at the woodshed, an old board-and-batten structure with only a narrow aisle between the stacks of split rounds. "The cats have taken out a few. They leave them on the doorstep."

"I didn't know cats would hunt snakes."

Another harsh image from his past seared Monks's brain—the cats on the hood of the Bronco, leaping and howling in the moonlight, while on the front seat a cobra weaved from side to side, trying to strike at them through the venom-smeared windshield.

"These cats will," he said.

They walked on, past the workout shed. It was almost dark, cool and still now, with the jays quiet. Higher up, a breeze rustled the redwood fronds and madrone leaves. A few tree frogs were tuning up for the night's concert. He walked slowly and she kept pace with him, swinging her leg without complaint. But on this rough and hilly terrain, she would get tired quickly. Monks stopped again, on the edge of the gully that led down to the creekbed.

"That old cabin down there?" he said. The neighboring place had been abandoned decades ago and had mostly fallen into the creek, a couple hundred yards down the steep hill. "I forbade the kids to go near it, but of course it was a magnet. One day, I'd worked all night and was trying to get some sleep, and I heard this shriek. I ran down there and found poor little Stephanie, she was maybe eight, scream-ing bloody murder. She'd jumped off something and landed on a rusty old fence post, broken off to a point, sticking a couple inches out of the ground. Went right through her tennis shoe and clear up through her foot."

Stephanie, his daughter, was now in medical school at UCSF. She and Martine had gotten quite close.

For a minute or so, Martine was silent. He could see her head moving, her gaze wandering the woods, but not turning to him.

Then, abruptly, she said, "I don't *think* I want a kid. My *mind* doesn't. I don't even think my body does. I don't know what it is."

She was forty-three. Monks was long since vasectomized and out of the child-raising mode. He did not consider that he had done all that good a job the first time around.

"Sorry I can't help you there," he said.

"No, you're not."

"You're right. I'm not."

"Have any of your women ever told you you're too honest?"

"No," Monks said. "You're the first."

"Liar."

He smiled gravely. They turned and started back. He knew, and supposed she did, too, that this had been a last-ditch attempt to woo her—offering the things that made him what he was.

When they had first been together, there were words of passion, each assuring the other that this was what they had been waiting for. But it was useless to invoke that. The problem was not any single one of the obstacles, or even all of them together. The affair was just something that had run its course, and this was like the point in a really great party that had gone on most of the night, when a silence touched the room, and everybody knew that there might be a few more drinks and laughs, but the good-byes were going to start soon.

If he hadn't pushed, it might have lasted longer— maybe quite a while. But Monks could not leave things like that in general, and she was right. Today's events had put him in the mood to have it out. He could have pushed it the other way, and asked her to marry him. But that would only be trying to bind her, to keep her from what she wanted— another chance at the kind of life most people considered normal, the kind of life that he had pretty much let go.

He had not thought he would ever live with a woman again. But once he had started, he had come to realize that when she was not here, he felt a sour gnawing absence.

They managed to keep up small talk while they ate. She asked more questions about what had happened today and Monks told her, but it was dutiful from both sides. Afterward, with his belly full and drowsiness coming quickly, he turned on the TV and settled back on the couch, head in her warm lap and her hand stroking his hair.

"I do love you," she murmured. "You know that."

Monks nodded. "I love you, too," he said, in a voice that was thick with exhaustion.

11

Her voice leads you to a different street, another doorway. It's darker and quieter in here than the last place. The bottles lined up on the back-bar shelves glitter with dusty colored light.

She's a silhouette, alone at the bar, posed for you.

She gives you a quick smile when you walk up next to her. She's in her late twenties, thin, wearing a tank top and jeans. She's probably been hit on several times already tonight, by men and women both. You look better than most of what she sees.

You order a glass of wine, a Clos Pegase merlot this time. Then you admire the bracelet on her right forearm. It wraps around, a silver and turquoise snake crawling up her skin. The silver seems liquid, but not from the room's light. From her.

"Where'd you get it?" you ask.

"In LA. It's Navaho."

You touch it, feeling her warmth shoot up through it into your finger.

"It looks alive," you say. She smiles again and tosses her hair.

She tells you she's from the Midwest. She's been traveling, working part-time here and there, crashing with people she meets. Her name is Lynn. You tell her a name, too, and let her know right away that you're a doctor.

Her eyes flicker. That could mean drugs.

She chatters on, but you listen past her words to what her voice is telling you in your head—what has hurt her all her life. She's almost pretty, but her chin recedes, and her nostrils flare at the tip.

You'll start with a rhinoplasty—remove a little cartilage from the base of each nostril, then tighten them together. Then implants in the mandible to move the chin bone forward. When it's finished, her face will have a beautiful balance. She'll wish you'd found her years ago.

"Are you really a doctor?" she asks teasingly. *Are we really talking drugs?*

"Really." You show her your medical license, making sure she also sees plenty of credit cards and crisp cash.

Then you lean close, lips just brushing her ear,

and say very quietly, "Look, we're both grown-ups. Let's not be coy. I like to party, and I've got a whole pharmacy at my clinic."

She doesn't say anything, doesn't even look at you, but it's just what she wanted to hear.

"Why don't we talk it over in my car?" you say.

You're parked several blocks away, and the two of you don't talk much on the walk. She's wondering whether she made a bad move.

But when she sees the car, her eyebrows rise.

"Nice," she says.

You unlock the passenger door for her. As she's getting in, you press a folded hundred-dollar bill into her palm.

"Just a little fun money," you say.

She acts surprised, even offended. "This isn't really what I do. What do you—you know—want from me?"

"Maybe you can help me with a fantasy."

"Well, maybe," she says warily. "But nothing weird, okay?"

"Of course." You start the engine. It has a smooth, reassuring purr.

"You mind if I smoke?" she asks.

"Go ahead."

She takes cigarettes from her purse and lights up, then relaxes back into the seat. This is looking good. There's money and drugs.

You're a doctor. You can give her what she wants.

12

When Monks woke up, the house was dim, with the only light coming from down the hall. He was still on the couch, covered with a blanket. Memory of the earlier hours began to return, and then, the fear that Martine had gone home.

But she was still here, a small mound in his bed, buried under covers in the now cool night. He put a hand on her lightly to assure himself and heard a slight pause in her breathing before it evened out again. Omar, the big Persian, was curled at her feet, looking almost half her size. There was the sense that he had been posted as a guard while the other two were out taking care of nightly cat business.

Monks went to the bathroom to urinate, rinse his

face, and brush his teeth, then back to the kitchen to put out fresh spoonfuls of cat food in their bowls. He turned out the light. The green LED numbers on the microwave clock said 1:08 A.M. The previous day's events were flickering through his mind like a videotape now.

He stood in the dark room, grappling with the urge to start drinking again, to blast on through the night, to reach that feverish black edge between this reality and a further one that lured, promising that it was realer still. He had been there many times, but not in several years.

He walked back down the hall to the bedroom. When he undressed, he realized, with surprise, that he was half-hard. He lay down beside Martine and touched her small breasts, an exploratory caress, not sure how welcome he would be.

But she stretched luxuriantly, then turned and cupped his tightened scrotum, hefting it curiously, as if judging its weight. Her hand moved to stroke his shaft, using the inside of her wrist, then pricking it with her fingernails.

Her touch was exquisite. He adored her. He tried to concentrate all his being on her, knowing that this would soon be gone, too.

And yet some lewd uncontrollable part of his mind kept playing the image of Eden Hale as she had been in that film, luscious, intense, braced on hands and knees and wide open to the ramming bursting need of men.

13

The night is yours now. You move through the pitch-dark woods without light or sound. The trail is steep and overgrown, but your steps are sure. Power surges through your veins and pounds inside your skull, burning and brilliant and supreme. You are beyond all limits.

Inside the plastic bag you carry is a warm limp weight.

You come to a deep cleft in the mountainside, a spring that was diverted years ago, to fill the swimming pool for the mansion below. No one comes here anymore. You pull away the rocks and brush that you had piled in the entrance. A strong odor seeps out, but musty, like copper and wet earth. The lime has done its job.

This is where you keep the leftover parts.

You lay her down on top of the others, then remove her silver-and-turquoise bracelet and wind it around your own arm. It burns with her heat, right through your skin.

Your body is tired, but your mind is full of her song, a song of worship, for the beauty you have given her.

14

Monks arrived back at Mercy Hospital before eight o'clock the next morning. He had slept poorly—had lain awake beside Martine for a long time after making love, finally dozing a little. But the memory tapes had kept playing in his head, and he was wide awake by six. He had gotten up, showered and shaved, and driven to the city.

He stopped first at the Emergency Room to check for messages. There were two. One, a hand-scrawled note from Roman Kasmarek, just said, "Stop by."

The second was an official hospital message, typed by a clerk and computer-printed: "Dr. D'Anton wishes to extend the courtesy of examining the

records of Eden Hale. Please call at your conven-
ience."

Monks rolled the paper up and tapped it against
his thigh as he walked down to the morgue. There
were such things as changes of heart, but by and
large they made him suspicious.

The hospital's cafeteria food was good and usually
tempted Monks, but this morning he settled for a
scoop of scrambled eggs and toast. He and Roman
found a table in a corner. The place was busy, filled
with staff in different colored uniforms and a few
visitors who were early, or who had spent an anxious night waiting with an ill friend or relative and
were not done with their vigils yet.

"The initial tox screen is in," Roman said. "And I
had a chance to look at the body before the city took
her. This isn't all official, but here's what I'm sure
of." He held up his forefinger, ticking off points.
"She had a relatively high level of Valium in her system, but nowhere near lethal. There's no direct connection to the death." A second finger appeared.
"You were right about the DIC. She bled out. That's
what killed her."

Monks felt a measure of relief. His diagnosis had
been correct.

But there remained the question of his treatment.
"What caused the DIC?"

Roman's ring finger rose to join the other two. "I
saw no evidence of surgical infection. No preg-

nancy, no obvious signs of trauma, carcinoma, any of the other usual causes. It's possible they'll turn up on autopsy, but I doubt it. But there was an infection. We found salmonella in her bloodstream."

"Salmonella," Monks said, laying down his fork. "Salmonella doesn't cause blood clotting. Just the opposite."

Heads at nearby tables turned toward them. Monks lowered his voice.

"She might have *had* salmonella, but I can't believe that's what did it," he said.

Roman's hand opened, palm out, for patience. "Take it easy, Carroll. I'm just telling you what the tests show."

"Have *you* ever known salmonella to act like that?"

"Not the common stuff, *enteritidis*," Roman said. "Which is what this is, or at least what it looked like. There are other kinds."

"You're sure it's not typhoid?" Monks said. "I thought about that." Typhoid fever was caused by a type of salmonella, and he feared that he might have missed it after all.

"Almost positive. I'm doing cultures, so we can verify it. But there are no other indications of typhoid, and it doesn't fit with the DIC."

Monks waited.

"But we've got to keep in mind, there are new strains of everything cropping up all the time," Roman said. "It's possible that this is some form of salmonella that looks like the regular thing, but has a much more severe effect."

"Do you really buy that?"

Roman shook his head. "I'm stumped," he admitted. "Maybe some other factor. Maybe a preexisting condition that's not obvious."

"I'm going to look at her records today," Monks said. But he doubted that D'Anton would have missed something like that.

"There's only one other thing I can think of that might have had that general effect," Roman said. "Some kind of toxic substance."

Monks focused a click. Toxins had been listed as a possible cause of DIC, but he hadn't given it much thought. So soon after the surgery, Eden would have eaten little or nothing.

"Such as?" Monks said.

"I thought about a contaminated drug."

So had Monks. "Everything the paramedics brought in was prescription, or looked that way," he said. "Pharmaceutically stamped pills." A bad batch was possible but highly unlikely. She might have taken something homemade. But both men were very familiar with the effects of street drugs, including those cut with dangerous fillers, like strychnine in heroin. And anything common would have shown up on the tox screen.

"What else?" Monks said.

"Not something you'd find around the house. I'd recognize anything from cleaning fluids to rat poison. Maybe in agriculture, or industry. She wasn't involved in anything like that, was she?"

Monks felt the insane urge to laugh. "Industry, but not that kind."

"What do you mean?"

"She was an adult film actress. Look, she was recovering from surgery. She'd have gone straight home from the clinic. She wouldn't have been out wandering around."

"Any indications that she was suicidal?"

Monks had never spoken with Eden Hale, never seen her really alive. There might have been a dark, despairing side to her. But it didn't jibe with what he knew, and it didn't seem to follow that a woman who had just gone through an expensive, painful treatment to become more beautiful would want to kill herself immediately afterward. Particularly in a protracted, agonizing way.

"No," he said. "Not yet, anyway."

"Well, I'm afraid that's not much help," Roman said. "I can run more tests or request the city coroner to. But it's tough when I don't know what I'm looking for."

"You think anything will turn up on the autopsy?"

"It'll bear out the DIC, Carroll. But I wouldn't hang too much on anything more." Roman hesitated, then said, "Just on the off chance it did turn out to be some particularly virulent strain of salmonella, was your treatment consistent with that?"

Monks pushed his plate away and leaned his elbows on the table, pressing the heels of his hands into his eyes.

"The intial phase was," he said. "Somebody comes in dehydrated and bleeding in an unknown location, you start by replacing fluid volume, then blood. Next step is to locate the source of the bleeding and treat that—if you can. That's where I diverged."

"Diverged how?"

"There was no way to treat it, except to try to break up the clotting. I gave her heparin."

"Seems reasonable to me," Roman said.

"If you look at it that way, yes. But going by the book—about the last thing you want to do with something like salmonella is thin the blood."

Monks took the elevator up to Baird Necker's office. This time he was uninvited.

His mind was stepping up its analysis, reviewing what he knew, eliminating some possibilities and considering others further. It was a little more satisfying with the new information, although still frustrating as hell.

Salmonella was a bacteria, a prime cause of what was generically called food poisoning. There were several exotic strains and modes of infection, but by far the most common cases seen in the States came from ingesting tainted food. Poultry was a major carrier.

Salmonella didn't cause clotting, but the opposite—if it was advanced enough, there was copious intestinal bleeding, discharged via characteristic bouts of bloody diarrhea. Usually there wasn't much that could be done, beyond replacing fluids and blood, and keeping the patient stable until the attack ran its course. With proper treatment, the disease was rarely fatal.

In short, if he had not given Eden Hale the heparin, he would be safely off the hook now. She would have died anyway, and the cause of the DIC might remain forever a mystery. But no one would be able to point a finger at Monks and accuse him of doing the wrong thing.

It was futile to think about whether he could have stood there and let her go, without trying *something*. That way lay madness.

But he had seen plenty of salmonella, and whether this was some new super mutant or the plain old garden variety, he still couldn't believe it was responsible. Something else, some terrible unseen pump inside her, had driven all her bloodstream's clotting factors into the smaller vessels, leaving the larger ones to bleed unchecked.

He thought about what Roman had said. His mind turned the word *toxin* over and over. But how the hell would she have gotten into something that virulent, and rare enough that it wouldn't show up on the tox screen, or be recognized by a highly experienced pathologist?

He had to admit: if he was looking at himself objectively, he would have seen a man clutching at straws.

"There's a new wrinkle," Monks said to Baird, and told him about the conversation with Roman.

"Salmonella, huh?" Baird said. "I wouldn't think she'd have been hungry, that soon after surgery."

"It only takes a taste. She probably wasn't thinking too clearly, with the Valium. Maybe she nibbled at something, chicken salad from a deli that she'd kept too long. Maybe her boyfriend will know. Did you know he was supposed to stay with her at least twenty-four hours, but he left her alone?"

"He seems like a putz, no argument there. But that doesn't have anything to do with us. This is escalating, Carroll. The young lady's mother and father were here yesterday. They're stunned. They didn't even know she was having the breast surgery."

Monks felt another heavy brick settle onto the load. He had a troubled son of his own, last heard of living on the streets of Seattle. But so far, no one had called on Monks to tell him that his child had died in a hospital far from home and family.

"I got the pretty clear sense that they're not going to make things easy," Baird said. "I told them there were complications that haven't been identified yet. Her father got seriously pissed off. They more or less walked out."

"I could explain it to them more clearly."

"I don't think that would do any good. By the way, one of your nurses has also commented that she didn't think the heparin was appropriate. She says she questioned it at the time."

"With all due respect to Mary Helfert," Monks said, "she's not a physician, and she's certainly not qualified to provide an emergency diagnosis. She didn't know what DIC *was*."

"It's another thing that doesn't help," Baird said. "I'm starting to look at damage control. If it comes to that, I hope you'll cooperate."

"Meaning, stand still and take the blame?"

"Nobody said anything about blame. But if we had to settle out."

"Before we start convicting, Baird, let's wait till the jury's in. Autopsy, final lab, and tox screen. Her history, any preexisting conditions. And there's still a possibility that this is related to the surgery."

Baird looked away, drumming his fingers on his desk. "D'Anton called me again—told me you went by his clinic. I wish you hadn't done that."

"Why the hell not? Physicians consult with each other when they're treating the same patient. Besides which, the surgery's going to be examined in the postmortem. It's not like there's any secret involved."

"I don't want to bring him into this."

A sour taste rose in Monks's mouth. "An ER doc is expendable," he said. "But not your golden boy–cash cow plastic surgeon?"

"I've got to think of the hospital, Carroll. He's world famous."

"There doesn't seem to be any doubt in anybody's mind about that. Especially his."

"He's bringing in millions of dollars' worth of business to this place. Which helps cover what the ER loses."

Monks's eyes widened in outrage. "The ER's in the business of healing the sick. Not scheduled elective surgery."

"Knock off the self-righteous bullshit. Are you telling me reconstructive surgery's not important?"

"I have all the respect in the world for reconstructive surgeons," Monks said. "But D'Anton caters to rich women's vanity. Period."

"People are entitled to any kind of health care that makes them feel good."

"As long as they can pay for it?"

"This hospital cannot operate as a charity," Baird said, speaking the words one angry syllable at a time. It was a line Monks had heard him say many times.

"Not to mention the fact that the ER provides sixty percent of all admissions, plus lab and other spin-offs," Monks said. "Which makes it possible for this hospital to survive, no matter what your bean-counter computer programs say."

"If they come in electively, they pay for what they get." Baird's forefinger jabbed at Monks's chest, an imaginary skewer. "But in the ER, we've *got* to take them whether they pay or not. So a lot of the time, they don't."

"We should start letting them die in the streets? Have the feds and the state close us down?"

There was a pause. Monks realized that they had both almost been shouting.

Baird pushed his chair back and stood up. "Let's cool off. This isn't doing either of us any good."

Several responses flashed through Monks's mind, but they all rang of adolescent bluster. Baird was right—this was not doing any good.

He left without speaking, went outside, and leaned against the building in the shade. It occurred to him that a red beer would taste just fine. He heaved himself off the wall and started walking to a bar called Charley's, just two short blocks away.

Charley's was an old-fashioned tavern, a long narrow room with a scarred bar, a burger grill, and worn vinyl booths. It was quiet, dark, inviting, the kind of place where you could easily spend a day or three.

But by the time he was inside, Monks had calmed down. There was too much going on. He could not afford a dull mind. He got a club soda and took it to a booth at the back.

He tried to decide which was justified—his anger at being sold down the river, the queasy feeling that he might, in fact, have mishandled the incident—or the even queasier one that a slick attorney could make it *look* like he had. He started assessing potential targets of liability.

First, chronologically, came D'Anton. But Roman had ruled out a surgical infection. The possibility of some other condition that D'Anton had not checked for, or had ignored, was not likely.

D'Anton had given Eden the Valium. It had probably factored in, by keeping her sedated—she might have called for help earlier, otherwise. But there was no direct connection to the death. His prescription was within reasonable limits, and it was not his responsibility to see that the drugs were used properly after she left the clinic.

Unless something damning turned up in the records or the autopsy, D'Anton was in the clear.

Next came Ray Dreyer, the fiancé. He had agreed to care for her for twenty-four hours after the surgery. But he was not a professional, not operating under any license or bonding. He might be liable to some degree, but on a personal level.

Then there was Monks.

For lawyers, the issue was clear. When someone undergoing medical treatment was injured or died, someone else was to blame. The simple rule for malpractice went: there had to be negligence, there had to be injury, and the negligence had to have caused or contributed to the injury.

Assuming that the DIC was, in fact, the cause of

death, Monks was also in the clear legally. Nothing he'd done had contributed to that.

But if a procedure was seen as questionable or simply unnecessary—such as administering the heparin—that was still sufficient grounds for an attorney to file a deep-pockets lawsuit, in the hopes that the hospital would settle out, for a hefty sum.

And Monks's name would be entered in a national registry of physicians who had tacitly admitted to negligence—tarred forever by that brush.

He walked back inside to a house phone and put out a page for Dick Speidel, the chairman of the Emergency Room's Quality Assurance committee.

Monks was in luck—Dick Speidel answered the page. Speidel was also an ER doc, so he didn't keep regular hours, and he wasn't on shift today. But he acted as liaison between the emergency group—a self-contained corporation that contracted with Mercy Hospital—and the hospital's administration, so he tended to be around quite a bit on business.

Monks met him in front of the ER's main entrance. Speidel was about Monks's age, a big bearlike man with thick dark hair and kind, cynical eyes. Like most longtime emergency personnel, he was under no illusions about textbook situations versus bloody, desperate, real ones.

"I need to make it clear, I'm speaking to you in your capacity as QA chair," Monks said. This made the conversation official business: the information exchanged was not available to any outsider, except by subpoena.

Speidel's eyebrows rose. "Nuclear secrets? Terrorist attacks?"

"I've got a Death Review coming up."

Speidel nodded. Word had already gotten around.

The hospital's Quality Assurance system, QA for short, reviewed all internal mishaps and mistakes, from medical errors to people slipping and falling. Everything that happened under its auspices was undiscoverable by the courts—its privacy was protected, including, especially, from lawyers. All personnel, from the chief of staff on down through janitorial, were under a strict injunction of confidentiality. Bribery and ratting did happen, but not often. This maintained rigorous honesty without vulnerability; it was the hospital's method of self-policing and self-educating. Like all systems, it had its flaws, but in Monks's experience, it worked remarkably well.

Eden Hale's Death Review was going through the QA system's standard channels. It was clearly the Emergency Room's case, and up to the ER committee's chair, Speidel, to assign another, nontreating ER physician—not Monks—to review it. The Medical Records department would provide all pertinent information. That physician would then fill out a form, answering three questions: Given the circumstances, was the outcome predictable? Was the treatment within the standard of care? Does this case need review by the full QA committee?

Monks wanted to know what his peers thought—what they would have done in his place; whether he was justified or damned.

"I'd like you to expedite the review, Dick," Monks said. "If it does go to committee, to do it this month instead of next."

Speidel frowned. "That's next Monday, Carroll."

"I know it's a lot to ask."

"Are you kidding? Most guys would put it off indefinitely and hope it went away. I just meant I'm not sure if I have time. I haven't even assigned it yet."

"If I screwed up, I want to know it," Monks said. "The hospital ought to know it, too. There are rumblings about litigation."

Speidel gazed off at the ocean. Monks knew that as liaison and QA chair, he would be acutely concerned about any situation that might reflect badly on the ER.

"All right," Speidel said. "If you don't have any objections, I'll do the initial review myself."

"That's more than fine with me."

"I'll let you know tomorrow morning."

Speidel went back inside. Monks stayed there for a minute, deciding what to do next. A distant fog bank was forming on the horizon, like a mirage. It offered a teasing promise of cooler air. That would be a blessing.

*   *   *

Ray Dreyer's phone number wasn't listed. But he had logged in at the ER desk yesterday. Monks coaxed the charge nurse into looking up his address and phone.

It was almost nine A.M. now, but he was reasonably sure that Dreyer was not an eight-to-fiver. If anything, the call might wake him up.

After four rings, a digital voice answered. *"The person you are calling is not available right now—"* It seemed that Dreyer wanted to stay anonymous.

Monks waited for the beep, then said, "Mr. Dreyer, this is Dr. Monks. I attended Eden Hale—"

The phone clicked, and a male voice said, "Yeah, I remember."

So Dreyer was screening calls, too. His tone made it clear that he was not feeling any friendlier. Monks decided to forget about social graces and get right to it.

"It turns out that Eden had salmonella in her bloodstream. Food poisoning. Any ideas how she might have gotten that?"

"Hey, I don't know what she ate," Dreyer said. "She had stuff in the refrigerator."

"You didn't stop anyplace after the clinic? A deli, takeout?"

"Uh-uh. We went straight back to her apartment."

"Did Eden keep anything around, like chemicals?"

Dreyer's tone turned wary, probably from worry

about recreational drugs. "What kind of chemicals?"

"Insecticides?" Monks said. "Photography equipment, heavy-duty cleaning fluids?"

Dreyer laughed thinly. "She never cleaned anything in her life, except when she took a bath. There's about five tons of makeup, if that counts."

It was a tender sentiment for a lost love.

"What about drugs?" Monks said. "This is just between us. Did she take anything besides the Valium the doctor gave her?"

"No way, man. All she wanted to do was crash."

And so she had, Monks thought.

"Okay, thanks," he said. "We're still working on this."

"So am I," Dreyer said mysteriously.

Monks hung up, walked back out to his battered Bronco, and drove to D'Anton's clinic.

15

The clinic's parking lot was almost empty this morning, but the front door was unlocked. When Monks pushed it open, Gwen Bricknell was busy at her desk—exactly as he had last seen her yesterday, except that she was wearing an eggshell-colored dress of light, fine cotton. Monks was not much of a judge of women's clothing, or men's for that matter, but he had a feeling that it was the kind of simple attire that was very expensive. The room was otherwise deserted. When he walked to the desk he caught the scent of her perfume, very faint, musky rather than sweet.

He did not expect her to be friendly, and he was

surprised when she smiled and said, "Good morning, Dr. Monks."

He murmured hello, struck again by her sheer beauty. If there was any flaw, it was flawlessness—as if, when D'Anton had sculpted her face, he had razored off the imperfections that lent humanness.

But her eyes, dark like olives, were alive—wary, but not hard with hostility. If anything, she seemed a little frightened. The shock of Eden Hale's death had had time to sink in, he thought. This was not the ER; losing a patient was not something that happened with inevitable regularity.

"We're closed, officially," she said. "I'm just rescheduling appointments."

"Dr. D'Anton was going to leave some records for me. Sorry if this is bad timing."

"No, no, it's fine. Welles—Dr. D'Anton—is taking a couple of days off. He asked me to make you at home. He apologizes for being abrasive yesterday. He was very upset."

"Understandable, of course," Monks said.

"I know this is awkward, Doctor," she said, surprising him again. "I don't mean for it to be."

"I appreciate that, Ms. Bricknell," he said. "I don't like it either. But I need to find out what happened to that young woman."

For the next couple of seconds, Monks had the eerie sensation that whoever was behind Gwen Bricknell's eyes had gone—that he was looking at an absolutely still body whose owner was someplace else. By the time he was aware of it, she was back.

"I'll get the records," she said. She stood and opened the door into the rear office, started to step through, and stopped abruptly.

Monks realized that the nurse, Phyllis, was walking past, just on the other side of the door.

Gwen's shoulders sagged in exasperation. "Phyllis, you are everywhere I *turn*."

"I cover a lot of ground," Phyllis said crisply. "Somebody has to."

"There's really no need for you to be here today."

"There's always a need for me to be here." Phyllis marched swifty on, a squarish, formidable presence. Gwen glanced back at Monks, rolling her eyes.

"She surprised me, too, yesterday," he said.

"She's incredibly competent. She does most of the low-level procedures. It's almost like having another doctor. But sometimes she decides she's in charge, especially when Welles isn't around."

Gwen went on into the office, leaving the door open. Monks glimpsed another figure, down the hallway that opened onto the procedure rooms. It was the maintenance man, Todd, apparently still at work on the air-conditioning. He raised a hand in cheerful greeting. Monks returned it.

Gwen came back a minute later, with a manila folder clasped in her hands. Her fingers were long and slender, tipped by crimson ovals. She did not wear a wedding ring.

134

"I wish I had such devoted staff," Monks said. "Coming to work when the clinic's closed."

"Todd's a gem," she said. "He can fix anything. That's how we found him. He was working at Bayview Hospital, and Welles came out one day and his Jaguar wouldn't start. Todd just happened to be there and got it going. Now we can't do without him. He's like that character on *M*A*S*H*, what's his name? Who always knows what everybody needs ahead of time?"

"Radar," Monks said.

"Well, that's Todd."

She walked ahead of him to one of the screened-off waiting rooms. Her dress was almost translucent, clearly outlining her body. It was an odd sensation, following her past the nude photos of herself on the wall. They had obviously been taken years ago, but she did not seem to have changed much. Eden Hale must have coveted those breasts, Monks thought. They were peach-sized, high and firm. No doubt, they, too, had been enhanced by D'Anton's touch.

At the waiting room's door, Gwen turned to him and offered him the folder. But she held on to it for just a second, so that there was a curious little tug of war between them before she let go.

Monks was reevaluating fast. Apparently, she did not hold grudges.

He sat in one of the comfortable chairs and opened the folder. It contained a standard sheaf of medical records. He paged through Eden Hale's history. It was clean, as they tended to be with young affluent patients; even things like chickenpox and measles rarely appeared these days. She had had persistent ear infections, requiring occasional draining and antibiotic treatment, until age eleven. There were no allergies or adverse reactions to drugs, no operations or broken bones. Her blood work showed her to be O positive, with no diseases, and white cell count well within the normal range.

A copy of D'Anton's chart from the breast procedure confirmed that it was an augmentation, using saline-filled implants, inserted through endoscopic incisions in the armpits. Most of the chart was a checklist, in technical jargon and abbreviations. Monks was not familiar with all the terms, but D'Anton's terse, handwritten notes at the bottom confirmed that the procedure had been routine and had gone smoothly. All in all, the records were thorough and excellent, the work of a top-notch professional.

There was a copy of her discharge form, the same form that the paramedics had found in her purse. It contained postoperative instructions—no strenuous activity, sponge baths only for five to seven days, sexual relations permitted to resume after that time provided the breasts were treated gently—and it stipulated that the patient must be cared for by a competent adult for at least twenty-four hours afterward. This was signed underneath with a scrawl that

Monks was able to read only because he already knew the name: Raymond L. Dreyer.

Finally, there were photographs—several of her face, both full on and in profile, others of her nude upper body, and a few close-ups of her breasts. Another set of images, computer-generated, appeared to be the projected results. These showed the breasts enlarged, shapely, prominent. They also showed a modified face, with nose and cheekbones sculpted into graceful lines—eliminating the hint of coarseness Monks had noticed.

It seemed that the planned makeover on Eden Hale had only started.

He looked again at the discharge form, under method of payment. It was checked CASH.

Monks stacked the sheets and put them back into the folder. There was no suggestion of anything other than that Eden had left here healthy. He hadn't really expected there to be. Any possibility that the records had been altered was extremely unlikely.

He walked back to the desk and gave Gwen the file.

"I'm sure you get told this a lot," he said. "I've seen your face many times. TV, magazines."

She raised a hand and pointed, with a *voilà* gesture, at the room's photo display of nudes.

"Yes?" she said, with just a hint of a smile now—a model advertising something intimate. "It seems like you've gotten a pretty good look at the rest of me, too."

"I'm an admirer of beauty," Monks said.

Her expression changed subtly, with a flicker of pleasure passing across her eyes before they lowered. It was a shameless thing to say, Monks knew. But, even calculated, it gave him a pleasant shot of electricity.

He'd spent a fair amount of time last night, during those sleepless hours, remembering his clear sense that Julia D'Anton had known Eden Hale, and that Gwen had wanted to hide it.

He did not want to confront her. It was probably nothing, and he would probably never see her again. But just in case there turned out to be some little scratch on D'Anton's Teflon surface after all, Monks wanted to keep Gwen Bricknell friendly, willing to talk.

"I'm glad we were able to help you, Dr. Monks," she said, her gaze returning to meet his own. "If there's anything more I can do, let me know."

16

Monks drove to North Beach, following Stover Larrabee's directions to a meeting place. Today, that place was a beat-up blue van with ON THE SPOT PLUMBING lettered on the side, parked on Stockton, a couple of blocks north of Columbus. Several lengths of copper and PVC pipes were strapped to the rack on the van's top. The back was filled with scarred toolboxes and bins of fittings. A couple of pairs of greasy Carhartt overalls hung from hooks.

That was all cover. The van was also outfitted with camcorders, telephoto equipment, a parabolic microphone, bugs and sweepers, and a full set of lock picks.

Larrabee was hunched forward with his forearms over the steering wheel when Monks got in. He had a pair of Leica binoculars in his lap. A small TV set with the sound off was playing the *Today* show. A couple of crossword puzzle books and paperbacks lay on the floor, along with a thermos of coffee and a trucker's jug to urinate into. The van was positioned to give a good view downhill.

"Fucking surveillance," Larrabee said. "Every time I take one on, I swear, never again."

It was only midmorning, but the streets were already happening, with crowds cruising the cafés and souvenir stores. With the warm weather, there was much flesh on display. Obvious tourists tended toward shorts and tank tops or T-shirts of the *I'm with Stupid* variety. Local skin was likely to be pierced or tattooed, and topped by hair of colors not found in nature. It occurred to Monks that this was an alternative plastic surgery, for those on tight budgets or who wanted to make a more radical statement.

"What's the venue?" Monks said.

"This guy comes to me. Ernesto, he's Panamanian, a little hotheaded. He's got some bucks, and a good-looking wife. But he goes to a business convention, and meets another babe he decides is the love of his life. Comes back home and tells his wife he's leaving her. This all happens within a week, now.

"So needless to say, his wife, she's Latina, too, she goes ballistic, and *she* goes out and picks up a

musician, a guy who lives down there"—Larrabee
pointed at a row of apartment buildings downhill—
"and fucks *him*. He's ten years younger than her, but
it seems to actually take—it's been going on a couple months now.

"Meantime, the husband starts to realize that
maybe the new babe isn't it after all. He decides he
wants his wife back, but she tells him to piss up a
rope. On top of that, he figures he's going to lose his
ass in the divorce. So he hires me to follow her and
photograph her with her guy. That way, he can claim
she's the one who broke up the marriage."

"He can?"

"If he can get divorced in Panama, which is what
he's planning, maybe," Larrabee said. "I don't particularly care. He's paying me a thousand bucks a
day plus expenses. But sometimes, I get involved in
this kind of idiot shit, I think of a lot of other ways I
could have made a living." Larrabee shook his head,
face wry. "So? What's going on with you?"

Monks brought him up to date. When he finished,
Larrabee turned off the TV. He put the binoculars to
his eyes and focused on the building where Ernesto
hoped to catch his wife and her paramour in fla-
grante delicto.

"Has it crossed your mind that this might not
have been an accident?" Larrabee asked.

Monks blinked. "You mean murder? No. Not
really."

"I'm just putting together what you've told me,"

Larrabee said, still scanning through the glasses. "She was a healthy young woman; she shouldn't have died. The DIC thing is very mysterious. Dr. Kasmarek thinks it could have been caused by a toxic substance, but it would have to be an unusual one—like, somebody deliberately chose it so it wouldn't be identified. She was alone the last several hours, and dopey, so it would have been easy to slip it to her."

He lowered the binoculars again and slouched back in his seat.

"And it sounds like those women at the clinic know more than they're telling," he said.

"It's still a long way from there to murder."

"This girl was not exactly Suzy Creamcheese," Larrabee said. "Not criminal, but money trouble. I ran quickie background checks on her and Dreyer. Bad credit reports, and they ran out on their rent in a couple of places down in LA. I keep wondering where she was getting all that money. Paying cash for the city's most expensive plastic surgeon."

"You think she could have been blackmailing somebody?"

"All I think so far is that there's several things that are *off*," Larrabee said. "What do you say we go take a look around her apartment?"

"A look for what?"

"Just a look. I doubt we'll find anything. It's a place to start, is all."

"Her fiancé said there were no chemicals—nothing like that."

"You can't take that guy's word for anything. Remember, he was the last one with her."

"It doesn't make sense that he'd have wanted to hurt her," Monks said. "He talked about her like she was his bank account. He was outraged that he'd been ripped off."

"You never know. Could be he's smarter than you're giving him credit for, and that's what he wants everybody to think. Maybe she was cheating on him, or costing him money some way he couldn't get out from under."

"You're not figuring on breaking in, are you?" Monks said warily. He had helped Larrabee do so in the past, and it had scared the shit out of him.

Larrabee grinned. "Relax. Her boyfriend said the building had a super, right? For a doctor and a private investigator—I'm betting he'd open it up."

"What about the lady you're supposed to be surveilling?"

"I've already got several photos of her and this guy together on the street. I was hoping maybe they'd get frisky this morning and leave the shade up, but there's nothing happening in there." Larrabee shrugged. "Ernesto wants more, that's another thousand bucks."

They drove to Eden Hale's apartment, on Twenty-fifth Avenue, near Irving Street.

* * *

The building was not luxurious, but it was nice—
several stories of whitish concrete, post-war, with a
glass-doored lobby and small but-well kept grounds.
Most of the apartments had a view, with the north-
facing ones overlooking Golden Gate Park.

"What do you figure these go for?" Larrabee said.
"Couple grand a month, minimum?"

Monks nodded. Minimum.

They rang the outside bell for the superintendent.
He appeared after a minute, an earnest-looking Hispanic man who could have been forty or sixty.
Monks and Larrabee showed him their respective
licenses, while Larrabee explained that they would
like to look around Ms. Hale's apartment for just a
few minutes. A twenty-dollar bill was artfully pre-
sented, and accepted, in the process.

The super took them up to the third floor and
down a quiet hallway. "Her mother and father came
here yesterday," he said, taking out keys. "They took
some things, her personal stuff, you know. They
gonna send a mover for the furniture." His serious
brown eyes looked from one to the other of them.
"There some kind of trouble here?"

"No," Larrabee said. "Just some questions we're
trying to clear up. Wait, if you want. We won't take
long."

The apartment was a one-bedroom, beige-
carpeted, with a couch, coffee table, dining set, and
a few other pieces of furniture. There was a home

entertainment center, with TV, VCR, and stereo, and two cordless phones, one in the front room and one by the bed. It was all good quality, and new. But it was oddly impersonal, giving the feel of a waiting room rather than a place where someone actually lived.

If there had been any photographs or other personal touches, they had been removed. The queen-sized bed had been stripped and the bathroom and medicine cabinet cleared. Monks kept an eye out for bloodstains, in case the paramedics had underreported her blood loss, and the salmonella had been more advanced than it had seemed. But there was nothing he could see on the carpet, and the couple of faint small stains on the mattress had the look of dried menstrual bleeding.

There was nothing under the sink but dish soap, a couple of sponges, and a spray bottle of 409. The refrigerator was empty, and the plastic trash can contained only a few crumpled, makeup-smeared tissues. Monks suspected that these had come from Eden's distraught mother. Whatever Eden might have eaten to give her the salmonella was gone.

Only two things remained that gave a sense of Eden herself. One was her reading material— dozens of issues of *Cosmopolitan,* other women's magazines, and fashion catalogs, stacked on tables or just lying around. The other was her clothes. One closet was stuffed, bristling with outfits that looked wild, sexy—on the cutting edge of fashion, he supposed, for the circle she had moved in. At least twenty pairs of shoes spilled out of a basket and littered the floor, with spike heels and boots predominant. Her lingerie drawer was another echo, packed with bras and panties that tended toward the colorfully skimpy.

But the other closet was a surprise. It had only a dozen outfits, dresses and blouse-skirt combinations, neatly hung. These were much more conservative, the sort of things professional women picked out carefully at exclusive shops. They looked mostly unworn, with the tags still on.

Larrabee looked at this closet longer than he had the other one. Then he turned back to the super, who was waiting politely in the doorway.

"Has anybody else been here?" Larrabee asked. "Besides her parents?"

The super shook his head. "Just the ambulance guys."

"How about her boyfriend? He said he talked to you that morning."

"Yeah, but I just told him what happened and he went straight to the hospital."

"You're sure he hasn't been back since?" Larrabee said.

"He don't have keys."

Larrabee stared. "No kidding? The guy she was going to marry?"

"She didn't want him coming around all the time.

She told me. I think they fought about it, you know?"

"I guess they would," Larrabee said. "How long did she live here?"

The super thought about it. "Maybe four months."

"Any other regular visitors?"

"It didn't seem like it. I'm not here all the time, you know. But I don't think she had, like, girlfriends or anything."

"Do you know where she worked?"

"She told me she's a model. But it seemed like mostly when she went out, she went shopping. Or at night."

"With her boyfriend?"

"Sometimes. Sometimes alone."

"No other men friends?"

"Nobody I saw."

Larrabee nodded, apparently satisfied with what he had gotten. "Okay. We may be back." Another twenty-dollar bill appeared and disappeared. "Thanks again."

"*Nada,*" the super said.

Outside in the van, Larrabee started the engine. "Looks to me like she was trying to change her life," he said. "Going from a bad girl to a good one. A new, upscale wardrobe. And no key for the old boyfriend."

Dreyer had used the term *fiancé*, but that could mean a lot of things, and it was looking like it had meant something different to him than to her. Or he might just have been lying. It seemed clear that she had been distancing herself from him.

"I got that, too," Monks said. "But not much else."

"Yeah, but there's something that *wasn't* there. An answering machine."

"Her parents could have taken it," Monks said. But he remembered that the phones themselves were still there. It seemed odd that they would take just the machine.

"Maybe," Larrabee said. "Or she had one of those voice-mail services. But if she *did* have a machine, especially if it was digital, which just about all of them are these days, the messages are likely to be recoverable, even if they've been erased."

"What are you saying?"

"Just my evil mind at work. Wondering if somebody else snagged it—afraid their voice might get identified."

"Dreyer?"

"Maybe there was something on there he got worried about. Like they'd argued, and he threatened her. He could have taken it that night, while she was knocked out. Or made copies of her keys, and come back when the super wasn't around. You got his address?"

Monks checked in his shirt pocket and pulled out the slip of paper he had copied from the Emergency Room.

"Haver Street. Looks like a few blocks west of Van Ness."

Larrabee leaned out the window to check the side mirror, then pulled into traffic.

"I can't wait to meet him," Larrabee said.

17

Ray Dreyer's building was a very different order of business from Eden Hale's—an old Victorian that had been chopped up into apartments, like a lot of others in the area, and like many of them, down-at-heels. The street was lined with distinctly unglamorous cars, the sidewalk cracked and gummy. The apartment windows were not open to the light and filled with plants, like in some of the city's other areas. Most were heavily curtained. In the entry, there was an old intercom system that looked defunct. Dreyer's name was not listed next to any of the buzzers, anyway. Only a couple names were.

They got back in Larrabee's van and punched

Dreyer's number on the speakerphone. The same machine answered as last time.

"It's Dr. Monks, Ray. Pick up if you're there. This is important."

The phone clicked. Dreyer said, "Yeah?" in a tone that managed to sound both indolent and impatient.

"I'm outside your place," Monks said. "I want to come in and talk to you."

"What about?"

"Eden."

"We talked about Eden. I got nothing more to say."

"Some new questions have come up," Monks said.

"You can tell them to my lawyer. You're going to be talking to him anyway."

"*I'm* going to be talking to *your* lawyer? What about?"

"I'm filing a wrongful-death suit against you, dude."

Monks stared at the phone in his hand, then dropped it on the seat and yanked open the van's door. Larrabee grabbed his arm.

"Hang on," Larrabee hissed into his ear. "You can beat the shit out of him as soon as we get inside."

Larrabee picked up the phone. "You're going to need a lawyer all right, Ray, but not for the reason you think."

"Who's this?" Dreyer said suspiciously.

"I'm a private investigator who used to be a cop, and I can have you in jail within an hour."

"That's bullshit." His voice was scornful, but working at it.

"She was murdered, Ray, we're sure of that now," Larrabee lied.

"*Mur*dered?"

"And you were the last one with her."

"You're fucking crazy," Dreyer said.

Larrabee did not speak. The silence lasted perhaps ten seconds.

"What good's it going to do me, talking to you?" Dreyer said.

"I'm sick of sitting out here. Open the door, or not."

Monks watched the building door steadily, his brain on hold.

"I'll buzz you in," Dreyer finally said. "It's number seven, third floor."

The stairway was scarred old oak, spacious, and once even grand, but now musty with the smell of invisible lives. The door to apartment number seven was open. It was a studio, with worn, stained carpet of a bilious green, an unmade Murphy bed, and a few pieces of cheap old furniture. There was a lot of stuff strewn around.

Ray Dreyer was standing in the middle of it, arms folded, head cocked to one side—challenging. He was wearing the kind of nylon jogging suit favored by those who never jogged and had a cigarette toward the corner of his mouth, in a sort of James Dean imitation.

Monks went in first and walked toward him, in a steady, even stride. On the last step, he swung his open left hand from his waist, coming hard off that foot, pivoting his hips with the swing, and then snapping them back. His palm landed across the side of Dreyer's face with a jolt Monks felt to his shoulder. It picked Dreyer up in the air, half turned him, and set him down facing the other direction. The cigarette went flying across the room and bounced off a wall. When he landed, he lurched another couple of steps with the momentum, hands flailing for something to grab. He caught hold of a threadbare couch, used it to turn himself clumsily around, and came scrabbling back toward Monks.

"You cocksucker!" he screamed, fists clenched. "I'm having you arrested!"

Monks stood without moving, hands ready, breathing heavily.

Larrabee, unperturbed, walked to the smoking cigarette and ground it into the carpet with his heel. Then he sat on a corner of a table, one foot dangling. He opened his wallet and held it at eye level, showing his license.

"Let me explain to you how this is going to go, Ray," Larrabee said. "First off, Eden dumped you to move up here. Wouldn't even give you a key to her new place. You came after her anyway. That's called stalking.

"Then you let her die. If you'd been with her, like you were legally obligated to be, she'd have gotten to the hospital on time.

"And now, you're trying to turn a *profit* on it. You got any idea how all that's going to look?"

Dreyer clapped his own hand to the reddening side of his face, then stared at it, as if he expected to see it dripping with blood. The look in his eyes was extremely ugly, but he was not making any more moves to fight.

"We're your *friends*," Larrabee said. "We might be able to help you, *if* you tell us the truth. Believe me, the cops won't help. They like things to get tied up nice and neat."

"I'm very afraid, man," he spat out with bitter sarcasm.

"I would be if I was you," Larrabee said. "And in prison, Ray, a good-looking guy like you—let's just say your dance card's going to stay full."

"Hey, I didn't *do* anything. She was my fiancée."

"Yeah, you keep saying that. Seems like she saw it differently."

Monks was feeling better. In fact, a lot better. He relaxed, stepped away, took a look around the place. Among the litter of clothes and junk, there was a fair amount of photography equipment. One corner of the room was piled waist-high with stacks of contact sheets and photos. Not surprisingly, most of the ones Monks glimpsed were of women.

"I can't believe this," Dreyer muttered.

"Believe it," Larrabee said. "Let's start with something simple. Did you take the phone answering machine from her apartment?"

"Why the fuck would I do that? Are you telling me somebody did?"

"I'm *asking* you if *you* did," Larrabee said. "Just like the cops will."

"The last time I was in there was when I took her home from the clinic. Everything was just the same as always."

"Where'd you go when you left her?"

"Why is that important?" Dreyer said. His belligerent gaze shifted evasively.

"It's called an alibi," Larrabee said patiently.

Dreyer sat abruptly on the couch, shoulders sagging. His hands clasped together between his knees, fingers pulling at each other.

"There's this woman, an actress. She's fan-fucking-tastic, drop-dead gorgeous. You'd recognize her name."

"Why don't you tell us?"

Dreyer hesitated, but then said—proudly, Monks thought—"She goes by Coffee."

Larrabee nodded, but Monks drew a blank. "*I* don't recognize it," he said.

Dreyer snorted in disgusted disbelief.

"Coffee Trenette. She made a big splash about ten years ago," Larrabee explained. "A movie called *Take Me*. Haven't heard much about her since."

"She had a little drug problem," Dreyer said.

"She came up to San Fran to get away from it. I'd worked with her a few times, back when. She called me up, the day Eden had the surgery."

"How did she know you were in town?"

"Eden ran into her somewhere, a couple months ago."

"Okay, she called you. And?"

"She'd found out her boyfriend was messing around. She said, 'I'm in the mood for a revenge fuck. Is it going to be you?' I told her I had to stay with Eden. She said, 'Then I'll find somebody else.'

"I told her, whoa, wait, I'll be there. Eden was out of it anyway. I figured I'd slip over to Coffee's for a couple of hours. But she wouldn't let me go home. Kept cutting lines of coke. Coming up with more sex things she wanted to do."

"A really *thorough* revenge fuck, huh?" Larrabee said.

"It was thorough, dude." Dreyer smirked. "Believe me."

Monks walked to a window and leaned against the jamb. It overlooked a scrabbly, garbage-strewn dirt yard where even the weeds seemed to be having a tough go of it. A decrepit wooden fence topped with razor wire surrounded it, but enough boards had been kicked out to make the yard a no-man's-land anyway.

You couldn't actually say that lust had killed Eden Hale, but it was a decisive link in a chain. In fact, it seemed to figure into several links.

Larrabee said, "Where did you think Eden was getting the money for her apartment?"

"She said she inherited a chunk. A rich aunt."

"And instead of cutting you in, she moved out."

"She *wanted* me to come up here. I wasn't stalking her, for Christ's sake. We were still *together,* she just needed some space."

"Were you still managing her?"

"I was trying, but it's been tough. And she was taking time off for the surgery. I've mainly been marketing my images." Dreyer flapped his hands in frustration. "I've gone all over this town, knocking on doors. Back in LA, I was connected. But I can't make shit here, and the rents suck. Look at this dump. Twelve hundred bucks a month."

"That's not so bad, if you're going to run out on it anyway."

"Hey, *fuck* you, man. Where'd you get that bullshit?"

"From back where you were so connected," Larrabee said. "What was Eden planning to do next?"

"Same thing she'd always done. Acting, modeling."

"Did it ever occur to you that she wasn't being straight with you? About that money?"

"What do you mean?" Dreyer looked from one to the other of them. If he knew the truth he was doing a good job of hiding it. "Jesus Christ, what are you talking about?"

Larrabee ignored the question. "Anybody else who might have had a serious problem with Eden? Think hard, Ray. Fingering somebody could be important for you."

"Nobody with *that* serious a problem."

"How about from the old days, when she was doing the porn?"

"That's history. Besides, we didn't fuck anybody over. The other way around."

Larrabee stood. "You better give us Ms. Trenette's address. We'll need to confirm that you were with her."

"Oh, *man,* do you have to? She'll never talk to me again."

"Yeah, well, you'll have your memories."

"Do me a favor and make sure her boyfriend's not around, okay?"

"Don't worry, that'll be our top priority."

Larrabee and Monks walked to the door. Dreyer heaved himself off the couch and followed.

"I'm not done with you, fucker," he told Monks.

"If I hear another word about you, Ray, I'll see to it that you get brought in for questioning and kept in for a nice long visit," Larrabee said. "I strongly suggest you fall off the planet."

Outside on the street, Monks said, "Do you believe him?"

"Unfortunately," Larrabee said, "I do. But I've got a little problem with Coffee just happening to decide to jump him, out of the blue, that one particular night. Let's go see if she's home. Just in case we can get another spin on it."

Coffee Trenette's place was very upscale, at the far west end of Lake Street, in a posh little enclave set in the hills above China Beach. It had a view of the rust-colored hills of the Marin headlands, sloping down into the Pacific, and of the great red spires of the Golden Gate Bridge. The front yard was enclosed by a high masonry wall, forming a court-yard, like in Europe. The yard was landscaped, with border gardens edged with stone, artfully placed trees, and hedges that once had been barbered into topiary. But it had gone weedy and was littered with dead foliage—the way a place looked when there were no longer people paid to take care of it.

"Is that movie she made any good?" Monks asked.

Larrabee grunted. "So good, it's been made about five hundred times. She plays a hooker with a heart of gold, who falls for a hit man who's trying to get out of the business, but he's forced to take on one last job and he gets double-crossed and they have to go on the run together."

"She hasn't done anything since?"

"There were a couple of others that didn't amount to much," Larrabee said. "The way that tends to happen, they get into drugs, they get atti-tude, they get unreliable and hard to work with. The people in charge find another hot young star. I don't think she'd be living up in San Francisco if she had anything going."

The black iron gate was unlocked. They walked to the front door and rang the bell. A woman wearing loose white pajamas answered it immediately.

Monks did not have to be told that this was Coffee herself. She was beautiful, all right—sinewy body, coppery skin, and a thick silky mane of ebony hair that fell halfway down her back. She might have been African, Latina, Eurasian, or any combination.

But he sensed something cold, almost dead, back in her eyes—a knowing look that was beyond cynical, an awareness that from where she was, there was no place left to go. He had seen it in the eyes of junkies.

"Ray called me and told me you'd be by," she said. "I'll do this once." She did not move out of the doorway or invite them in.

"We'd just like to confirm that Ray Dreyer spent the night before last with you, Ms. Trenette," Larrabee said.

"Confirmed. Anything else?"

"We'd appreciate a chance to chat a bit. About your acquaintance with Ray and Eden, that sort of thing."

"Why in the world," she said scathingly, "would I *chat* with people like you?" She turned away and closed the door. It did not slam, which somehow resounded even more loudly than if it had.

Walking back to the van, Monks put his hands in his pockets. "My bad karma, catching up. I should have gone to her movie."

Larrabee nodded distractedly. "I'm thinking about where to go with this. There's nothing to take to the cops, yet. Just suspicion, and that's worthless. Especially—" Larrabee paused, and cleared his throat.

"Especially coming from a doctor who's feeling the heat?" Monks said sourly.

"Sorry. But yes. You got anything planned for this afternoon?"

Monks shook his head. "Sit around and chew my own liver."

"How about visiting Eden's parents? Sacramento, what's that, an hour-and-a-half drive, maybe two?"

"I'm not so sure they'd want to talk to me," Monks said.

"I can't see that you've got anything to lose."

Monks exhaled, then nodded. People had told him that before.

They reached the courtyard's iron gate. They paused, looking the place over once more. It was still, empty, almost desolate. Monks supposed that movie stars, especially ex–movie stars, led often-quiet lives, just like anybody else. But this place had the same feel as what he had seen in her eyes.

"Coffee looks used up," Monks said.

Larrabee closed the gate quietly. "That's a good way to put it," he said. "Used up."

18

They bought deli sandwiches and took them back to Larrabee's, eating while he tracked down the address of Eden Hale's parents. Monks opted for Italian meatballs in a thick red sauce, messy but just the ticket. He finished every bite, swabbing the plate with the last bits of bread. He had not realized he was so hungry. The Hales lived in Citrus Heights, an area of Sacramento. Larrabee called and spoke briefly to Mrs. Hale, asking if she was willing to meet. Monks gathered from what he overheard that she was reluctant—apprehensive at why a private investigator wanted to talk to her. Larrabee assured her, with professional skill, that he would explain. He did not say anything about Monks coming along.

They exchanged the van for Larrabee's Taurus, a car he liked because it was so inconspicuous. The drive to Sacramento was a straight shot on Interstate 80, across the Bay Bridge, through Berkeley and the suburban sprawl east, out into the open of Fairfield and Vacaville. Even though it was early in the summer, the fields and foothills were already brown and parched.

Traffic was bumper to bumper, most of it traveling at eighty miles an hour or trying to, and squeezing even tighter together over the long narrow causeway into West Sacramento. Monks had a musty memory of a lesson learned in physical chemistry classes—that molecules forced closer together by heat and pressure would move faster and faster, until they finally boiled over or exploded.

Neither of them was familiar with the freeways in Sacramento proper. The spiderwebs of interchanges turned into an all-out free-for-all that had them battling their way through the maniacally confident locals. Signs would appear with the suddenness of flashcards, sending them careening across several lanes of traffic, desperate to make an exit or else they'd end up trapped in the speeding streams to Stockton, Tahoe, or Reno.

Finally, with relief, they found their way to Citrus Heights and joined the relatively normal street traffic. It was just before two P.M.

Tom and Noni Hale lived in an upscale area—a tract, like most of the city's suburbs, but older, built in the late fifties or early sixties, and more gracious. The house was ranch style, long and low with a stucco exterior and a red tile roof. It was weathered to a soft brindle color that helped give it a Spanish feel. But most of the comfortable quality came from the yard, large and private, closed in by oleander hedges and a vine-wreathed fence. Monks glimpsed orange and lemon trees in the back. He had a brief mental image of a laughing little girl, the picture of innocence, playing underneath them.

They got out of the car and walked to the door. It was significantly hotter here than in San Francisco—over a hundred, Monks was sure. The air had a different feel to it, an infinitely fine grit that seemed to abrade his skin and teeth. To the east, the snowcapped peaks of the Sierra Nevada looked like clouds through the hazy air. The Sierra foothills looked bone-dry, too.

A woman answered the bell. She was fiftyish, attractive, with carefully applied makeup and coiffed hair tinted auburn. A loose tunic covered a suggestion of spread around her waist, but tight pedal pushers showed off calves that were still slim and firm. Her face was tense with stress.

"Mrs. Hale? My name's Larrabee. I called earlier."

Her mouth made a little grimace. "Yes," she said, and stepped back to let them in. Larrabee did not move.

"This is my associate, Dr. Monks," he said.

She blinked, and then her eyes widened.

"You're—not—the one who—"

"I attended your daughter in the Emergency Room," Monks said.

"I can't believe you had the nerve to come here." Mouth trembling, she wheeled around and called, "*Tom.* This is that doctor!"

A man came striding into the room from another part of the house. Tom Hale had the look of a jock gone to seed, with thinning hair and a once powerful body turned shapeless. He was wearing a golf shirt and pleated white shorts. His face was red from sun, anger, and possibly booze.

"I did everything in my power to save your daughter's life, Mrs. Hale, and I've been saving lives for more than twenty-five years," Monks said. "I wouldn't dream of coming here if I couldn't say that."

Tom Hale ignored him and glared at Larrabee. "Is that what this is really about? You told us you had questions, but you brought him here to try to soften us up? Well, forget it."

"I came here because I'm willing to explain in detail what happened in the Emergency Room," Monks said. "I'll also tell you that the case will undergo a review by a team of medical specialists in the next few days. If they find that I was negligent, I'll quit practice."

Larrabee glanced at him, astonished. Monks had

not known he was going to say that until he did. But
he meant it.

Noni Hale's face had gone from outraged to
doubtful.

"I did come because I have questions, Mr. Hale,"
Larrabee said. "Not to try to soften you up."

Slowly, Noni moved aside from blocking the
doorway. "You have to understand, this is very hard
for us," she said. Monks and Larrabee followed her
into the house.

The living room was immaculate, with a leather
couch and chairs and a dozen *Sunset* magazines
fanned out in perfect order on the glass-topped coffee table. The photos of two young men were on
prominent display. One was wearing the dress uniform of a marine lance corporal; the other was in a
tux, with his arm around his beaming bride. They
were all clean-cut and good-looking. There were no
photos of Eden.

"When you took home Eden's things," Larrabee
said, "did you take a phone answering machine?"

"I don't think so. No." Noni turned to her still
glowering husband for confirmation. He shook his
head sullenly. "I don't remember seeing one," she
said.

"Do you know if she had one?"

"I'm—not sure. I suppose so."

Monks remembered that the parents had not
known about Eden's breast surgery. It did not sound

like there had been much communication between them.

"Did she have a source of income, besides her work?" Larrabee said. "From you? Or an inheritance, anything like that?"

"No. We used to help her out now and then. But not for years." Noni looked puzzled now.

"She must have been doing pretty well, judging from her apartment."

"She'd been on TV. *Days of Our Lives, General Hospital*, some others. But we don't really know much about that part of her life. The whole acting thing—it wasn't what we wanted. We tried our best to get her into something more respectable. She was very smart, but she didn't care about school."

Larrabee cleared his throat. "Are you aware that she was involved in, ah, adult films?"

Tom Hale, pacing at the room's far edge, made a choked angry sound.

Noni folded her arms. "Eden made some mistakes."

"I wasn't passing judgment," Larrabee said.

"That was years ago," she said, still sharp-edged. Then she sagged. "Some of our friends found out about those films, I don't know how. People at church. It was awful. They wouldn't say anything, but—the way they'd look at us."

Tom Hale's face was getting increasingly ugly. "What's the point of this?" he demanded.

"I'm trying to put together a picture of your daughter's life," Larrabee said.

"Why? What difference does it make now?"

"We're considering the possibility that Eden's death was caused by a toxic substance," Monks said. "Our hospital pathologist—a man I respect a great deal—suggested that."

"Toxic substance? What do you mean?"

"A chemical, probably."

"Something that poisoned her, is what you're saying," Tom Hale said.

"It would have had that effect, yes."

"What does that have to do with the phone machine?"

Larrabee gave Monks a look that plainly said: *It's up to you.* Monks hesitated, trying to weigh the Hales' grief against his own need to push this.

"We're also considering that it might not have been accidental," Monks said.

Noni Hale looked like she had been hit in the face. Tom stepped past her with his jaw thrust forward. His eyes were furious, the skin around them screwed up tight.

"What? Why the goddamned hell aren't the police in on this?"

"We haven't approached them yet," Monks said. "We're trying to establish whether we have cause to."

"So you *don't* have any cause to?"

"What we have at this point is speculation, based on medical knowledge."

Hale pointed a shaking forefinger at Monks. "You know what I think? I think this is a hoax. You let our daughter die, and now you're trying to weasel out of what you've got coming. Get out."

"Tom, *wait*," Noni said. "I want to know about this."

"We're not saying another word without our lawyer." The finger stabbed at Monks again. "You'd better have one, too."

"I'd advise you to keep everything you took from her apartment," Larrabee said. "Store it carefully, especially medicines, chemicals, anything like that. Oh, and bedding. Towels. Clothes she'd worn recently. It may need to be examined."

Tom Hale stomped out of the room. At the door, Larrabee offered Noni a business card.

"This is not a hoax, Mrs. Hale," he said quietly. She hesitated but took it.

Monks trudged through the heat to the Taurus. All in all, it had gone about as he had expected—no better, no worse. He wondered how much of Tom Hale's anger had to do with losing his daughter, and how much was because the family's dirty laundry was getting an airing.

They were about to pull away from the curb when they saw a young man come hurrying out of the Hales' backyard, at the far end of the house. He was waving at them. He trotted to the car, glancing back over his shoulder as if he feared that someone would stop him.

"I heard you talking to my parents," he said. His speech was hesitant, with some of the syllables forced. Monks got the impression that he had learned not to stutter. His eyes were earnest and filled with appeal. "Eden *did* have an answering machine."

So—this was one of Eden's brothers. But Monks was pretty sure he was not one of the faces in the living room photographs. He was twenty-two or -three, tall and gangly, with a long, pale face and a vertical crown of hair four inches high, dyed gold. One ear sported a stud that looked like a real diamond.

"When did you talk to her last?" Larrabee asked.

"Just a few days ago." He glanced nervously at the house again.

"What do you say we take a drive?" Monks said. "Come on, hop in."

He got into the backseat and sat with his hands clasped between his knees. Larrabee eased the car out into the street.

"I'm Carroll, and this is Stover," Monks said.

"Josh. Hi."

Eden and Joshua, Monks thought, recalling Noni Hale's concern about her church. The names did suggest a biblical theme. Although in Eden's case, it had taken a twist that clearly had not been foreseen.

"Any place in particular you'd like to go, Josh?" Larrabee asked. "Get a burger, maybe?"

"No, thanks." His lips started to tremble and his eyes dampened. "I can't believe she's dead."

"It's tough, really tough. Were you close?"

"We were like sisters," Josh said, watching their faces anxiously. What he saw, or didn't see, seemed to reassure him. "Well, it's not any secret. I played with her dolls and wore her clothes when I was little. My parents tried like heck to change me, but—"

But they finally started pretending you and Eden didn't exist, Monks thought.

"It sounded like your folks weren't getting along with her," he said.

"They stopped speaking to her after they found out about those movies. Now—they're totally freaked."

"That's sure understandable," Larrabee said. "When you talked to her, what kind of a mood was she in?"

"Good. She seemed happy."

"Not worried about anybody or anything?"

"She was getting ready to have the surgery, and she was a little scared about that. But excited, too." Josh gazed down at his clasped hands. "Do you really think somebody might have k-k-killed her?"

"It's a possibility. Can you think of anybody who might have wanted to?"

"Noooo," he said hesitantly.

"How about her boyfriend?" Monks said. "Fiancé, whatever he is. Ray."

"Well—he's a lowlife."

"I gathered that."

"You know him?" Josh asked, surprised.

"We met. He's a lowlife, but—" Monks prompted.

"He really got off on her being an actress. She used to joke that she never had to worry about him beating her up, because it might hurt her looks."

"Did she ever take advantage of that?" Larrabee asked. "Fool around with other guys, make him jealous?"

"She had sex with people sometimes, to help her career. But Ray didn't care about that. He'd even help set it up. Like those porn movies."

"Ray set up the movies, huh?" Larrabee said.

"When they were living in LA. It was a favor to somebody who was going to give her a part. It was supposed to be kept secret. She used a different name."

"Did she get the part?"

Josh shook his head sadly.

Larrabee cruised on through the curving side streets, where there was not much traffic to require his attention. Sacramento was essentially flat, but they were high enough here to get glimpses of its expanse, mile after mile of tree-lined streets cut by the blue bands of its confluent rivers and the speeding glittering glass and metal streams of the freeways.

"There's one big problem with all this, Josh," Larrabee said. "Your sister was all of a sudden spending a lot of money. She told Ray she inherited it from an aunt. Is that true?"

Josh lowered his eyes, then shook his head again.

"Where'd she get it, then? Do you know?"

He did not answer. His fingers twisted each other anxiously.

"I'll be real straight with you," Larrabee said. "When the police get in on this, the first thing they're going to look for is whether she was blackmailing somebody."

"No!" Josh looked up, starting to go teary-eyed. "She wasn't like that at all."

"How can you be so sure?"

"Eden was sweet, she really was," Josh said, suddenly defensive. "But she believed what she wanted to. Ray latched onto her when she was still in high school. She was the prom queen, and he came on like this big photographer, who was going to make her career. After that, she couldn't get away from him. He talked her into things, like those movies, but just loser things. She never would have done anything really *wrong*."

Monks hoped it was true, and allowed himself to feel a little better. If this was, in fact, the end of his career, maybe it had not been wasted on a hard-hearted gold digger.

"But something was going on with her, huh?"

Larrabee said. "Come on, you knew her better than anybody else. Suppose somebody did hurt her. You'd want to help us find out who, right?"

Josh squirmed in his seat. "She made me promise to keep it secret."

"It doesn't matter to her now, Josh. Sorry to put it like that, but it's true."

Finally, he seemed to make up his mind. He glanced somewhat theatrically to both sides, then leaned forward and said in a confidential whisper: "It was the man she went to San Francisco to be with."

"Could you be a little more specific?"

"Her plastic surgeon. Dr. D'Anton."

Larrabee, to his credit, kept driving smoothly, but Monks swiveled in his seat. Josh shrank back, looking a little frightened at his intensity.

"Eden was having an affair with Dr. D'Anton?" Monks said. "Are you positive, Josh?" As he spoke, he remembered her discharge form from the clinic, with method of payment marked: CASH.

"Oh, it was more than an affair. He was making her beautiful." Josh sounded dreamy now—maybe seeing himself in her place. "It wasn't just a fantasy. He had the power to really do it. And then, she was going to be *somebody*."

The air-conditioning was on in the car, but Monks rolled his window down anyway. The fresh air, hot and gummy though it was, felt good sweeping across his face. He was starting to want a drink.

19

They got back to San Francisco about five P.M. Monks picked up the Bronco at Larrabee's office and started the drive home. The rush-hour traffic was thick, and he spent a slow twenty minutes on Highway 101, getting through the floodgate of vehicles pouring on and off the Richmond Bridge. Even the two-lane country roads past San Rafael toward the coast buzzed with manic tailgaters. With relief, he pulled into the dirt parking lot of his favorite place to shop.

It was one of the few old general stores left along the coast, with scarred wooden floors and the palpable aroma of decades of meat, fish, sausage, and cheese. It was bigger than you thought when you first walked in, with counters of dry goods at the back—jeans and wool shirts, boots, fishing and camping gear, first aid and automotive supplies—a basic selection of just about anything you might need to get by. It was cool and dark and quiet. The owners were an extended Portuguese family, the stumpy beret-wearing padron, his always-black-dressed wife, and a fluid collection of children, grandchildren, cousins, and nieces and nephews.

The wife was behind the counter when Monks walked in. She greeted him with eyes that seemed sad, even reproachful.

"Dr. Monk. You don't come see us no more."

Monks realized guiltily that Martine had been doing most of the shopping for the past several months, and his usual twice-a-week visits had fallen off.

"I'm sorry, Mrs. Lisbon. I've been terrifically busy. I'll do better, I promise."

She nodded slightly, accepting the excuse, if not entirely satisfied.

By way of reparation, Monks bought more than he had intended to: a large salmon fillet, chunks of brie and Jarlsberg, a Genoa salami and a string of linguica, a loaf of fresh sourdough bread, the makings for an avocado salad. He threw in half a dozen bottles of Carmenet wine, mostly cabernets, but two of the sauvignon blanc that Martine favored, just in case.

And liquor. It was more expensive than at the

chains, but early on in the twenty-some years that he had been coming here, he had understood that there was an importance to this sacrament that transcended money—an arcane link between him and a way of life that had a kind of profundity, a connection to the way things were on some essential ancient level, that was missing in his own.

As he was about to make his selection, the padron came in the rear door with his heavy stumping walk. He spent most of his time at his bocce court out back, working on his game, or socializing with friends, or just sitting. But he always seemed to appear for this part of the ritual, whether by radar or something as mundane as a buzzer system. His wife faded back at his approach.

"What today, Doctor? The usual?" His face was the color of saddle leather, deeply creased, sprouting a gray stubble of whiskers. He had the worst teeth Monks had ever seen. They were exposed by a knowing grin, an understanding between two men of the world.

"Better throw in a couple extra, Antonio," Monks said.

"How many you want? Three, four?"

"Make it six or eight. Hell, make it a case."

The old man's grin widened. His wife backed farther away, eyes anxious, lips moving slightly as if she were saying a rosary. Antonio's thick-fingered hands carefully placed bottles of Finlandia vodka into an empty carton.

"A little drink is good for a man," he said. He said it every time.

Monks made the requisite response. "It keeps the blood flowing."

He was back in the Bronco, just starting it up, when the store's front door opened and Antonio came huffing out, waving, with something in his hand. Monks realized it was a net sack of lemons.

"You almost forgot," Antonio called.

The lemons were beautiful, fragrant and smooth-skinned, promising succulent juicy flesh inside: the perfect complement to the vodka.

"Christ, thanks, Antonio," Monks said. He lifted up in the seat, reaching for his wallet.

"No, no," the old man said, waving the money away. "On me."

Stover Larrabee was in his office drinking a can of Pabst when the phone rang. The caller was a cop named Guido Franchi, who had been a rookie with Larrabee on the SFPD. Franchi was still on the force, a detective lieutenant now.

Leaving Sacramento, Larrabee had decided it was worth checking whether Dr. Welles D'Anton had ever had any involvement with the police. Like a lot of private investigators, Larrabee had an informal and not always legal arrangement of sharing information with several cops. He had left a message for Franchi, asking him the favor.

"What do you say, Deadeye?" Franchi said.

Larrabee smiled. The same incident that had gotten him thrown off the police force—shooting a mugger with a 9mm pistol, from roughly sixty yards, at night—had won him the respectful nickname from his colleagues.

"Thanks for calling, Guido."

"How's the glossy life of the private dick?"

"No benefits or pension, that's how. You?"

"I'm retiring in three years and twenty-seven days," Franchi said with conviction.

"Not so good, huh?"

"You wouldn't like it any better than you used to, let's put it that way. On top of all the other bullshit, there's too many young cops full of steroids and attitude."

"I guess we were, too," Larrabee said. "Attitude, at least."

"Yeah?" Franchi said doubtfully. "I don't remember *liking* it so much. Anyway, what I got here, you never heard it from me, right? One thing I don't need right now is to piss off somebody like a big-time surgeon. I want these next three years to go real quiet."

"Capisce."

"Okay. D'Anton's name doesn't show up anywhere on the computers. I asked a few of the old-timers. Sergeant Tolliver remembered something, back about ninety-seven."

"He would," Larrabee said. Tolliver was a thirty-year veteran, a massive black desk sergeant who quietly ran things while the waves of politics swept and crashed all around him. His memory was legendary.

"I dug up the report," Franchi said.

"I'm going to owe you some drinks, I can tell."

"There's not much. Routine missing person, a young woman. No real connection to D'Anton, just a sideline. Still interested?"

Larrabee slid into his desk chair and reached for a pen. "Real interested," he said.

Julia D'Anton awoke in the late afternoon. The window shades were drawn in her bedroom, to shield her from the westering sun. She was disoriented, groggy from a long nap, and from the Vicodin she had taken. She got up, put on a robe, and went to a window to see if anyone else was home.

The only other car in the drive was Gwen Bricknell's red Mercedes convertible. Gwen usually stayed at her own apartment in San Francisco, but tomorrow they were entertaining here, and there was a lot of preparing to do.

Julia walked outside, thinking that Gwen might be swimming. The house was in a secluded little valley in Marin, near the coast, an old family place that she and Welles had expanded into a luxury getaway. The swimming pool, filled from a spring that flowed from the mountainside above, had been crafted to look like a natural rocky grotto.

But there was no one in it. Julia turned back and

went into the house, through the living room, and up the stairs to Gwen's pied-à-terre here. Julia knocked, and waited, hearing the rhythmic thump of music inside. This was Gwen's private place, securely locked when she was not here. Only cleaning maids and occasional lovers were allowed in, both under her strict supervision.

Gwen opened the door, flushed and sweating, drying her face with a towel. She was wearing a spandex outfit. Her hair was pulled back in a tight ponytail. A large-screen TV showed several shapely women, also spandex-clad, dancing in swift precise unison. Like Gwen's apartment in San Francisco, like every place she had lived, this one was fitted out with an exercise studio—Nautilus weight-lifting equipment, a NordicTrack, videos of aerobics and Mari Winsor workouts and bun busters. Most mornings she was up at five A.M., putting in a fierce hour-long regimen before dressing to go to the clinic, with extra stints when she had time. She was just as careful with other aspects of her health. There were cabinets filled with vitamins, the finest skin-care products, estrogen and collagen cremes. She had tried them all, in all combinations, even getting ingredients directly from the clinic and mixing them herself.

Then there was the medicine that fueled her fierce energy—a plate with several lines of cocaine, waiting on a dresser.

"Sorry to interrupt," Julia said.

"It's fine. I was just getting ready to shower."

"I was wondering about tomorrow night. Whether Welles is coming." D'Anton usually came to the parties here, dispensing Botox injections to his female guests.

But now, nothing was as usual.

"He'll make an appearance," Gwen said. "He knows he can't let his adoring fans down." She waited for further questions, her face politely inquiring—the same look she used on women at the clinic, to put them in their place.

Julia felt her anger stir but resisted the urge to rise to the bait. She turned to go, then asked, as if by afterthought, "Did that Dr. Monks stop by?"

"Yes. I showed him Eden's records. He seemed satisfied that everything was all right."

"He's not going to be a nuisance, then?"

"I don't know about that," Gwen said. She stepped back into the room and picked up the cocaine plate, offering it to Julia.

Julia waved it away. "What do you mean?"

Gwen bent over the plate and inhaled through a plastic straw, a long shuddering breath into each nostril. She came back up with eyes bright and intense.

"I got a phone call right before I left the clinic," Gwen said. "Dr. Monks thinks Eden might have been murdered."

20

This evening, Martine was not there when Monks got home. He knew it before he pulled up the driveway and saw the empty spot where she usually parked her car, before the edge of his vision caught the disappearing tail of the black cat, Cesare Borgia, no doubt plotting revenge against his truant humans.

But then, there was no reason she should be.

There was a single message on his answering machine. He had a feeling he knew who it was going to be, and he was right.

"Carroll!" Baird Necker's voice roared. "That girl's father called up screaming that you'd come by, talking about murder. Are you fucking crazy? If you pull anything else like that, I'll kill you with my own hands!"

Monks put away the groceries. Then he opened a fresh bottle of the Finlandia vodka and sliced a lemon into wedges. He poured the liquor into an old-fashioned glass, watching it smoke slightly over the ice. He gave it a minute to chill, then raised the glass to his lips. The first taste brought goose bumps.

Ordinarily, he would have worked out first, but tonight he was not even going to pretend. He had been scheduled to work the day after tomorrow, but he had called Vernon Dickhaut and arranged for Vernon to take over for him. Monks had not given a reason—just said something had come up. He had not wanted to explain that he might not be coming back to work ever again.

It had been a long time since he had felt like this.

He finished the drink in three strong swallows and poured another one to take with him to the shower. He stayed in for a long time, as if the almost scalding water could wash away the past two days. Then he dressed in clean jeans and a sweatshirt, poured a third drink, and took it out onto the deck.

Pacing, drinking steadily, he went through the story in his head, piecing together the information that he and Larrabee had coaxed out of Josh Hale.

Eden and Ray Dreyer had been living together in Los Angeles until several months ago. On a visit to San Francisco, through some connection, they had attended a party at the home of Dr. D. Welles D'Anton. There, Eden had caught the eye of Julia D'Anton, the doctor's wife.

Julia was a sculptress—Monks recalled her strong hands, work clothes, and the stone chips he had seen in the back of her SUV—and a patroness of the arts. She had asked Eden to pose for her.

Not long after that, Eden had started an affair with Dr. D'Anton. It must have been a hot one. She had moved to San Francisco, receiving quite a bit of money from him—along with free cosmetic surgery. It seemed that D'Anton planned to make her into a showpiece.

And Eden was trying to change her life accordingly. She was getting rid of Ray and her connections to his sleazy world. She was upgrading her wardrobe. There was something childishly wistful about it—the belief that by changing her clothes and body, that would change her being, too.

Never mind that the trigger for it all was an affair with a married man, which, given its intensity, seemed likely to end in divorce. Eden may have been sweet and naive, but she obviously had no compunctions about taking D'Anton away from his wife.

Monks wondered if that was why Gwen Bricknell had lied about Eden being "just another patient"—if Gwen had known about the affair and was trying to protect D'Anton. If the news came out, it would make for a juicy scandal.

But while it might be unethical for a physician to have sex with a patient, it was not illegal. And none of the information put Monks any closer to knowing who might have murdered Eden Hale, or why—or even *whether* that was, in fact, what had happened.

Still, some potential motives were starting to appear, like shapes in fog.

Maybe D'Anton had wanted to end the affair—in spite of what Eden had told her brother Josh—and Eden *had* blackmailed him.

Or Julia D'Anton, fearing that her marriage was being destroyed, might have decided to remove the threat.

Ray Dreyer—jilted as a lover, and losing his long-term investment—was still on the charts, too.

There were many other possibilities that might or might not ever come to light. Including the damnable one that the salmonella in Eden Hale's bloodstream *was* what had killed her. That if Monks had recognized it and treated it differently, she might have lived. And all the rest of this was a waste of time and effort, a pathetic attempt at exoneration—an epilogue to a ruined medical career.

He went back inside and poured another drink, noting that the bottle was more than one quarter empty. He took the drink and the cordless phone back outside with him.

Martine answered on the third ring.

"It's me," he said.

"Hi." Her voice sounded remote.

"I just wondered what you're doing."

"Nothing. Fixing dinner."

Monks thought he heard talking in the background. It was probably the TV.

"Any developments?" she said. "On your—situation?"

"Yes," he said, but then stopped, unable or unwilling to continue, at this remove. "Is there somebody there?"

She sighed. "No, Carroll."

"Just asking. It will be good for you to make new friends."

"Are you drinking?"

"Yes." He took a long swallow, clinking the ice close to the phone so she would hear it.

"You really want to know what I'm doing?" she said. "I'm watching movies. The kind you were watching yesterday."

Monks's forehead creased. Martine had occasionally brought a rented video home, but he was pretty sure they had not watched any in the past week or two, and he had not been to a theater in years.

"Yesterday?"

"Porn," she said patiently.

"You're watching *porn* movies?"

"I never really have before. But—I don't know. I keep thinking about that young woman. What all that's about."

"Are you learning anything?"

"You wish," she said wickedly. Then, serious again: "I'm trying to imagine myself doing those things. Like, with two men at once, or even three."

Monks was not sure he liked where this was going. "So, your interest isn't completely academic?"

"I don't know what it is," she said. "Just looking at a different world. No, that's not all. There's some—prurience—is that the word?"

"One of them. Does it arouse you?"

"Some of it. Not much. It gets repetitious pretty quick."

"There are only so many permutations," Monks said.

"The dialogue's unbelievably bad."

"I expect they improvise a lot."

"Do *I* make sounds like that?" she said.

"Yes. But they're very musical."

"You're blessed with the blarney, Monks."

"Do you wish you were here?" he said.

"Yes. No. Carroll, I want to make this as easy as possible."

"Of course, Martine. That's the right way to look at it."

"Oh, go away." This time, she sounded like she was starting to cry. The phone clicked off.

Monks thought about calling back. Instead, he finished the drink and poured another one. It occurred to him just how precise was the term *heavy heart*. When things started to go wrong, they seemed to go like an avalanche—first a few rocks that you might be able to dodge, but then the whole mountainside tearing loose and coming down on your head.

He drank, remembering, unwillingly, the other time in his life when he had been in a similar situation. The year was 1988. Monks was chief of emergency services at Bayview Hospital, in Marin County. He had been losing popularity there for some time: with some other physicians, because he would not look the other way at certain good-old-boy practices, such as uncredentialed procedures; with staff, because he had no tolerance for various forms of slackness that were considered perks in big hospitals.

One night Monks had monitored, by radio, a team of paramedics in the field who were attending an elderly seizure victim. The senior of the medics was certain it was a heart attack and that a shot of adenosine would save the elderly lady's life. Monks, miles away and unable to see the victim, had only pulse rate and blood pressure to go on. These, together, suggested that a heart block might be the only thing keeping her alive. Adenosine would remove it.

He forbade the shot, clearly, twice. Radio contact was then mysteriously lost from the paramedics' end. When it was reestablished, some eight minutes later, the shot had been administered and the patient was dead.

The senior paramedic then claimed that Monks *had* ordered the shot. His partner, and the hospital staff who had been there in the ER, seemed uncertain.

The radio tape was hard evidence of what had really happened. But the paramedics were well connected to the sheriff's department—and the tape disappeared en route to the evidence room.

Monks, the Emergency Room, and the hospital had been sued. Then, as now, the hospital's administration had wanted to settle out of court. That would have saved money and bad publicity, but Monks would have been left tagged by the tacit verdict of negligence. He had fought it, and eventually won.

Or at least he had won that aspect of it. In between, he had discovered hard and fast that he had been mistaken about many things, and people, that he had taken for granted. It had precipitated a tailspin that had been building anyway, with him first giving in to it and then pushing it. When it ended, some four years later, he was no longer employed, no longer married, and largely a stranger to the world he had lived in before.

He finished the drink and poured another one, then walked down to the Bronco. He unlocked the safety-deposit box he had bolted under the driver's seat and took out the pistol he carried there, a Model 82 Beretta, 7.65-millimeter, double action, simple blued steel. He carried it back up to the deck.

The Beretta was a little smaller than his open

hand and weighed just over a pound. It had a nine-shot clip, with room for another round in the chamber. That was an important thing to remember about automatics. When a revolver's cylinder was empty, so was the pistol. But even when the clip was out of an automatic, the gun had that one more bullet, hidden, right there in firing position. A lot of people had been killed through failure to recognize that.

The 7.65's weakness was that it did not have much stopping power. The trade-off was that he could slip it in his back pants pocket. He kept a .357 Colt Python in his house safe, which would blow a hole in a car engine, but it was heavy and bulky. There were some higher-caliber automatics available that were not much bigger than the Model 82, and from time to time he thought about moving up to one of those.

But then, he had never fired a weapon at a living thing, and never intended to.

The pistol still had a light sheen of oil from the last time he had cleaned it. That had been more than a year ago, after the last time he had actually carried it and the closest he had ever come to using it, against a pair of junkie muggers deep in the Mission District.

The next dawn was when he and Martine had first become lovers, right here on this deck.

The pistol had a good weight, a *feel,* and when he chambered a round, there was a satisfying metallic click. Monks could see why guns were so popular.

When you had one of these in your hand, you were somebody.

He made sure there were no cats around and aimed at a dead tree about thirty feet away, downhill toward the creek, away from neighbors. In the past, he had been a surprisingly good shot. Larrabee claimed it was the same steady nerves and hands that made him solid in the ER.

The gun cracked with a sharp little sound like the pop of a whip, jerking slightly in his hand. He fired the rest of the clip, then walked down to the tree. He could see that several of the slugs were imbedded in the wood, but probably not all. It was hard to hit anything more than a few yards away with a barrel this short.

The .357, with a six-inch barrel, was a lot more accurate.

He went inside and got it out of the safe. His glass was empty again. He poured another drink on his way back out.

The .357 made a lot more noise than the Beretta, too, a big hollow boom that echoed up and down the canyon through the evening air. Monks squeezed off the rest of the cylinder's six shots, blowing fist-sized chunks of dead wood out of the tree. This time, there was no need to go down there and see if he had hit.

But if you really wanted to get down to business, a 12-gauge shotgun was your man. Monks got out the Remington from its hiding place, behind a panel in the hall closet. He stepped back out onto the deck, raised it to his shoulder, and blasted off the four rounds in the magazine.

When the last echoes died, the tree was cut almost in half and the forest was very still. Monks was breathing hard. He laid the shotgun on a table beside the pistols and drained his glass again. He went inside and poured another.

Dusk was verging on night by now. In the thick woods that stretched down to the creek, moonlight glowed off the sinuous trunks of the smooth-barked madrones. The chorus of tree frogs was rising toward full swing, a soothing singsong pulse that would last until dawn. Monks could hear the rushing wings of bats, welcome because they cleared the air of mosquitoes, although at times they crawled inside the house's walls and talked in whispers that sounded eerily human. Somewhere, a dog barked, a sudden baying of alarm. It was picked up by another dog a quarter mile farther away, and then another, a canine telegraph that might stretch all the way to the Mississippi River, a dogless barrier too wide for sound to cross.

He knew that he had come to that long-gone but so familiar edge, where too much of what lay behind was pain and nothing ahead mattered, where black rage ruled him, and one little step would put him over. The last time he had been there was the night he had almost strangled Alison Chapley with her own scarf. He had never let himself get that close since.

He realized that the phone was ringing. He picked it up and said hello.

"Hello," a woman's voice said. For those first seconds, he assumed it was Martine's. Then she said, "You probably don't remember me. It's Gwen Bricknell."

Monks was more than surprised. He made a hard effort to change realities.

"Indeed I do, Ms. Bricknell," he said.

"Gwen. Please." Her voice had a confiding tone.

"All right. Gwen. I'm Carroll."

"Am I interrupting you?"

"Not at all," Monks said. "Glad to chat. Or is there something I can do for you?"

"Maybe. Maybe I can do something for you, too."

"Oh?"

"I have a soft spot for men in pain."

Monks blinked, taken off balance again.

"Am I in pain?"

"Oh, yes," she said gently.

"How do you know?"

"Sometimes I can just feel things. Sort of like reading minds."

"Really? What am I thinking right now?"

"You're wondering what I'm wearing."

This was not true, but Monks said, "Well? What?"

"Not very much. Let's leave it at that." Several interesting images of the superb Gwen appeared in his mind. "But before, a minute ago—you were thinking something very different," she said. "Dark, dangerous. There was someone in the past, that you had a terrible moment with."

Monks held the phone away and stared at it, trying to be sure he had just heard what he thought he had. Hairs had lifted on his neck.

"Am I right?" she said.

"Yes," he said shakily.

"That's why I called. To help you out of that."

"Thank you."

"I can do more, much more. But there is something I want to ask you."

"Of course," Monks said. He was still trying to get grounded.

She hesitated. "This is confidential, in terms of the clinic."

"I'll do my best with that."

"We got a phone call this afternoon. It was Eden Hale's father. He said you'd come to his house, claiming she'd been murdered."

This time, Monks was not entirely surprised. Tom Hale had called Baird Necker to complain, too. Apparently, he had grabbed the phone and broadsided his outrage.

"That's somewhat distorted," Monks said.

"He wanted to know what we knew about it. I told him it was the first we'd heard of it."

"Sorry to put you in an awkward spot."

"Will you tell me why you think that, about Eden?" she said.

"I don't think it. It's just a possibility."

"What if I told you—this sounds crazy—what if I said I've been thinking about it, too? It won't go away."

Monks pushed aside everything else that was running through his head.

"You must have a reason," he said.

"It's one of those things I feel."

"Like you just did with me?"

"Like that, yes. But—I don't know exactly how to put it. It's almost like it's a different color, except it's not a color at all. With you, it was pain and anger. This is hate. Someone who wanted her gone."

Monks was not as skeptical as he would have been a few minutes earlier.

"Who?" he said.

"I don't want to plant anything in your mind. I'd rather have you come watch—this person—for yourself. If you notice something, too, then I won't think I'm crazy."

"I'm the farthest thing from psychic, Gwen." Although Monks had often noticed that he had an uncanny ability to make stoplights turn red just as he got to them.

"You don't need to be," she said. "I'm talking about a possessiveness you can see. It's creepy."

Possessiveness of whom? Monks wanted to ask. *Why did you tell me that Julia didn't know Eden? Did you know about Eden's affair with D'Anton?*

But she had gone from hostile to friendly to

offering information. He decided to let her keep moving at her own pace, at least until the time came when it might be necessary to push.

"All right," he said. "Where do I see it?"

"Welles and Julia host events." She pronounced the word like it began with a capital E. "Like parties, but more—focused. There's going to be one tomorrow night. Will you be my date?"

It seemed that there was not going to be any mourning period for Eden at the D'Anton household.

"I'd be honored," Monks said.

"Will it feel awkward to you? Being with a woman who's—well, you know. Been exposed a lot."

"My guess is I'll like it fine."

"You *do* say the right things," she said, and now her tone was sultry. "Let me give you directions."

He got a pen and wrote them down. The place was near the Marin coast, south of him—a private, very choice area of real estate.

"My God, I hope it cools down," she said. "I'm beaded all over with sweat. What about you?"

"It's actually not bad here. I'm up in the redwoods."

"I meant, is there anyone *you* suspect?"

"Everyone," Monks said.

She laughed. "You must stay very busy. I'll see you tomorrow, Carroll."

Monks put down the phone, still trying to process

what had just happened. The guns lying on the pic-
nic table brought back the enormously different
reality of a few minutes before. He felt like he had
been walking down the hall to a familiar room, but
suddenly found himself in another city. Abruptly, he
feared it might be the onset of a malaria attack. But
they almost never came anymore, and he had not
felt any warning symptoms.

He tasted his drink. It had gotten watered from
melting ice. He dumped it over the railing, went
inside, and poured another one. The vodka bottle
was past the half-empty point.

When he walked back out, a man's voice said,
"Doc?"

Monks jerked around, spilling the drink.

"Hold your fire," the voice said. "It's Emil."

"Emil," Monks said, opening his arms expansively. "Come on up."

The voice's owner came into view, a thickset
grizzled man in his late sixties. This was Emil
Zukich, a neighbor from a couple of miles up the
road, the master mechanic who had given Monks
the Bronco, then rebuilt it when it had been savaged
by gunshots.

"I didn't see your lights," Monks said.

"Mrs. Fetzer called me about some shooting
down here. Thought maybe I'd better come in
quiet."

Shame touched Monks. Mrs. Fetzer was his closest neighbor, a reclusive middle-aged widow. He

had not considered that the shooting might alarm her or drag Emil out to check on him.

"Everything's fine," Monks said. "Just a little target practice."

"Target practice? This time of night?"

"I've got some fine vodka."

"I can't stay. How about if I help you put those away?" Emil nodded toward the guns.

Monks was suddenly very tired. He walked to a chair and sat down heavily. "I'm sorry, Emil," he said.

"I ain't going to ask if you're all right, 'cause I can see you're not. That's a bad mix, Doc. Booze and guns."

"I know."

"Maybe I should take them with me."

"I'm all right now."

"I'll just check them, then."

Emil cleared the weapons one at a time, making sure they were unloaded, not forgetting to open the Beretta's chamber. A Korean War vet, he had fought at Pork Chop Hill. When he finished, he put them back on the table.

"Anything I can do?" Emil said.

"No. I just need some sleep. Sorry again."

"Not to worry. Things can get that way, I know." Emil faded into the night like a bandit.

It came home to Monks, with force, that he was alone again.

He went into the kitchen and swilled vodka from

the bottle. It was warm and its fine flavor was lost to his taste, but he drank it anyway. He pulled food from the refrigerator, salami and cheese and bread, and tore off chunks with his teeth, aware as he bolted it down that he was ravenous.

When his belly was quiet, he made his way down the hall, lurching a little. He stopped in the bathroom to urinate and brush his teeth. Then he fell into bed.

As he reached to turn out the light, his gaze was caught by an illustration in an open book on his nightstand, a work of medieval history. Martine had probably read in it last night, while her deadbeat lover slept on the couch. The picture was an old woodcut by Dürer. Several women in a rustic kitchen, surrounded by leering imps and familiars, were brewing a cauldron of magical potion, then flying up the chimney to join the hordes of their sisters, riding their broomsticks through the turbulent moonlit sky to a *Walpurgisnacht* orgy.

The witchcraft terror had exercised a tremendous hold on the medieval imagination. In Europe, between about 1300 and 1700, tens of thousands, almost all women—some estimates put the number at over a million—were executed for this ultimate heresy, selling their souls to the powers of evil, joining forces with the enemy of mankind.

In practice, beneath the genuine superstition of the times, there were far more tawdry motivations at work: misogyny, cruelty, and greed. The elderly,

eccentric, and deformed—offensive to righteous cit-
izens and helpless to defend themselves—were
often targeted. But being young and pretty could be
dangerous, too. A man suffering from unrequited
lust might decide that this could only be because the
desired one had cast a spell on him, and have the
revenge of seeing her punished for rejecting him.
Someone who coveted a neighbor's property might
swear that they had seen that neighbor make unexplained trips into the forest at night; the victim's
possessions would be confiscated, and given or sold
cheaply to the accuser. Many suffered, as at Salem,
from the lies of spiteful children.

Once the victims were accused, they were guilty
until proven innocent, which almost never happened. Typically, they were tortured into confessing
whatever lurid scenarios their inquisitors dreamed
up, then burned alive. They were also forced to
implicate others, so the process mushroomed. Vil-
lages were decimated; victims' entire families were
considered contaminated; children were tortured
into accusing their parents, then burned along with
them. It was all done with the utmost piety.

There was evil in the world, Monks had no doubt
of that—pervading human life, in different guises,
in every era. During the witch-hunts, it had worn the
judges' robes.

The oblivion of sleep came to him with merciful
swiftness.

21

The laser printer in Stover Larrabee's office whooshed quietly, adding more information to the stack that was accumulating. Larrabee was not an office person, and he had not grown up in the computer generation. He was more comfortable working in old-fashioned ways. But there was no denying that computers saved a lot of time, phone calls, and miles.

Guido Franchi, his SFPD detective friend, had provided a tantalizing piece of information. In 1997, a young woman named Katie Bensen had been reported missing. A routine police check turned up a common scenario. Katie was in her early twenties—no one knew her age for sure, or even if that was her real name. According to what she told friends, she had run away from home in her early teens and drifted ever since. She had no trouble finding places to crash; she was attractive, and willing to trade sex for money or drugs.

Katie had never been found. The police were unable to locate any family. She joined the ranks of young women who frequently went missing like that—drifters, druggies, girls who came to San Francisco looking for something or to get away from something else, living in a shadow world beneath the radar. Usually, they moved to another city because of legal or personal trouble, often changing names. Overworked police departments could not spend time and resources chasing girls who wanted to stay disappeared. But they could easily become throwaways—victims of that dangerous world, which included predators who sought them out.

One thing set Katie apart. She had claimed, to her friends, that she had been a patient of Dr. D. Welles D'Anton. For a young woman who had been living one step above the streets, this was, to say the least, unusual.

There were no more details in the police report. It was only noted that D'Anton's office had been contacted, in the hopes that they might have a current address for her. They did not. That was that.

Franchi was right—the case went nowhere, and it was several years old. Most likely, Katie had lied about her connection with D'Anton to impress her friends, and just skipped town.

But if not, she was another young woman whose unexplained death was linked to D'Anton.

The police report did mention the name of a nurse in D'Anton's office, one Margaret Pendergast. Tracking her was no problem. Ms. Pendergast was an upstanding citizen, at least on paper. She had bought a house in Anaheim in early 1998.

Which meant that she had left D'Anton's employ not long after Katie Benson's disappearance.

Larrabee found her phone number, but got no answer. He left a message on her machine, then started focusing on Dr. D. Welles D'Anton himself.

The standard background check information on D'Anton came up readily, including his license to practice in the state of California. But Larrabee realized that none of it dated back farther than twenty years. This was astonishing: his medical education should have been a matter of public record.

Larrabee started to entertain the incredible notion that D'Anton might be a fraud. He accessed a CD-ROM directory of board-certified medical specialists and looked again, scrolling carefully down the list of names.

His finger stopped tapping the key. He grinned.

The credentials were impressive—M.D. from Johns Hopkins, surgical residency at UCLA, back to Hopkins for plastic surgery certification—

But they were for one Donald W. Danton. Born in Youngstown, Ohio, November 3, 1952. Married Julia Symes in 1983. The dates jibed with a man of fifty. It had to be him.

The usual reasons for a name change were obvious—a criminal record, bad debts, adopting a stage persona. But this apostrophe had turned him from Donald Danton of Youngstown, Ohio, to Dr. D. Welles D'Anton of San Francisco, plastic surgeon to the stars.

Next, Larrabee found that the name Symes was old California money, with plenty of alumni from Stanford and USC. The LA branch of the family included several financiers and producers in the movie business. Julia Symes, D'Anton's wife, was from San Francisco but had gone to college at Pomona. She would have been an undergraduate there at the time Danton—now D'Anton—was doing his surgical residency at UCLA. They had married the year she graduated.

Larrabee was getting the feeling that D'Anton had orchestrated his career very carefully—acquiring the proper medical credentials, a wealthy wife who was connected in the film world, and a new name and persona.

A quick online search turned up no allegations of malpractice or negligence against D'Anton, with the apostrophe or without. But very often, cases didn't show up on those kinds of records because they never got that far. A physician who was threatened with a lawsuit, or a misconduct complaint, would inform his or her insurance company immediately. The company's attorneys might then persuade the complainant not to pursue it, or an agreement would be reached privately. There would be no official record of the matter.

Larrabee had put out feelers for several other avenues that might turn up these kinds of incidents. The personnel at ASCLEP, the malpractice insurance company that he and Monks worked for, might have heard about them—or other physicians, lawyers, and newspeople, of whom Larrabee knew quite a few.

But the best bet was D'Anton's own insurance company, Pacific Doctors Mutual. If any complaints had ever been lodged against him, they would be in the files. But those were highly confidential, jealously guarded from outsiders.

Hacking was beyond his level of skill. But he knew just the person for the job, Tina Bauer. He called Tina and spoke with her briefly, arranging to stop by her apartment. The day had already been a long one, with the drive to Sacramento and back. But this was business that needed taking care of.

Larrabee locked up and walked through the old building's hall, ears attentive to familiar sounds, alert for possible intruders. It was zoned for commercial use only; legally, he was not supposed to be living there. But the owners were glad to have their own private security force and looked the other way.

The building housed another dozen offices, mainly small shipping companies and wholesalers. It was a throwback to an older era, like a stage set of musty offices and aging personnel moving slowly in their little enclaves, oblivious to the frenzied digitized world outside their doors. By this time of evening it was deserted.

It was after eight and getting dark when he walked outside. He liked the night, and he always felt better when he got out on the street. The San Francisco sky was a shade of midnight blue he had never seen anywhere else, and the great buildings of the skyline glimmered with elegance and power. There was no place like it. Where he had grown up—Flint, Michigan—seemed like another planet. His name, Stover, came from his mother's maiden name of Stoverud, Norwegian loggers and farmers. His father had worked the assembly lines in Flint, until that bitter closing had cost the town the little it had. By the time Stover was twenty, there was not much else to do but leave.

Traffic this evening was relaxed; rush hour was over and the Giants were playing out of town. A few human shapes carrying garbage bags or pushing shopping carts were moving, with the deliberateness of having no destination. There were a lot of street people in the neighborhood, down toward the east end of Howard Street. Pac Bell Park, new and splendid, was a fine addition to the city. But the surrounding gentrification, blocks and blocks of upscale condo and office buildings, had pushed the homeless toward the older areas. Larrabee knew the ones who had been around a while and always kept a sheaf of folded dollar bills in his pocket to hand out when he met them. This maintained a respect for him and his property, and even a sort of loyalty between him and those denizens of a world that was like a halfway house to death.

But there were always newcomers, drugged to craziness or just not giving a shit. Confrontations were still rare, and the few times that violence had seemed likely, he had been able to head it off by opening his jacket to show his pistol. But the probability kept looming larger that a gang member with his own gun, or a junkie pulling a knife out of nowhere, was going to catch him unprepared. It was a no-win situation—if he defended himself successfully, he was probably in serious trouble with the law, and if not, he was dead—and while he hated to give in, he was thinking about moving. Growing up, he had hated the grimy industrial buildings that surrounded him, and wanted only to get away. But now they brought a strange comfort.

He got in his Taurus, pulled out onto Howard, and headed toward Castro Street. This was where he had started as a rookie cop, in the Southern District south of Market Street, flanking the Mission. In this heat, there were a lot of people out—a little world on each street corner and several in between, interacting and clashing, hookers, gangbangers, drunks, addicts, the halt and lame and many insane: a micro-cosm of predators and victims.

Larrabee had spent more than ten years wearing the SFPD's blue uniform, and another year and a half under cover. One night he had shot a particularly vicious mugger who was preying on tourists near Fisherman's Wharf. But it was dark; the mugger had managed to ditch his pistol so that it was never found; and his defense lawyer successfully argued reasonable doubt that Larrabee had shot the right man. He had been suspended without pay. He might have been reinstated eventually, but the beating he had taken at the hands of the system that he had risked his life to protect left him bitter and disgusted. Instead, he had decided to go private.

He worked mostly alone, without the sophisticated equipment or networks of the bigger agencies. His cases were rarely dramatic; most of his income came from investigating malpractice insurance claims for a doctor-owned company called ASCLEP. This was how he and Monks had met. Monks was a case reviewer and expert witness for ASCLEP, but his medical expertise was a help in fieldwork, too, and sometimes it was good to have another body. Larrabee paid Monks back in kind when he could. Once, it had almost gotten him killed.

But there was more to the partnership, and more than friendship. Monks fascinated him.

Larrabee was under no illusions about himself.

He was smart, but not intellectual. He cared, but that caring was tempered by a hard edge, a self-preservation instinct that kept his brain in control of his feelings. It wasn't something he had to work at. It was built in.

But Monks—Monks was something else. He was a South Side Chicago mick who'd spent years laying his hands on damaged bodies and dealing with all the troubles that came with that. He was not shy about fighting, physically. But underneath, Larrabee sensed another quality, much harder to grasp, that showed through in glimpses. It was like some gentle thing that was trapped in a cruel cage, desperate to break free. Sometimes it came across as childlike, sweet, and clear, or hurt and incomprehending. But other times, that desperation turned destructive, even berserk, and he sensed, too, that Monks had spent a lot of his life fighting it, trying to channel that fierce energy. He had a hard time keeping going. And Larrabee, for reasons he himself did not fully understand, was determined to make sure that he did.

The heart of the Castro District was gay and trendy. But west toward Twin Peaks, there was a more conservative maze of curving hilly residential streets that seemed to lead only to others like them. As well as Larrabee knew the city, he still got lost in there. The houses were small and set close together, not fancy, but well kept. There was a sense of watchfulness about the area.

Tina Bauer let him into the house she shared with her partner, Bev. She was a small woman in her late thirties, bony, flat-chested, and mousy. Her hair was a neutral brown, bobbed, and she wore cat's-eye glasses. You could not call her pretty, although there was a certain girlish appeal. Bev thought so. Bev weighed over two hundred pounds, worked as the night dispatcher for a trucking company, and was insanely jealous.

Except that she was wearing a T-shirt and sweatpants, Tina looked like she could have been an accountant, and in fact, she had been. But she had the sort of mind that grasped things differently than other people's, especially in the realm of electronic information. Fifteen years earlier, married, recently graduated from UC Berkeley, and working for Pacific Gas and Electric—the epitome of straight—she had figured out a way to shave a tiny fraction off of pennies of the utility's incoming revenue and deposit it in her own numbered account. The missing amounts were so minuscule individually, and spread so thin, they were barely noticed. By the time they added up enough to catch the accounting department's attention, she had accumulated several hundred thousand dollars.

This had launched her on a road to self-discovery, starting with two years in prison. Not surprisingly, her marriage had collapsed, but she had not liked men all that much to begin with. Over the next years, she had refined her skills to the point where she could operate with near invisibility, and she kept it small-scale. Occasionally she was questioned, as when a bank discovered that funds had been electronically moved from a place they knew about to a place they did not. But nobody had been able to make anything stick.

"What have we got?" Tina said. She was very serious and matter-of-fact. He was not sure he had ever seen her smile.

Larrabee handed her a printout with the pertinent information about D'Anton.

She scanned it, eyebrows rising. "You're going after a big fish."

"Know anything about him?"

"Just his reputation. Lifter of famous boobs and booties."

"I want you to check his malpractice insurance company files," Larrabee said. "Pacific Doctors Mutual. Any kind of complaint or irregularity that shows up."

"Did somebody's tits explode on an airplane?"

"It's nothing that simple."

"Okay," she said. "I should be able to do it tonight. Insurance company firewalls usually aren't much."

"You want some money up front?"

"We know where you live."

As he was stepping out into the hall, Tina said, "Hey, Stover." She was standing with her hands on her hips, watching him thoughtfully. Her face was stone serious, as always.

"I wouldn't mind blowing you once in a while," she said.

Larrabee had thought that he was pretty good at turning a compliment, but this one left him speechless, twisting in the wind.

"Don't worry, Bev's at work," she said. "But it would feel too weird here anyway. I could drop by your place."

"That's, uh, a lovely offer, Tina. I'm incredibly flattered."

"It's the only thing I miss, with guys. I'm very oral. Dildos aren't any good for that, I like it to feel alive. But I don't want to, you know, ask just anybody."

"No, that wouldn't be smart."

"You have to keep it secret. If Bev found out I even thought about it, she'd kill me."

"I believe you." He did.

"And you can't come in my mouth. I don't like that part."

"I promise."

"Yeah, and the check's in the mail," she said. "Keep it in mind."

In fact, it was impossible not to.

There was one more place Larrabee wanted to look at tonight, a restaurant that Eden Hale had talked about to her brother Josh. Apparently she had painted it in glowing terms—a classy establishment with an upwardly mobile clientele, a different order of business from the sorts of places where she had hung out with Ray Dreyer in her earlier life. Larrabee wondered how much time she had spent here, and if she had made any acquaintances. She had to have done something with her time, besides shopping and carrying on her affair with D'Anton.

The place was called Hanover Station. It was located several blocks west of China Basin— another industrial building that had been abandoned as industry died. Dot-commer entrepeneurs had refurbished it and opened it at the crest of that money wave, five or six years ago. Larrabee had never been inside.

When he walked in, he saw that it had been turned into a single space the size of an airplane hangar, ringed by a second-story balcony for dining. The brick walls had been left uncovered, the old hardwood on the main floor refinished. The back bar was antique, cherry or rosewood. All in all, it was not bad, although the nut must have been fearsome. The room was nowhere near full now, and he suspected it was in jeopardy, with the crashing of the markets that had built it.

He ordered a Lagavulin scotch, straight up with an ice-water back, at the bar. He paid for it with a twenty and got five back. That came as no surprise, but the drink was short. For a place that was losing business, that was the wrong direction to take. The bartender was a slick, good-looking young man, brimming with unconcealed self-admiration.

Larrabee decided there was no help there for what
he wanted.

He stood and sipped, casually watching the
scene. The crowd was all young, mid-twenties to
thirties, well-dressed, confident, used to spending
money. Two cocktail waitresses circulated among
the tables. Larrabee made his choice, left his empty
glass on the bar with no tip, and sat at a table in her
area.

She came over immediately. He had picked her
because she didn't really fit this place—she looked
like she would have been more at home in North
Beach or the Haight. She was about thirty, tall, and
very slender, dressed in close-fitting black, with
long straight dark hair. She wore at least one ring on
every finger, and many bracelets, all silver. She was
quite attractive, although there was a certain Morti-
cia Addams quality.

"What can I get you?" she said.

"I'd like to buy you a drink."

She rolled her eyes. "Sorry. I work till two, and
I'm going straight home. Alone."

"I didn't say you had to have it with me." He laid
a twenty-dollar bill on her tray.

"What do I have to do for that?" she said warily.

Larrabee handed her three photos of Eden Hale
taken from the Internet, face shots with different
angles and hairstyles, that he had chosen from her
films. "Recognize her?"

The waitress touched one of the photos with a

long-nailed fingertip. "There was somebody who used to come around, who looks like this. I think her name was Eden?"

"That's her."

"I haven't seen her for a while."

"You won't," Larrabee said.

The bored glaze in her eyes went away. Her mouth opened a little.

"Have you got five minutes to talk to me?" he said.

"You a cop?"

"Private." He opened his wallet and showed her his license.

She was starting to look interested. "I'll meet you out front," she said.

He waited outside the front door. A sea breeze was springing up, and the moon was dimming behind thickening fog. There was not much traffic on the streets, but a few blocks away, the stream of headlights on the skyway of Interstate 80 was steady, an unending fuel line of human fodder for the city's guts.

The waitress came out and stood by him, fishing nervously for cigarettes in her purse. Larrabee took her Bic lighter from her fingers and held it while she leaned into the flame, cupping her hand against the breeze. She inhaled and stepped back, crossing her arms, one hand cupping the other elbow.

"Thanks," she said. "She's dead, that woman?"

Larrabee nodded.

"Murdered?"

"It's looking that way," he said.

She shivered. "What do you want to know?"

"What she was like. Who she hung out with. If there was anybody in particular."

"She was nice enough. She always came in alone, and I never saw her leave with anybody. But she got hit on a lot."

"She was a good-looking girl," Larrabee said.

"Yeah, but it was more than looks. There was just something about her that said 'fuck me.' I'd see the guys watching her; it was like they were back in the jungle—wanted to throw her down on the floor right there. She'd play into it, but it wasn't really even like she was prick-teasing. It's just the way she was."

"You ever overhear her talking? Figure out her story?"

"Just a little. She said she'd been an actress, but she was getting into modeling. There was something else, too. Wait a minute."

The waitress put her hand to her forehead, concentrating, with the cigarette smoking between her fingers.

"She was going to work for some famous surgeon, something like that. Seems like maybe she hinted she was going to marry him."

Larrabee's eyebrows rose. "Marry him, huh?"

"I *think* I heard that. I didn't pay much attention, really. I hear so many people talking about all the stuff they've got going, and I think, then why are you sitting in here trying to impress everybody?"

She inhaled deeply on the cigarette, watching him. Her eyes were softer now, the early toughness gone. It was something that happened, an odd bit of psychology, like transference. People wanted to please their interrogators, to contribute something important. People who were not criminals, at least.

The suggestion that Eden had talked about marrying D'Anton was a choice bit of information. But there wasn't much else he did not already know, and he doubted there would be much more.

"One more question," he said. "How did she dress?"

The waitress shrugged. "Like everybody else here."

"Like a businesswoman? Not flashy?"

"Like she'd just come from the office."

"Did that seem strange, with her acting slutty?"

She snorted with amusement. "Are you kidding?"

Larrabee handed her one of his business cards. "Keep thinking about it, and ask your friends, huh? If anything turns up, give me a call."

She reached into her purse again, head ducking as her fingers searched, hair spilling around her face. It made her look more vulnerable still. She found the twenty-dollar bill and offered it back to him.

"You didn't have to give me money," she said.

"Come on. I've been keeping you away from your tips."

"I don't make twenty bucks in five minutes."

"Neither do I," Larrabee said.

She smiled and tossed her hair. "Maybe we should have that drink sometime."

He left with her name, Heather, and her phone number written on another one of his cards.

There were many available women in San Francisco, and Larrabee encountered them frequently through his work. That also gave him a romantic gloss that was more imagined than real. He got his share of come-ons, with the offer of sex usually there more or less immediately. This was fine with him, although, by his own lights at least, he never exploited it. But the need was there in him just like anybody else, particularly when he was in between longer relationships. Like now.

The last one of those had been Iris, the stripper with the stage name Secret, who had left two years ago to dance in Vegas. At first she had come back to stay with him often, and there was a time when it seemed like the relationship could have gotten solid. But she had slipped into another world, or maybe hardened into what she was destined to be from the beginning, with the dancing giving way to hooking and drugs. He had not heard from her in a while.

He was thinking seriously about Tina's offer. The sheer weirdness of it was intriguing, and he was reasonably sure that she wanted exactly what she said and nothing more. As for the waitress, Heather—he had been in those sorts of situations many times, and he doubted he would go for this one. The way it usually went, there would be a few nights of entertaining discoveries about each other's lives, accompanied by energetic lust. Then the unraveling would start—the realization that there were no real common interests or compatibility—and it would take its course, probably with a fair dose of pain and trouble.

Although there would be those first few nights.

He got into the Taurus and punched the number of D'Anton's former nurse again.

This time, a woman answered.

"Mrs. Pendergast? Margaret?"

"I'm not interested. And take my name out of your computer." She sounded middle-aged, with the sharp-edged reply of someone weary of endless solicitations.

"I'm not trying to sell you anything, Margaret. My name's Stover Larrabee. I left you a message earlier."

"Oh? I haven't checked, I just got in."

Larrabee was relieved. At least there was no overt hostility, yet.

"I'm a private investigator. Calling you from San Francisco."

"What about?" she said, cautious now.

"About a young woman named Katie Bensen, who went missing back when you were working for Dr. D'Anton. Do you remember that?"

There was a longish silence. Then she said, "I do. But I don't especially want to."

"Will you give me just a minute, Margaret?" he said quickly. "So I can explain to you why you should?"

Larrabee lowered his voice to a confidential tone, just the two of them in on this delicate and crucial matter, and plied his trade.

22

Late, after midnight, you find yourself driving toward the clinic. In the past you've returned to the operating room—to linger, to replay the event, moment by frozen moment, in your mind.

But tonight, you drive past. Things have gone very wrong: the word *murder* has been spoken. It's not about last night, or even the other times. It's what they think might have happened to Eden Hale.

That Monks is prying, and that will bring the wrong kind of attention around. The thought of this—of *him*—sets off the old fear. You realize you've been grinding your teeth.

You pull over to the curb and close your eyes.
Concentrate.

It starts to come to you. What to do, how to set
things up, so they'll look at someone else.

You think about who might fit.

23

Monks slept a surprising ten hours, a sign that he had been exhausted as well as drunk. He awoke hungover, no doubt about that, with his senses operating through a grainy screen. But the sleep made him feel a hell of a lot better than he otherwise would have.

Herded by cats darting between his ankles, he walked down the hall to the kitchen. He put out fresh food for them, started water heating for coffee, then checked the blinking light on his phone machine.

The message was from Larrabee. "I've got something good. Come on down here as soon as you can."

The call had come last night, and it was still early,

not yet seven A.M. Monks decided there was time for breakfast. He scrambled eggs with cheddar cheese, browned half a can of corned beef hash, topped it all liberally with jalapeño sauce, and washed it down with strong black French roast. By the time he shaved and showered, it was just eight A.M.

Monks called Mercy Hospital to see if Dick Speidel, the Quality Assurance chairman, had come in yet. He had.

"I looked the case over last night, Carroll," Speidel said. "Personally, I lean toward your side, but I'm going to recommend that it go to committee. It's so unusual, and she did die."

"Fair enough."

"The bottom line is, it seems pretty clear that she was beyond help when she came in. You took a wild swing. I'd probably have done the same, if I'd even thought of it. But you're going to be up against some purists who might consider it an inappropriate procedure."

"I already am," Monks said.

"Well, you won't have long to wait. I've sent out copies to everyone. You're on the docket for Monday."

"I appreciate it, Dick."

"See you then. Good luck."

Monks put down the phone, feeling better than when he had picked it up.

His guns were still on the deck, glistening with dew, a silent accusation of last night's excesses. He dried them, wiped them down with an oily rag, and put each one away, where it belonged.

The fog that had been hovering offshore had moved in during the night, shielding him, at least for a few hours, from the hammering sun. Grateful for its cover, he got into the Bronco and drove down to the city again.

Stover Larrabee was just getting out of the shower when the phone rang, a little after eight A.M. He was groggy, not used to the hours. He usually stayed up late and slept late.

The caller was Tina Bauer. "I found something," she said. "Just a reference to a file, but the complainant's name's on it."

"I'll come get it. When's good?"

"I could bring it over, if you want."

"Well—if you're sure it's no trouble, Tina."

"I've got to run some errands anyway. Half an hour?"

"I'll be here."

While he dressed, he replayed the tape he had made last night, on the phone to Margaret Pendergast—D'Anton's former nurse. Strictly speaking, it was illegal to tape a conversation without the other party's permission, but sometimes expediency outweighed everything else.

It had taken some time to get her going, but Larrabee was a professional sympathetic listener, and Margaret, like a lot of people who hold on to a troubling secret for a long time, was glad for a chance to unburden herself at last.

"I don't think I did anything illegal," Margaret's recorded voice said nervously. "Not really, anyway. But what if I did? Would you turn me over to the police?"

"I don't have any reason to, Margaret. I'm just trying to get information that might help my client. I mean, you didn't do any bodily harm? Rob somebody, nothing like that?"

"Certainly not! I just—knew something I didn't tell. I don't even know for sure it was important."

"In that case, I seriously doubt it's an issue," Larrabee said. "How about this? You tell me what happened. I'll give you my professional opinion on whether you broke the law. If there's any problem, we can discuss it."

He heard her sigh, a thin, spinsterish sound. "It's not just the police," she said. "I was very disturbed. But—" The sentence lingered, unfinished.

"But it's time to make peace with it, huh?"

"I *would* like to get it settled," she said.

"Margaret, I do this all the time, and I can promise you, a lot of people it wouldn't bother. But you, I can tell you've got a real conscience. Believe me, you'll feel much better."

She sighed again, then started remembering out loud.

Margaret had worked for D'Anton for about two years, from 1995 to 1997. She had been in her forties then, never married, a highly competent nurse with a great deal of administrative experience. She had been wooed to D'Anton via a head-hunting agency. Her stay had by and large been a smooth one. She didn't have much personal contact with D'Anton—he tended to be brusque, and mainly ignored his support staff. His anger could be ferocious. The clinic was not a relaxed or friendly place, but it was run at a high level of competence, and pay and prestige were excellent.

She remembered the girl who had disappeared, Katie Bensen, because street-smart Katie had been very much out of place among D'Anton's other, affluent patients. But the staff did not ask questions. Katie's procedures had been simple, a couple of light skin peels to remove traces of adolescent acne.

About two months later, a plainclothes SFPD detective came in. Margaret was handling the desk. He showed her a photo of Katie and asked if they had a current address for her. He was polite, apologetic for bothering the august Dr. D'Anton, and it was clear that he did not really expect any help—this was just a space that needed to be filled in on a report.

Margaret looked up Katie's records. Her address was the same one the detective had, an apartment in San Francisco. To make sure, Margaret checked the billing records. There she found something surprising. Katie's bill had, in fact, been sent to a different address—D'Anton's Marin County house.

Margaret thought it must be a mistake. The billing was done by a separate office, an independent contractor that handled many other physicians. Someone there must have been looking at D'Anton's address for another reason and carelessly typed it in.

She told the detective that the clinic had the same address for Katie that the police did. He thanked her and left.

Then, wanting to correct the mistake, Margaret went to D'Anton and told him what had happened.

She had never seen him get flustered before. He stammered out an explanation—Katie had modeled for his wife, Julia, and the procedures were partial payment for that.

Then he got angry. The police had no right to come around casting aspersions on *him*. And Margaret had no business giving out information without a subpoena.

She was taken aback. It was nothing medical, or confidential, she pointed out—just confirming the address the police already had. D'Anton barked a few more sharp words about loyalty and priorities, then turned his back and stalked away.

D'Anton ignored her for the rest of the week. Then he surprised her again, by asking her to meet with him privately—to stay late, on a Friday evening, after everyone else had gone home.

He ushered her into one of the operating rooms and closed the door behind, even though the building was empty. There was a cold intensity to him that frightened her. She had violated his strict policy of clinic confidentiality, he told her; she was being dismissed. If she agreed, without argument, he would give her an excellent recommendation and three months' severance pay. Otherwise, she would get neither.

She moved to Southern California soon afterward and found a new job.

"I should have gone to the police and told them," she said to Larrabee. "I'm not proud of it." Then she added, defensively, "But—you know. I was a nurse, a woman. He was the great surgeon. He'd have gotten rid of me anyway, with a bad recommendation and no money."

"Why do you suppose he got so upset, Margaret?" Larrabee asked.

He waited through her long silence, aware that this was the question that must have gnawed at her through the years.

"All I can think," she finally said, "is that he didn't want anybody to connect him, or his wife, to a girl who'd gone missing."

Tina arrived at Larrabee's right on schedule. She was wearing blue jean cutoffs, a tank top, and sandals. Her legs, he realized, were really pretty good.

She handed him a sheet of paper, a computer printout. It read:

Case file # 3184-E 06: entry # 14 on this document
Opened: 7/25/98
Insured: D. Welles D'Anton, M.D.
Complainant: Roberta E. Massey / 1632 Paloma Ct / RC
Allegation: Professional misconduct
Status: No further action taken by complainant.
Statute of limitations expired: 7/25/99

The reference was to an actual file, the kind kept in a folder in a cabinet, in the insurance company's offices. It would contain specific information about the case—but getting to it, at least legally, was next to impossible. Professional misconduct could mean many things, and it was possible that the claim was frivolous and had just gone away.

But D'Anton might have paid somebody off, as he had Margaret Pendergast. Apparently, the matter either had been dropped or settled informally—directly between the complainant and the physician, with no action from the insurance company.

"You're a gem, Tina. What do I owe you?"

"Call it three hundred. It didn't take long."

He gave her three one-hundred-dollar bills.

She folded her arms. With the cutoffs and purse slung over her shoulder, she looked like a hooker from the neck down. But her face, with the cat's-eye glasses, still belonged in the world of fluorescent-lit offices.

"So?" she said. "You want me to do you?"

Larrabee hesitated, touched by something like superstition at disrespect to this serious business. But it wasn't tough to shake off. He glanced at the clock. Monks wasn't due for another hour.

"Well—sure, if you're sure," he said.

"You worried it'll fuck up our professional relationship?"

"Not from my side. You're not using me as leverage to break up with Bev, nothing like that?"

"Nope. We're tight. It's just something she can't give me."

"I feel a little funny about it being one way."

"That's okay. This way, I'm not really cheating." Tina unslung her purse and set it on a table, swinging into business mode.

"How do you like to, uh, operate?" Larrabee asked.

• "You go sit on the couch."

He did as he was told. It was like being under the watchful gaze of a nurse.

She took a small tape recorder from her purse and clicked it on. Then she got beside him on the couch and curled herself over his lap, like a cat. She was a good warm weight, with perfume that suggested lilacs.

The tape started playing, the strumming of a

folksy guitar, then a husky male voice talking. Larrabee realized, with some surprise, that it was an old episode of *Prairie Home Companion*.

"We used to listen to it in the joint," she said. "His voice turns me on. Wow, I haven't done this in a long time."

"I imagine it's like riding a bicycle."

"You can touch my breasts."

He slipped his hand inside her top. They barely existed, palm-sized areas of soft flesh, but the nipples were surprisingly large.

"That's nice," she said. "Maybe next time I'll bring my vibrator."

She went to work with that same businesslike competence, still wearing her glasses, occasionally raising her head to giggle at a joke from the tape. It was the first time Larrabee had ever heard her laugh.

The deep voice in the background was unsettling, like having another man in the room, and from time to time other voices chimed in. With the vibrator, it would be a full-fledged chorus.

But then, you could get used to just about anything.

24

"**S**he sounds batshit," Larrabee said. He was speaking of Gwen Bricknell. Monks had told him about the phone conversation last night.

"I hate it when you sugarcoat things, Stover."

"She got some bad vibes from somebody, so she thinks they killed Eden?"

"That's what she said. *I* don't know." In the gray light of day, what had seemed eerily intense last night now seemed improbable, even silly.

Monks poured half a cup of coffee. It wouldn't quell his hangover, but it shoved it around some.

They were in Larrabee's kitchen, which, like the rest of his apartment, was technically not supposed to be in his office-only building. That showed. There was a single small counter with a stainless sink, a minimalist refrigerator and stove, and a few prefab cabinets hung on the walls. An over-under washer and dryer completed the utilitarian effect. But as with most kitchens, a lot of living got done there, and for Monks and Larrabee, a lot of their work. Two large windows let in north light and breeze, and the big old oak table was good for spreading out papers.

"You better go to that party—excuse me, *event*—and check it out," Larrabee said.

"I intend to."

"You just might be in for some very high-class affection. Soft spot, huh?" Larrabee grinned.

"Christ, she's not interested in somebody like me."

"Oh, no? She made a point of telling you she was almost naked."

"That wasn't quite how she put it."

"It's what she *meant*."

"It was hot, that's all," Monks said.

"What, she can't afford air-conditioning?"

"She probably talks to every man like that. Maybe it's a model thing."

"Jesus, Carroll, give yourself a break. A lot of women would think you're a pretty good catch."

"There's one who doesn't."

Larrabee's face got serious. "Trouble on that front, huh?"

Monks exhaled. "You know how it is. You take a turn somewhere back there. Somebody comes along who wants you to untake it, but there's no way."

"Martine's a very smart woman. Let her go shake loose a while; she'll come around. Face it, you've ruined her for anybody else."

"It'll help if I still have a job."

"If she really loves you, she'll support you," Larrabee declared. "Meantime, you don't have to be talking about a walk down the aisle with this Gwen babe. I'd guess she just wants a workout. She doesn't seem to be hooked up with anybody. She's through modeling, and she probably doesn't meet many guys at that clinic. Along you come. You're interesting. You're not bad looking, if the lights aren't up too high."

"You're a regular Dear Abby this morning."

"It's just one of those days when love's in the air, old buddy," Larrabee said expansively. "It's giving me a kinder, gentler feeling about the fact that we might be talking about more than one murder."

The phone number of the insurance complainant, Roberta Massey, had changed several times over the years, although the address, a trailer court in Redwood City, was the same. That usually meant a series of disconnects, for nonpayment of bills.

The woman who answered had the husky voice

of a smoker and a hopeful tone, as if every call might be the one about the winning lottery ticket.

"I'm calling for Roberta," Monks said.

"She's working, at the church. You want to leave a message?"

"I'm a doctor, Ms.—?"

"I'm Bobbie's mother," she said, sounding worried now. "I didn't know she'd been to a doctor."

"This is about something that happened a long time ago," Monks said. "With Dr. D'Anton. I'd like to know about the complaint Roberta filed against him."

Monks waited.

"She's tried to forget about that," Mrs. Massey eventually said.

"A young woman died in my care, Mrs. Massey. She'd been a patient of Dr. D'Anton's, too."

"Well, I'm sorry. But what's that got to do with us?"

"If he's been involved in any wrongdoing, your information could be very important."

"*I* wouldn't mind seeing somebody go after that Dr. D'Anton," she said, sounding tougher now. "He should at least pay Bobbie something, after what he did to her."

"You mean, he hurt her?" Monks said.

"Yeah," she said harshly. "And then weaseled out of it. The bastard."

Monks glanced at Larrabee, who was listening

intently on the speakerphone. Larrabee gave him a nod.

"I can't promise anything, Mrs. Massey," Monks said. "But there is the possibility of legal action. I need to hear Roberta's story. When would be a good time?"

"She gets home about three. But I have to tell you, she might not want to talk about it. She's worked very hard on forgiving."

"I respect that," Monks said. "But she might be able to keep somebody else from getting hurt. Ask her to think about that, will you, Mrs. Massey?"

He thanked her and ended the connection. Larrabee sat back.

"Sounds like Roberta might be thinking about Jesus, but Mom's thinking about money," Larrabee said. "My guess is, you're going to get the story."

Redwood City was about a half-hour drive from San Francisco, down the peninsula. That left almost three hours to fill. Larrabee went into his office to take care of other business. Monks got a pack of index cards and returned to the kitchen table. Years ago, he had discovered a technique that was a great help in malpractice investigations. It worked well for criminal cases, too. It was a little bit like reading tarot cards, except that it was based on facts.

He started by writing down the major pieces of information they had so far, one point on each card, concentrating on what had started all this—Eden Hale's death.

> *Eden Hale dies in ER of DIC*
> *Roman Kasmarek suggests possibility of toxin*
> *Ray Dreyer propositioned by Coffee night of Eden's death*

Then he started shifting the cards around, looking at different combinations, trying to read the past. Questions, contradictions, and lapses would stand out, and a part of his brain beneath the surface of consciousness would worry at them. Often—and often during sleep—the knots would start to dissolve.

He worked at it for more than an hour, stopped for a sandwich of cold cuts from Larrabee's refrigerator, then returned to put the information into a concise summary in his head.

Right off, there was the problem that they were trying to investigate a murder, even though they weren't sure that it *was* a murder. The main reason for suspecting so was Roman Kasmarek's bafflement at what had caused the DIC. Roman, a much-experienced pathologist, had suggested a toxin as the only thing he could think of that might have had that effect, but it was nothing that showed up on tests, or that he recognized.

If Eden had been poisoned, it was almost certainly intentional and carefully planned—not something she had taken accidentally. That was another problem. The substance could have been administered hours before she started to get sick, by someone she did not even notice.

The single tangible indication so far that strengthened the possibility of murder was the disappearance of her answering machine. It might have been taken by someone who feared that a recorded conversation would identify them. That pointed to someone who had access to Eden's apartment, and who she had talked to. But it was also possible that her parents had thrown the machine in with the other things they had taken and just not remembered, or it had been moved in another innocuous way.

The intangibles weighed more heavily in Monks's own mind—primarily, that there *were* people who might have wanted her dead. The more he was learning, the more his list was expanding.

D'Anton was still at the top. He was a physician, familiar with medicines and chemicals. He certainly had the opportunity to administer poison. As for motive, he had been spending a lot of money on her. She had even suggested to acquaintances that he was going to marry her. He might have decided he wanted out of the relationship, and she refused—maybe threatened to expose him to scandal.

But as things stood, D'Anton was untouchable.

Ray Dreyer also had opportunity and motive. His jealousy might go much deeper than he admitted, especially if he realized that he was losing Eden for good. He could have given her poison, and still spent his night of passion with Coffee Trenette. And it was just possible that he was smarter than he wanted anyone to think.

Julia D'Anton had to be considered. If she knew about Eden's affair with her husband, she might have acted to protect him, or her own glossy life. And there was another bit of information that might conceivably enter in. Eden had posed for Julia to sculpt. Julia's models were also sometimes her lovers. Could she have been jealous at losing Eden—especially to her own husband?

There was the suspect Gwen Bricknell had hinted at. And he dutifully added Gwen herself to the list. As D'Anton's assistant, she had reason to be protective of him, too. Monks didn't give this much weight, although it was going to put an edge on his date with her tonight.

He started wondering if the poison could have come from the clinic, and decided to include the other personnel there—the nurse, Phyllis; the maintenance man, Todd; clerks, janitors, anyone who might have had contact with Eden and access to supplies.

Then there were all those possible connections and reasons that there was no way to imagine—someone Eden had angered, an obsessed fan from her porn days, a rejected lover, a random psychopath. She was sexually arousing, the kind of woman that men would do stupid things over—and that other women would see as a threat.

Monks put the cards into an ordered stack and set them aside. The bitter truth was, he had a vested interest in murder. If it *was* a toxin that had caused the DIC, his use of heparin was going to be far more justified than if he had failed to recognize and treat salmonella.

But so far, intangibles were what all those factors remained. It would take hard evidence to push this into an official investigation.

He poured more coffee and took it to a window. Outside, the fog was burning off. The Embarcadero, skirting the Bay, looked festive with traffic and tourists.

Now that the up-to-date information about Eden was fixed in his mind, he turned his attention to what Larrabee had said earlier:

We might be talking about more than one murder.
Monks started a new set of cards.

Katie Benson disappears after treatment by D'Anton
D'Anton dismisses nurse who talked to police
Roberta Massey's mother claims that D'Anton hurt Roberta

He stared at that last card, trying to see into it, as if it were a door he could force open.

25

The trailer court where Roberta Massey lived with her mother was at the eastern edge of Redwood City, squeezed up next to the area's salt evaporators, huge greenish-brown fields of stagnant water that extended out into the Bay. It was hot here, almost treeless, with the sea air gummy and smelling faintly of processed sewage.

Monks was alone. He and Larrabee had decided that the two of them together might be intimidating to a reluctant witness—that a doctor, with a personal grievance against D'Anton, would have a better chance to win Roberta's sympathy.

The mobile homes were decrepit and crammed close together, and the maze of sticky streets was lined with junker cars. He felt himself being watched through dirty curtained windows as he cruised, looking for the address. He decided that if he left the Bronco here overnight, it would be gone by dawn—although treated with respect, becoming the personal ride of some biker.

1632 Paloma Court was a corrrugated aluminum single-wide that had once been aquamarine. Time and the salt air had reduced it to a dull flaky green. It was set back only about ten feet from the street, and surrounded by sparse grass struggling up through the sandy soil. A small dog inside started yapping when Monks climbed the rickety wooden steps.

The woman who came to the door was wearing a calf-length blue denim dress and a silver cross around her neck. Her dark hair was long and straight, with bangs over her forehead. She wasn't wearing much, if any, makeup, or other jewelry besides the cross. He guessed that she was about thirty, maybe younger, but with the unhurried movements of someone who had settled into an older pace. She was thick-bodied, pale-skinned, pretty in a puffy sort of way.

"Are you the doctor?" she asked through the screen.

"Yes. Roberta?"

She nodded shyly.

"Thanks for seeing me," Monks said.

"Mom's gone next door, but she'll be back."

Monks wondered if that was a warning, in case

he intended to try something. Letting people know they were being watched might be standard procedure around here.

She unhooked the door and opened it. The dog, a little dust mop with feet, jumped up on his shins and wagged its tail furiously, but then nipped his fingers when he bent to pet it. He stepped into a space that was clean but claustrophobic, heavy with the pall of cigarette smoke, and beneath that the less definable spoor of people who had been living close together for a long time. A large TV faced a much-used couch. The walls were hung with crosses and cheap reproductions of religious paintings, including a suspiciously handsome Christ.

"Mom told me what you said, about how I might be able to keep him from hurting somebody else," Roberta said.

"I'm glad you see it that way, Roberta. I know this is difficult for you. Will you tell me what happened?"

She bent her head down, as if she were praying, and swept the bangs back off her forehead.

Monks saw the scar, just at the hairline, going from the far right of her forehead to the center. His hand moved to touch it, his forefinger tracing the hard ridge of flesh.

"Dr. D'Anton did *this* to you?" he said in disbelief.

She nodded, her eyes still cast down. Then she turned away, bending over and hugging herself, with sudden wrenching sobs shaking her body. Monks put his arm around her shoulders. She turned again, toward him, and wept against his chest.

A few minutes later, calmer but with her voice still trembling, Roberta told Monks her horror story, in halting words that were a strange mixture of pious platitudes and street talk.

It had happened in the summer of 1998, starting when she went to a party in San Francisco. She was looking for drugs, preferably narcotics. She had no luck at first, but she met another young woman there who wanted the same thing. The second girl knew about another party, that same night—at D'Anton's house, in Marin County. She had been there once before, with friends. She hadn't been invited this time, but she thought that a couple of attractive young women might be allowed to crash. Things could get pretty wild, she said, and there had been plenty of dope around. But she needed a ride, and Roberta had a car.

They drove to D'Anton's house and blended timidly into the party. Many of the guests were older and obviously had money. Roberta felt very much out of place with them. But there were other young people, too, and no one asked her to leave.

And there were drugs—pot and cocaine being used openly, with plenty of liquor and good wine.

The two girls wandered apart. Someone gave Roberta a Vicodin. She started to get very high.

At some point, an older man spoke to her. She knew that this was the host, Dr. D'Anton—he had been pointed out to her—and she got nervous again. But he seemed interested in her and asked her about herself. He told her she was pretty, and then he did something that stayed in her mind—he reached up and spanned her forehead between thumb and forefinger, as if measuring it with calipers, then traced his fingertips across the frontal ridge above her eyebrows.

Her forehead *was* a little protuberant, Monks noticed, marring her attractiveness with a slightly beetle-browed look.

She only spoke with D'Anton for a minute. She kept partying, drinking too much. She got woozy. Things became unclear. She remembered trying to apologize to a woman who helped her to a couch in a quiet room. Then she passed out.

When she came to, she was on an operating table.

"I saw this light that came to warn me," she told Monks. Her voice was softly reverent. She was sitting beside him on the couch, her hands nervously petting the little mutt in her lap. "I was unconscious, my eyes were still closed, and it appeared in my mind. It was like a flame, like the pillar of fire the Lord sent to lead the Israelites. I started to wake up. And felt—" She shivered. "Felt something burning across here." Her finger touched the hairline scar.

"He was cutting your skin?" Monks said.

She nodded, swallowing dryly. "And then he

started pulling it down. Ripping it right off my face. I opened my eyes. There was blood running into them, but I could see those hands, with rubber gloves, and the knife he was holding. I screamed and started thrashing around. It must have freaked him out, because then he was gone."

She was starting to cry again. Monks patted her wrist. The dog growled protectively.

"Did you think he was going to kill you, Roberta?"

"I don't know. Maybe he was trying to fix what he'd looked at before, my forehead. But he's crazy, I know that."

Monks stood and put his hands in his pockets, listening as she talked on in her shaking voice, coaxing her to continue when she broke down.

Roberta had managed to get up off the operating table. She could feel the fold of loose skin flapping down her forehead, and she could hardly see through the blood running into her eyes. She found a towel, wiped her eyes and pressed it against her forehead to stem the blood, then stumbled through the darkened building, trying to find her way outside. She had no idea where she was; it might or might not have been D'Anton's clinic. She came to a door, but it was locked.

She was frantically trying to open it when someone slipped an arm around her from behind, pinning her own arms, and jabbed a needle into her shoulder.

She tried to plead, but she lost consciousness

within seconds. Her last thought was that she was going to die.

But she awoke, slowly, groggy and in pain. It took her some time to realize that she was in the driver's seat of her own car—slammed into a highway underpass bridge abutment. The windshield above the steering wheel was spiderwebbed, as if her head had hit it. The dashboard and hood were littered with shards of glass. Her face was sticky with congealed blood.

But except for the laceration on her forehead, she was unhurt.

It was still night, and deserted. She recognized the place as a wooded area of San Francisco near China Beach. She had no memory of the accident— no memory of having driven at all, since arriving at D'Anton's house.

What Roberta did next, Monks thought, defined a fundamental difference between the culture that she had grown up in and the one that he had. She had found her way to a pay phone—but instead of calling the police, she called her mother. Then she hid until Mrs. Massey and her boyfriend—an ex-con named Jerry—came to pick her up.

They went to the hospital in Redwood City. No one said anything about D'Anton—only that Roberta had been in a wreck. Her mother stayed with her, while Jerry called the police and reported the car as stolen.

A young ER doc stitched up Roberta's cut, warning her that this was only a temporary fix, to stop the bleeding. The scar would need to be repaired by a plastic surgeon, the sooner the better.

But that had never been done. In the months that followed, Roberta thought more and more about the light that had appeared to her and saved her life. She began to understand that it had been a call from Jesus. She had gotten involved with a local church that was active with the poor, and now she worked there part-time. She embraced her disfigurement as a sort of stigmata—deliverance from the vanity of physical beauty.

"It was a gift from Christ to signify my salvation," she said. "To share in His sufferings." She watched Monks, her face hopeful, as if pleading silently for absolution.

Monks said, "Why didn't you go to the police, Roberta?"

She lowered her eyes again.

"I was—you know. In trouble, drugs, mostly. On probation. I figured, if they found me in a wrecked car, fucked up—forgive me, Lord—I was done for. I'd already spent ten days in county. Those dykes in there—" She shivered again. "No way was I going back."

"But you decided to file an insurance complaint?"

"That was Jerry's idea. I didn't want him to do it, but he talked Mom into it because maybe we could get some money. He knew this lawyer and got him to go to the insurance company and threaten to sue Dr. D'Anton.

"Next thing we know, this big black shiny Mercedes pulls up outside, and this man gets out wearing, like, a three-piece suit. He told us he was Dr. D'Anton's lawyer. He looked at the place like he'd just stepped on a turd—wouldn't sit down or even come in. Just stood there in the doorway and talked for about ten minutes, telling us how he was going to bust our balls. It was like listening to the devil, man—he was so smooth, absolutely sure of himself. He said the lawyer we'd used wasn't really a lawyer; he'd lost his license. He said I was a known criminal and a druggie, and I was making up a filthy lie to get money out of this famous doctor, and I was going to go to prison, like, for twenty years.

"Then he says to Jerry, 'Attempted fraud, in partnership with a disbarred attorney, would be a rather serious violation of your parole, wouldn't it?' I still remember that exactly." She mimicked a cold, contemptuous voice. "'A rather serious violation.' Jerry was out of here pretty quick after that."

Monks's restless gaze scanned the room. A shelf of photos included a couple of a pretty, slender girl in her teens. There was no doubt that she was Roberta. She looked saucy, wearing low-cut blouses that thrust her young breasts forward proudly— ready for the world.

"That doctor who sewed you up," Monks said.

"Did he say anything about the cut looking unusual?"

She shook her head, surprised. "Why?"

Because lacerations from a broken windshield typically consisted of many shallow V-grooves, and a precise surgical incision that long would almost certainly have caught the attention of any emergency physician.

"Just curious," Monks said. "Did Dr. D'Anton say anything to you when you were in the operating room?"

"Nooo?" she said, drawing it into a question. Her eyes were starting to get wary.

"The more specific the things you can remember, the more weight it all carries," Monks said soothingly.

"I remember those hands," she said, and added, with unveiled sarcasm, "real specifically."

"What about his face, Roberta? What kind of expression did he have?"

"I didn't see his face."

Monks blinked. "Not at all?"

"Just his hands."

She did not seem to realize that this weakened her story even more. Monks decided not to point it out. He asked a few more questions, then thanked her, and promised her he would be in touch with her soon.

Roberta walked out the door with him. "It's not

easy, living here," she said. "There's a lot of sin around. I pray hard to keep from falling back in."

Monks glanced at the surrounding trailers, quiet, but brimming with the sense of secretive and illicit goings-on.

"I don't have any trouble believing that," he said.

"I pray for Dr. D'Anton, too. I haven't just forgiven him. I thank him for bringing me to Jesus."

"That takes a big soul, Roberta," Monks said.

Bigger than his, that was for sure.

Monks found his way back out through the trailer court's shabby maze to the endless strip of El Camino Real, then took Woodside Road toward Interstate 280, pondering this new pool of information.

He could accept that Roberta had not gone to the police because, in her world, they were even more frightening than someone who had tried to kill her. That nightmare was over. Being under the heavy boot of the law, unfairly or not, could last years, even the rest of her life.

But her story would still be worthless in court. Any decent defense attorney could convince a jury of exactly what D'Anton's lawyer had said—that Roberta had been drunk and drugged, had piled up her car, and had made up the incident in an attempt to get money. She didn't know where it had taken place. She hadn't even seen her attacker's face. The physician who treated her hadn't commented on the nature of the cut. And why had D'Anton let her live? He would have had to stage the accident, roughen the scalpel incision with glass. Had he abducted her in a moment of impulse, then come to his senses and realized she would be traced to the party? Regained a touch of humanity at her screams, or just lost his nerve?

Monks believed that Roberta *thought* she was telling the truth. He speculated about recovered memory—the kind of fantasy that abuse victims sometimes constructed, out of guilt, fear, the need to block out traumatic events. Surely she was familiar with rumors about girls who disappeared. Could she have incorporated that, in a drug-induced psychosis, into a rationalization for the accident and her behavior leading to it? Her religious conversion, soon afterward, indicated that guilt feelings were already present in her.

But it was so damned outlandish and, at the same time, grounded in real possibility. This was not about sex experiments on alien spacecraft, or human sacrifice at Satanic rituals. Even her admission of not seeing D'Anton's face added the ring of truth.

And then there was Katie Bensen. Who had been a patient of D'Anton's, and had modeled for Julia D'Anton. Who was also an attractive young woman of about Roberta's age, and also a free spirit who liked drugs and parties.

Who also had vanished, and D'Anton had been upset enough to get rid of the nurse who knew.

Interstate 280 was a pretty road along this stretch, if you ignored the fact that it ran right on top of the San Andreas fault. The area was hilly and wooded, with a miles-long wildlife refuge on the coastal side. Traffic was relatively light going north, with the thickening commuter momentum from San Francisco coming the other way.

Monks reached Burlingame within a few minutes, and then he did something he had promised himself he would not. He took the Trousdale exit toward Martine Rostanov's house. He wanted badly to see her, to be in her presence—to inhale the warmth from her skin and help take away the chill that had settled under his own.

He approached her driveway slowly and started to turn in. Then he stopped. Another car was parked in the drive behind hers—a handsome black Saab.

Monks drove on past and went back to the freeway, berating himself. He should have called first. He was acting like a teenager. It was insane to assume that the Saab might belong to a lover, and he had no right to expect otherwise, anyway.

The urge was upon him to pick up where he had left off last night—to check into one of the Union Square hotels near John's Grill, with its great portrait of Dashiell Hammett, and spend the evening at that fine bar. It was another thing he had not done in a long time.

But he kept the Bronco pointed north, up Nineteenth Avenue, through the greenery-laced Presidio, into the mist that had settled over the Golden Gate Bridge. The party that he was invited to tonight was at D'Anton's Marin County house—the same house where Roberta claimed to have been abducted. It would be good to get the feel of the place.

Monks started to realize that something in his mind was calling attention to itself—something Roberta had said that he hadn't paid much attention to at the time.

She had not been able to describe the person who had led her to the couch where she passed out. But she was certain that it had been a woman.

26

Monks arrived at D'Anton's Marin County house—the event site—just at dusk. He had driven the last few miles on a narrow asphalt road in the coastal mountains, north of Mount Tamalpais. The road followed a ravine, a creek bed that was dry like most this time of year, until it opened into a small secluded valley. He stopped at the top of the rise.

The air had the feel of the sea and the fragrance of the surrounding eucalyptus groves. The Pacific was another two or three miles west, glimmering with the day's last light, a hazy sheen of reflection and mirage streaked by the wakes of passing ships. The gray band of fog on the horizon would probably move in again tonight, then burn off by midday. Like the peninsula to the south, it was sunny here most of the year, and rarely too hot or cold.

The place looked like it originally had been a farm, with a barn and several outbuildings. The house was an ornate Victorian, replete with finely proportioned bay windows and intersecting roof-lines, and a veranda that wrapped around two sides. It was built against a cliff, a natural rock formation, and it was huge. It must have cost a fortune, like the real estate itself.

Lights showed through the windows and around the grounds, with sconces marking a pathway from the parking area. That was filled with cars, thirty or forty, a canopy of expensive burnished metal. A few people were strolling toward the house. It was a picture of affluence, luxury, the leisure of the upper class.

And it was the place where Eden Hale, Katie Bensen, and Roberta Massey had all been guests.

Monks drove down to join the party.

He parked, and was walking toward the house, when someone called, "Hey, how's it going?"

Monks turned and recognized Todd, the maintenance man from the clinic, unlocking the door of an older-looking cinder-block building. Monks glimpsed inside and realized it was a wine cellar, with hundreds of bottles in racks and cases stacked up against the walls.

"This is my third run in the last hour," Todd said. "They're going through it fast." If he was surprised to see Monks here, it didn't show.

"Gwen told me you're the man they can't do without. Are you the bartender, too?"

"Naw, I just help take care of the place. When they have a party, I set up tables, keep the supplies coming, all that."

D'Anton's devoted staff, Monks thought.

"This your first one of these?" Todd asked.

"Yes."

"Knock yourself out. There's a lot going on." Todd stepped into the wine cellar and picked up one of the cases, tucking it under a muscular arm. He was wearing a tight T-shirt and jeans, still in surfer mode. He was handsome, vital, and it occurred to Monks that Todd might attract a fair amount of attention from D'Anton's female clientele. And that he probably knew a lot about what was going on behind the scenes at the clinic.

"You've been with Dr. D'Anton several years now?" Monks asked.

"Going on six. Why?"

"You get to meet the movie stars, all that?"

"I'm not a toy boy." The words came out suddenly and sharply, with a hostile glance.

Monks was taken aback. "I wasn't suggesting anything like that. Just—you know. It must be interesting," he finished lamely.

"I've got my own interests," Todd said. He heaved the case of wine up onto his shoulder and turned his back, heading toward the party.

Monks followed more slowly. Flattery was usually an effective way to start probing for information, but apparently he had hit a nerve.

He nodded sociably to other guests, but no one offered introductions, which was fine with him. There was the sense that they all knew each other. The dress was informal but elegant, Armani jackets and open shirts for the men, summer dresses for the women, with a lot of jewelry on display. He had put on his one decent sport coat, a Harris tweed—hardly in this style range and a little warm for the weather, but serviceable.

He reached the house and stepped to a window, to see if Gwen Bricknell was inside. This was evidently the party's center, a large old-fashioned drawing room. White-clothed tables set with liquor, wine, and hors d'oeuvres lined the walls. The room was crowded with figures who looked posed in a tableau. Those at the periphery stood in pairs or small groups, talking, drinking, eating.

But at the center, a man and a woman presided, like a high priest and his acolyte at the altar. The man was Dr. D'Anton. The woman was the nurse, Phyllis, whom Monks had encountered at the clinic.

He realized that there was a gradient of the sexes in the room—mostly men at the periphery, more women closer to the center. He guessed that many of them were D'Anton's patients. Most were in their forties, or older, but their beauty was almost surreally enhanced. There was a lot of collagen and silicone walking around in that room.

Phyllis was preparing something with her hands. She turned to D'Anton, presenting the glimmering object to him solemnly. He lifted it to the light and inspected it, as if offering a chalice. Now Monks realized what it was—a syringe.

D'Anton leaned over a woman who was sitting in a chair, with her head tilted back. His hands, holding the syringe, moved to her face.

Botox, Monks thought. Party favors.

He stared, thinking about Roberta Massey. *I remember those hands, real specifically.*

D'Anton finished the injections and returned the syringe to Phyllis. The woman in the chair rose, and another postulant took her place, leaning back to receive D'Anton's blessing.

Monks moved on, looking for Gwen.

He could see another cluster of guests, outside, toward the far end of the house. The area was a large flagstone patio, discreetly lit, with more tables of food and drink. Monks heard splashing and realized that there must be a swimming pool there. He started toward it.

Then his gaze was caught by a figure, a woman, off to his left, moving away from the crowd, toward the shadows at the edge of the lawn. She paused, cupping her hands to light a cigarette. A nearby sconce highlighted her coppery skin and long mane of silky black hair.

She was dressed differently than she had been yesterday—soft sleeveless pullover, skintight flared jeans cut below her navel—but there was no doubt that this was Coffee Trenette.

Another link in that chain that kept leading back to Eden Hale.

The match she was holding flared. But Monks saw that what she was lighting was not a cigarette— it was aluminum foil twisted into a conical pipe. Whatever was on the foil glowed briefly as she inhaled. She shook the match out, then let her head hang back in bliss. Maybe crack, Monks thought. Maybe heroin.

He walked over to her. She was half turned away and didn't see him.

"Small world, Ms. Trenette," he said.

Her hand moved quickly to thrust the pipe into her purse. She turned to him, face cool. Then recognition came to her, and she jerked away as if she had been hit with an electric shock.

"What are *you* doing here?" she hissed.

"Nice to see you, too."

"Don't you fuck with me, asshole."

"All right, I'll get straight to it," Monks said. "Of all the guys out there, how was it you happened to pick Ray Dreyer on that one particular night? The way he tells it, you wouldn't have spit on his shoes before then."

Her eyes gleamed with the feral look of a threatened animal. Her cultivated air was gone, too.

"You got a problem with that, you better lose it," she said. "I got some people be pleased to deal with you."

"Eden was your friend, Coffee, and now she's dead. Doesn't that mean anything to you?"

"You don't *make* friends in that world." She spun away, her shoulders rising and falling rapidly with her quick breaths.

Then, with her back still to him, she said more quietly, "You think I don't feel bad? Eden was nice to me."

"Even though you got a break, and she never did?"

Her head moved, in a nod that might have meant yes. "She was too nice, you know what I'm saying? People walked on her."

"What really happened that night, Coffee?" Monks said. "After your fight with your boyfriend?"

"There ain't no boyfriend, honey," she said scornfully. "Unless you count the ones come around wanting smoke and pussy."

"Then why did you call Ray?"

She stepped away from him, her forearms rising to cross her breasts, hands clasping her slender upper arms. Then she glanced back to him, with her gaze cool again.

"Because I'm a bitch," she said. But it had the feel of bluster this time.

She walked away, toward the crowd around the swimming pool. Monks almost felt sorry for her. Under her hardness and arrogance, there was a girl who had been given too much too fast. It had gone to her head, and she had made bad choices. Like Eden, she was a casualty of a world that glittered on the surface but was lined with broken glass.

But his pity stayed at *almost*. There were too many real victims who had never had anything but bad choices to make.

So—there hadn't been any boyfriend or fight. Something else had impelled her to sleep with Ray Dreyer that night, and guilt about it was softening her. Monks decided that he and Larrabee would be calling on Coffee again.

"I didn't realize you two knew each other," a sultry voice said.

Monks turned to see another young woman walking toward him. Like Coffee, she was dressed very differently than the older guests, in a thigh-high leather skirt and black tube top under an open white blouse. A wide belt with a big brass buckle encircled her narrow waist. Her dark hair was done up in a tousled ponytail.

He realized, with astonishment, that this was Gwen. He had only seen her before in her professional mode, beautiful, but sedately dressed and clearly almost forty. Now, in this light, she could have been in her twenties.

When she reached him, she leaned forward,

offering her cheek to be kissed. Monks obliged, catching the scent of that same perfume she had worn at the clinic, deep and heady, musky rather than sweet.

"You look ravishing," Monks said.

"Tell me how you met Coffee," she said teasingly. "I need to know if I should be jealous."

"No worry there. My partner and I found out that Eden's boyfriend spent the night with her, while Eden was dying."

Gwen stepped back in shock. "My God, that's awful. That's why he wasn't with Eden?"

Monks nodded. "We asked her to confirm it. She did, but she wasn't happy about it."

"No, I don't suppose she would be. Coffee's not doing very well anyway."

"Drugs?"

"Big-time. And money. She's about to lose her house."

Monks remembered the air of neglect around the place. "I heard she had a very promising future."

"There's a million luscious young girls with promising futures out there, darling. Some of them get lucky, for a while. But only a few are good enough and smart enough to stay on top."

It seemed clear that Gwen included herself in that select group.

"Let's have a drink," she said. "I've got a bottle of Veuve Clicquot on ice. I've been saving it for a special occasion."

"I'd better stick with club soda for now," he said.

"Come on, just one glass. You'll be more fun if you relax."

"You mean, I'll *have* more fun?"

"No, *be* more fun, for me," she said. "I'm very selfish."

Monks smiled. "All right. Just one."

"It's inside. I'll get it."

She left him, walking to a side door of the house, her long slim legs flexing gracefully with a model's fillylike stalk.

Monks heard another loud splash from the swimming pool.

"It's great," a young woman's voice called invitingly. "Like a bath."

He moved quietly closer. The pool was like a grotto, springing out of a rocky cliff, lit by underwater lamps. It had a distinctly Mediterranean feel. Quite a few of the guests were standing around it, drinking and talking.

By now Monks had started to notice that there were two fairly distinct groups—the older and more affluent, and a younger set, dressed casually and even flamboyantly, like Gwen and Coffee Trenette. Tight jeans and tops that accentuated breasts or pectorals seemed to be the prevailing uniform. They were mostly quite attractive—they looked like they were, or could be, actors and models.

One of them, a man, was looking back at him pointedly—glaring, in fact. He had on wraparound sunglasses, and it took Monks a moment to realize that it was Ray Dreyer, Eden's ex-boyfriend.

Dreyer was wearing a black silk jacket over a T-shirt. Monks walked over to him.

"Thoughtful of you to dress in mourning," Monks said quietly.

"Fuck you," Dreyer mouthed. Monks braced himself, thinking that Dreyer might want to pick up their fight where it had left off. But he turned away and went the other direction, farther into the shadows.

Another old friend who was glad to see him, Monks thought.

Then he noticed a slight flare of light, from the other direction. The main front door of the house was opening and closing. A man was coming out.

D'Anton.

Monks walked quickly back that way and intercepted D'Anton as he reached the bottom of the porch steps.

"Good evening, Doctor," Monks said.

D'Anton glanced around impatiently. The glance turned to an icy stare as he recognized Monks.

Monks was very aware that he might be looking into the eyes of a man who was capable of mutilating a living human being.

"How *dare* you come to my house," D'Anton said.

"Gwen Bricknell invited me."

"And you actually accepted?" D'Anton said, with withering disbelief.

"I was watching you inside there. It must be quite a feeling, being surrounded by your own creations."

Unexpectedly, D'Anton smiled. It was filled with pity for Monks.

"Do you know what they would tell you?" D'Anton said. "What they *have* told *me*? That they belong to me. Any fool can give them money, but I can give them what really matters—youth and beauty."

"So you figure you have the right to do anything you want with them?"

D'Anton's smile vanished. "I don't know what you're getting at, but I have had enough of you," he said. "If you come around me again, you'll be hearing from my attorney."

"The same errand boy you sent to scare Roberta Massey?"

D'Anton recoiled, a tiny backward jerk and widening of his eyes. But he recovered instantly. Monks had to hand it to him.

"That name means nothing to me," D'Anton said.

"Oh, right, you're not good with names, are you."

"I remember yours, now." D'Anton held Monks's gaze with his own, steely and unwavering, for a few seconds longer. Then he turned away and continued his brisk walk, fading into the night.

D'Anton had recognized Roberta's name, there was no doubt about that. Monks considered that he might have played that card too early. But it would increase the strain on D'Anton, and strain could lead to mistakes.

Monks moved back toward the pool, but stayed a little apart from the crowd. In another couple of minutes, Gwen came back out, carrying two flutes of pale effervescent champagne.

This time, as she passed the crowd at the pool, she was accosted by a thickset, balding man in his sixties, who leered at her like a satyr.

"Jesus, sweetheart, you look like jailbait tonight," he said in a loud, raspy voice.

Gwen paused, glancing at him in amusement.

"I know you're an expert there, Ivan."

"That thing still as tight as it used to be?" he growled.

"*You* certainly didn't stretch it any."

A ripple of laughter sounded from nearby guests, watching the two of them like a circle drawn up around teenaged boys getting ready to fight. Monks was touched by an equally adolescent outrage, a schoolboy urge to step in and defend his girl's honor. But she seemed to be enjoying it thoroughly—keeping the loutish attacker at bay, like an exquisite fencer, with quick, sure barbs.

Maybe the preoccupation with youthfulness that he sensed here was catching, Monks thought, although there had been none of it in the brilliant adamantine intensity that emanated from D'Anton.

She moved away from the group, her head turning, looking for Monks. He raised his hand to catch her attention.

"There you are," she called, and came to him. "I thought I'd lost you."

"No chance of that."

She handed him one of the flutes. "What shall we drink to?"

"How about the hostess?"

"Oh, you are good. All right. The hostess decrees that we entwine arms, like in the movies. Gaze into each other's eyes. And drain our glasses dry."

Monks had to stoop forward a little to be able to entwine arms and still drink. The champagne was wonderful, dry and tart, with a sort of muskiness like her perfume. Her eyes were dark, warm, intent, and their faces were close. She brushed his lips with hers. He was bemused. He had not seriously believed that she might be interested in him, no matter what Larrabee had said, and romance did not seem like a good mix with a murder investigation. But he wanted to keep things going and, he admitted, it was highly enjoyable. He felt a touch of guilt about Martine. Then he remembered the black Saab he had seen in her driveway earlier. That helped.

She took the champagne glasses, set them aside, and then came back to his embrace.

"Shall we do that some more?" she murmured.

"A lot more," Monks said. "But first, why don't

you show me that person you told me about? The
one who's so possessive of Dr. D'Anton?"

The wary look that he had seen in her eyes at the
clinic came back.

"I've been trying to pretend this is just a party,"
she said quietly. "But that won't work, will it?"

Monks touched her cheek. "I'll be glad to pretend
with you. But I need to do my job, too."

She stayed absolutely still for two or three seconds. Again, he got that eerie sense that whoever
lived inside her had left.

Then she gripped his arm conspiratorially.
"Come on," she said, and led him toward the house.
She pointed in through a window. "There."

The nurse, Phyllis, was still in the center of the
room. It looked like she was putting away the Botox
materials. She was wearing a dark gray suit, jacket
and skirt, that made her square figure look even
frumpier in this gala crowd.

"Phyllis?" Monks said.

Gwen nodded emphatically. "She's very sneaky,
and very jealous of Welles. She has all these little
ways of letting everybody know she owns him.
There've been times I've *felt* her behind me, and I'd
have sworn she had a knife in her hand."

Monks added more weight to Gwen's suspicion
than he had given it before. He remembered his
sense that Phyllis was stealthy. And she certainly
had the skills and opportunity to administer poison
to Eden Hale.

He decided it was time to push.

"Did Phyllis know about D'Anton's affair with Eden?" he said.

Gwen turned to him swiftly, eyes wide. "How did *you* know?"

"It's not going to be a secret much longer, Gwen. Is that why you lied to me, about not knowing her?"

There was a pause. It had the feel of being timed for effect. Then she sighed.

"All right, that was stupid of me," she said. "I should have known you'd find out. But no, that's not why. If Welles gets dragged through the mud, he deserves it."

"Why, then?"

"It will make more sense if I show you something," she said. "And then I'll work on making you forgive me."

She took his hand and led him around the house, in the opposite direction from the swimming pool. The original old structure, its windows unlit, jutted out ahead of them like a wing.

"This place has been in our family more than a hundred years," Gwen said. "On Julia's side. I spent a lot of time here, growing up."

"*Our* family?" he said, startled.

"She and I are cousins. I'm sorry. I guess you couldn't have known that."

Monks wasn't immediately sure how this new factor affected the mix, but it seemed to tighten things another notch.

She pushed open a door and touched a switch that turned on an overhead light. The space was large, two full stories high and taking up most of the wing. Apparently, the interior walls and upper floor had been taken out. The old hardwood floor was strewn with dust and rubble. There were a couple of large wooden workbenches and racks of stone-carving tools.

And the space was crowded with sculptures. All were human figures, and they all seemed to be of women—busts, torsos, a few full-sized. There were some clay models, but most were of stone. The style was classical, the forms lifelike. As best as he could judge, the renderings were competent—no more.

"This is how these parties got started," Gwen said. "Welles and Julia like to entertain. His patients, their social circle. Then Julia started inviting some of her models. It took on a life of its own."

"It does seem like an odd mix."

She shrugged. "The older guests are rich. Some are connected, film, modeling agencies, that sort of thing. They like having young, pretty people around. And *they* need money and favors. Most of them don't have any real talent."

Monks noted that it was the second time she had disdained them. And yet she, the fortyish hostess, ultra-sophisticated supermodel, was dressed like one of them, and had clearly loved being the center of attention—sparring like a teenaged cock-tease with the satyrlike Ivan. Monks wondered if her costume was a whim, or if there was a deeper element involved.

She walked to a figure that was draped and lifted away the canvas. This one was full-sized, a nude of a woman reclining on her side. It was unfinished, but the stone had an intrinsic quality— a sheen, almost a glow, that seemed to come from within.

"Is that marble?" he asked.

Gwen nodded. "Carrera. Julia got it from Italy. Recognize the model?"

He did not, at first. The delineation of the face had barely been started. But this piece stood out from the rest. The body was graceful, the pose sensuous, with thighs parted slightly in enticement, and Julia D'Anton had managed to capture a taunting element in the tilt of the head.

Then it clicked. "Eden," he said.

"Julia was a little—" Gwen hesitated, then said, "All right, I'll say it. In love with her. Then Eden started up with Welles. It hurt Julia badly."

"In love with, as in having an affair?"

Another hesitation. "Yes."

Monks gazed at the statue, and abruptly he *saw* the sorrow it contained—the passion the sculptress had invested, shimmering out through the muted glow of the stone. Accomplished or not technically, it was charged with emotion.

"Julia can be cruel," Gwen said. "A lot of people know it. So that's the reason I fibbed. I didn't want anyone to think she might have done something to Eden, for revenge."

"How do you mean, cruel?"

"Emotionally. When she's angry, she'll take it out on people. She was like that when she was young, and she never outgrew it."

"Why are you so sure she *didn't* do something?"

"I just am. I've known her all my life, for God's sake." Gwen let the drape fall back into place.

Monks was getting confused. Her words seemed to be leading in too many different directions. But it was not just that. Something was happening in his head that he could not quite grasp.

"How about D'Anton?" he said. "How well do you think you know him?"

"Since I was seventeen, when he and Julia met. He refined my face and gave me these." She touched her breasts. "And I've worked for him for eight years. Why? Do you suspect *him*?" She seemed amused at the thought.

Monks had been working his way toward something, but it slipped out of his recall. Gwen was watching him, eyes warm and lips parted. He stared at her, struck anew by her beauty, then turned away, trying to concentrate.

Roberta Massey, and the other girl who had gone missing, Katie. That was it.

"Gwen," he said. "Did you know that the police came to the clinic?" His voice sounded thick and slow to his own hearing.

She stepped to him, put her hands on his hips, and very lightly pressed her pelvis against him.

"No. But can't it wait?" she said, arching up to be kissed, lips open this time.

Monks imagined that he could feel the heat rising from her, a shimmer of delicious sensation seeking to enfold him. He held her, entranced by this ritual of human beings exploring each other's mouths with their tongues. It was very strange. But it was *good*. He remembered feebly that he had been thinking about something that had seemed important. But yes, that could wait.

"I feel like getting wet," she announced.

Feel like getting wet. The words spun disjointedly in his head. That was a strange way to put things. How could a person feel like getting wet?

She led him back the way they had come. Monks inhaled deeply, feeling the scents of the night cut into him in a heady rush, the eucalyptus, her perfume, smoke that he identified as marijuana. Bits of the conversations they passed joined *feel like getting wet* in his mind, swirling and reverberating with hidden importance.

told her I'd never ever
he came around with
five thousand? bullshit maybe twenty

There were more swimmers now, fluid shapes moving through the water or hanging on the sides. Monks was close enough now to see that the underwater lights revealed bare feet, legs, asses. He looked at Gwen in astonishment.

"No suits in the pool," she said, with a slight smile. "That's the rule."

pool that's the rule

The marijuana smoke was thicker here, with glowing red dots traveling through the darkness a few feet at a time, pausing, traveling on. He had been catching more whiffs of the deep acrid smoke of harder drugs, too.

"It gives the young people a chance to get looked over," she said. "Arrangements get made."

Monks realized that almost all the swimmers were from the younger set. The older guests stood on the deck with drinks in hand, chatting or just watching.

He remembered what Gwen had said on the phone—*like parties, but more focused.*

Then he saw that one of the watchers was Julia D'Anton. She was alone, a little way apart from the crowd, wearing a long black dress and heavy dark eye shadow—another mourner for Eden. But she was gazing intently at the swimmers.

The term *chickenhawk* came into his mind.

As if he had spoken it aloud, Julia raised her gaze and met his. Her eyes seemed as dark and empty as a skull's. He looked away quickly.

He became aware of a couple clinging to the wall in a dark far corner of the pool, face-to-face, their steady underwater motions creating an eddy that rippled out across the water's surface and right through his skin, penetrating him in a *whoosh* as if his body was gone and only his raw nerves were left to feel.

And he saw, as he had seen the heartbreak glow from the statue of Eden Hale, but with an intensity so heightened it was almost unbearable, that this was a marketplace—that some commodity was being bartered away by the young to the old, in return for money, drugs, the hope of fame. It was not sex, or pleasure—that was only the medium of exchange. It cut far deeper, into the vitality of youth.

Coffee Trenette. Used up.

Focused.

Monks moved onward, lurching a little. Gwen walked patiently beside him. They came around the grotto's rock cornice, and he found himself staring at another tableau. A man was leaning against the wall, relaxed, complacent-looking. Monks recognized the satyrlike older man who had accosted Gwen earlier. He was clothed, but his trousers were open and his chubby member protruding, gripped in the hand of a pretty young woman. She was nude, her skin glistening with water, apparently just out of the pool. One of her knees was slightly bent, as if she was about to kneel.

But when she saw Monks and Gwen, she let go of him and stepped away, head turning aside and gaze going downcast, arms moving automatically across her body. Monks had once read somewhere that a Western woman, if caught unclothed by a strange man, would cover her vulva and breasts, but in other parts of the world, she would cover her face. There was a certain logic to that.

The satyr grinned at Gwen. "I keep telling you, baby, I got the power," he said.

"You got Viagra," Monks suggested distantly.

The grin dissolved into a hostile stare.

"Why don't you go back where you came from?"

"Impossible," Monks pointed out, frowning. "No space-time continuum can ever be repeated."

"You're a fucking wacko, you know that?"

"Not my fault. Schroedinger's."

"Get outta here!"

Monks backed away, shaking his head, trying to clear it. His brain seemed to bounce inside his skull.

Gwen came beside him again, catching his arm, steadying him. "Ivan likes to make sure everyone knows he's still virile."

"Poor girl."

"Don't worry, she's getting hers," Gwen said. "He owns a modeling agency."

Monks was starting to hyperventilate. Waves of pure sensation were washing through him. They were not unpleasant, but they were frightening.

Then he was aware that Julia D'Anton was standing in front of him. Her arms were folded imperiously.

"I see you found a date," she said coolly to Gwen, but her gaze stayed on Monks.

"I see you're looking for one," Gwen retorted.

Julia ignored her. "So you think someone murdered Eden, Dr. Monks? And that they might be here tonight?"

Things had gotten far more complicated than that, Monks thought, but the right words would not come.

"If thou hast blood on thy hands and shed more blood, wherewith shall ye cleanse it?" he asked, trying earnestly to explain. "For how shall ye wash off blood with blood?"

Both women looked startled.

Gwen murmured, "You'd better excuse us," to Julia, and helped Monks to a chair. He sat heavily.

"Something—is happening to me," he said.

"What kind of something?" Her fingers massaged his neck and shoulders.

"In my brain," he tried to explain. "The universe is getting scrambled."

She inhaled sharply. "Oh, my god. It sounds like ecstasy."

"Like what?"

"Ecstasy," Gwen said. "XTC."

Monks raised his head and stared at her.

"I wonder if someone slipped some in your drink," she said. "Sometimes they do that, to newcomers. It's supposed to be a joke, but this is awful."

Her fists went to her hips in outrage. "If I find out who did it, they'll never come here again."

The import hit him with numbing impact. "I can't believe," he said. "Can't believe—I need to get someplace." He tried to heave himself to his feet. Her hand held him down with surprising strength.

"But darling, you *are* someplace," she said. "Just sit still a minute. You'll calm down." She crouched beside him, her face close. Her eyes were luminous with passion. "I'll predict the future. A beautiful woman wearing black will fulfill all your desires. Soon."

"Black?" he said stupidly. Her blouse was white. The only thing black she was wearing, that he could see, at least, was the top underneath it.

"Come on. We'll go where we can be safe and alone."

"My car," he objected.

"Don't be silly, you can't drive. Let yourself *go,* Carroll. I'll take care of you."

This time, she helped him get to his feet. He stumbled along, holding her hand like a child.

She led him away from the pool and party, around the base of the cliff that abutted the house, and up a stairway of flat stones that had been set into the earth. It was quiet here, and dark except for the gibbous moon, topping the coastal mountains to throw its cold fire across the land.

Monks became aware of the musical sound of

trickling water, growing louder as they climbed. They came to a plateau, a hundred yards behind the house and a bit higher than its roof. The water was running down a rock face in a little fall, into a natural pool, about twenty feet across.

"This is the spring that feeds the swimming pool," she said. "Julia and I used to play here. Sit."

She eased him down onto a flat rock. Monks started to get his wind back. The dizzying surges were leveling off, leaving him bristling with unimagined perceptions. He turned his head slowly, seeing the swelling hillsides split into deep, secretive crevasses, watered by streams that emptied into the great sea. Trees burst from the earth with their fierce erect trunks, then gentled out into feminine branches that lifted long-tipped fingers in supplication to the sky. All of nature was fueled by this huge engine, the generator of life.

And everywhere within it, death was waiting—hidden, seething with menace, razor talons ready to strike.

"Are you ready for the lady in black?" she said.

He turned toward her voice. The blouse was gone and she was stepping out of her skirt, tossing it aside. Her fingers worked at a knot between her breasts. She unwound the garment sensuously, then tossed it around her neck. Monks realized that it was not a tube top. It was a black scarf.

Except for that, she was all flesh, shining ivory in

the moonlight like a pagan goddess. Her splendor filled him with worshipful awe.

She walked to him boldly, high full breasts shimmying with her steps, nipples taut in the crisp air. She was shaved bare as marble. He stared, entranced by the miracle of skin, its color that no image could ever quite capture, its smooth sheen so warm to the touch.

"How old am I?" she demanded.

Monks was confused. How could she not know?

"Thirty . . . nine?" he hazarded.

"No! I'm eighteen. And very naughty." Her hand moved to the back of his neck and urged him toward her. "Taste me."

Monks parted the delicate slick flesh with his tongue, finding the tiny bud within. Jewel in the lotus, he thought. Man in the boat. He felt her shiver, her fingers tightening in his hair. She shivered again, and again, and then tensed, thrusting hard against him.

Far away above him, he heard three soft cries, oh, oh, *oh*.

For half a minute longer, they stayed still, with his cheek pressed against her warm belly while her fingers stroked his hair. Then she sank to her knees.

"Now you," she said. Together, they tugged off his clothes. She pushed him back down onto the rock and fastened her mouth on him, liquid fire, quickly sucking him rigid. Then she slipped her

arms around his neck and straddled his thighs.
Monks slid slowly into delicious softness that went
on and on, and oh, man, holy angels, this was *it,* this
was what being born was all *about*—

"Can you feel my womb?" she whispered.

Whoa, she was at it again, picking his brain, but
could he *ever* feel it, a sweet soft rub right where it
counted, *rubadubdub*—

"*It* can feel *you.*"

Well, that was just wonderful, that was how it was
supposed to be, yep, the way it was all engineered,
he understood that now like he never had. He was
leaning back on his hands, sharp bits of gravel bit-
ing into his palms and buttocks like the teeth of
unseen watchers, goading him on, gleefully whispering unintelligible words. She settled into a slow
swaying of her hips, coaxing pleasure from him
until there was no longer a point where he stopped
and she started, with those wonderful breasts
bouncing against his chest, *oh my god I am heartily
sorry for anything bad I ever said about silicone.*
The black scarf was looped around her throat, tumbling down her back, and abruptly, a razor-edged
vision flashed into his mind of the night he had
almost strangled Alison Chapley with a black scarf
just like it. And he remembered that Gwen had
picked *that* out of his head.

"The scarf," he said thickly.

"Yes?" she panted.

"It's—how could you know—?"

"That it's special to you?"

"Not special," he managed. "Scary."

She quickened her movements, fingernails digging into his back. Her eyes were aglow, her mouth open, laughing, joining her voice to the invisible chortling chorus—

"Come in me!" she cried, and he did, in shuddering waves, roaring with the unendurable raw sensation.

Monks fell back onto the rock, pulse hammering, arms sprawled at his sides. He was drained, his soul as empty as his loins, nothing left of him but a sensory apparatus. She rose and stood over him, majestic, imperious, the insides of her thighs glistening with her conquest.

"Now I can heal you," she said. "What you're afraid of—I'll make it go away."

He wanted to point out that he did not really mind being afraid, that in some ways he much preferred it to being brave. But before he could find the words, she loosened the scarf from her neck and dangled it over him, as if teasing a cat.

"Take hold," she said.

He reached up and gripped it. It was silk, sending little electric shocks through his fingertips. She tugged, stepping backward, urging him upright, then to his feet. When she got to the pool, she stepped in, disappearing with barely a splash. She was still holding her end of the scarf, and its tension jerked him to the pool's edge. A few seconds later, the white column of her body appeared again, her head breaking the surface. The scarf was stretched taut between them.

She tugged. Monks resisted, listening to the voices in the night's gentle wind. They seemed to be promising that this was what every instant of his life had been leading to.

She pulled again, harder. Whether she forced him or he yielded, he was not sure. The water was cool, a harsh shock to his skin, and it was deep. His feet did not touch bottom, and his motions to swim were awkward, his body not reacting with its usual coordination. It was alarming, a sudden forceful reminder of how out of control he was. He let the scarf go, struggled to the pool's rocky edge, and clung there. He spent a few seconds catching his breath, then started hauling his torso onto dry land.

Gwen breaststroked easily over to him. Her movements were graceful, and she shimmered with strength, her body all lissome toned muscle.

"Not *yet*," she said. "You haven't given it a chance." She gripped his ankle and tugged playfully, pulling him back in. He was not prepared for it, and he sank below the surface again, thrashing, gulping water. He came up hacking, groping for the rim.

"I can't" —he coughed— "do this."

"Oh, yes. It's what you've always wanted."

She disappeared in a smooth swift surface dive. He felt her hands at his right ankle again. This time, when she came back up, something was looped around it.

The something tugged, pulling him toward the pool's center.

She moved backward, treading water, holding the scarf's other end, towing him. She was smiling.

"Give in to the embryonic fluid that surrounds you," she whispered. "You're being reborn."

"I'm drowning," Monks gasped.

He tried to eggbeater kick, but the scarf held his right leg useless, and the left just flailed. He paddled furiously with his arms, but they barely kept him afloat, and were tiring fast. The voices cawed in triumph now, like ravenous prisoners finally about to tear into a meal.

He understood, with terrible clarity, that the scarf linking him to Alison Chapley had returned now like a vengeful snake to strike back at him.

He thrashed toward Gwen, but she eluded him easily. She dove again, becoming a silvery shape flitting in the water's blackness. The scarf yanked at his ankle, hard this time, pulling him under. Monks fought his way back up, sucking air in shrieking gulps—understanding that this was the last time.

"Now ask yourself, was Eden really worth it?" he heard her say behind him.

Monks inhaled one more lungful of air, then plunged his face down into the water, doubling over to grip his ankle. The scarf was wet, tightened into a knot his fingers could not undo.

She yanked again, pulling his ankle from his hands. He found it once more, hooked his thumbs inside the loop, and pushed down with everything he had. The loop caught for a second on his heel, but then slipped free.

He broke the surface, clawing for the pool's rim, kicking back to keep her away. He felt her hands on his leg again, felt the tightening loop of the scarf. He lashed out savagely, a hard thrust with his heel. It connected, with a shocking impact, with her flesh. Then he was free.

He scrabbled out of the water on his belly, suddenly aware of a raging presence around him that wanted furiously to hold him back. The rocks' sharp teeth tore at his flesh as he rolled to his feet. He crashed into the woods and ran headlong, branches and twigs underfoot stabbing and slashing him, voices howling in his head. He missed a step on the steep hillside, stumbled, missed another, and fell rolling downward, the hard earth beating the breath from his lungs and clawing more skin from his flesh. He kept himself rolling, over and over, tumbling down until he crashed against a rotted fallen log. He dragged himself over it, into its lee, and huddled there, fighting to get his breath back.

After a minute or so, he heard her.

"Carroll," she called. "What's the matter, darling? I was only playing!" Her voice was sweet, anxious, concerned.

Monks raised his face just enough to glimpse over the log. She was standing on the hilltop at the edge of the woods, a silvery magnificent vision. Her hair was loose now, a wild, wet stream down her back and shoulders, shimmering as her head turned slowly to overlook the moonlit landscape.

"Are you hurt? Tell me, I'll come help you." She took a few tentative steps forward, brush crackling under her feet. Monks tensed, ready to flee again. But she hissed in pain and bent suddenly to grip her foot, then backed away, limping a little. He closed his eyes in thanks. The same sharp branches and stones that had fought him were his protectors now.

But the sense of menace was still thick around him.

"You can't stay out till morning—you'll freeze! Come to me, love. I want you again."

Monks waited.

Suddenly, in screeching fury: "You kicked me, you *bastard*!"

He bowed his head again and hugged himself, shivering. He had never heard a voice like that—it was the furious presence he felt, speaking through her.

"Do I scare you because I'm not a cripple, is *that* it?"

He closed his eyes. She had found that in him too,

not just Alison now, but Martine. Vengeance was descending for all that he had and had not done.

"I know you hear me," she called, voice low with wrath. "I can feel you. Go ahead and hide, but I've got you in me now. You're *mine*."

He opened his eyes in time to see her stalking away, her white shape fading into darkness.

Monks lay there trembling in his cold rebirth. Around him, the night creatures moved with tiny rustlings, stealthy, timid with fear or fierce with readiness to pounce. In the distance, an owl hooted, *whuh oo-ooo*. The presence hovered around him, electric with menace: Hecate, queen of the night, mistress of spellcasters. They had powered their magic with effluvia from the victim's body, believed to contain the vital essence—hair, nail clippings, menstrual blood. Semen.

Monks forced himself to rise. Getting out of *here* was what mattered most in the world. He could see the lights of the house downhill and steered himself by them, crashing naked through the brush, barking in pain from his tormented bare feet. The invisible fury fought him like a headwind, while the voices chittered in his brain.

The parking area was deserted. He trotted in a crouch to the Bronco, pausing to peer in the windows, to make sure it was empty, then dropped to the ground and pulled himself under the rear end. His fingers found the set of spare keys he kept wired there, hidden by a carefully applied clump of mud.

He got in and shuddered with relief when the big engine caught.

He found the narrow road and piloted the vehicle like a grandmother, hardly faster than a crawl, hands clenching the wheel at ten and three, staring wide-eyed through the windshield in the desperate effort to keep that winding line of pavement between the front tires. The overwhelming sense was that he and the Bronco were staying still. Everything else was moving, in a fluid shifting tapestry that obeyed no rules of physical order.

It got quickly unendurable. His panicked gaze searched for a place to hide, and spotted the moonlit tall tops of a eucalyptus grove across a field. He aimed for it, jarring his bones over ruts and hummocks, and finally pulled in behind the trees.

Little by little, the fury around him eased and the voices in his head receded. Awareness of cold seeped back in, and his body responded to meet its need, rummaging in the Bronco's rear for jeans and a sweatshirt. He went teary-eyed at their delicious warmth. He was feeling pain again now, too, from his cuts and bruises. Dark blood seeped from his flesh where the branches had slashed. But he knew that the healing had already begun—that invisible forces, like brownies in a fairy tale, were gathering to rebuild the torn tissue and replace the lost fluids. It was a marvel, this fleshly system that carried him around. As a physician, he was only a clumsy mechanic, able to guide the process a little. But the real work was taken care of on a molecular level, by some mysterious organic instinct that knew exactly what it was doing.

For a time he could not measure, he huddled in the front seat, drifting off into fantastic inner landscapes, getting hints of insights that seemed to have stupendous importance, then snapping back into watchful fear.

At last, he could feel that the drug was wearing off. The moon was near the horizon now. He guessed that four or five hours had passed since he had first arrived at the house. He got out and walked around for a minute to clear his head, then started the engine again. This time, things around him stayed put. He drove carefully, still a little shaky, but all right on the predawn back country roads.

Monks's mind was already filling with doubt. Had any of it really happened? Had she actually tried to drown him—or was that only a drug-induced fantasy, generated by a compounding of his fear, suspicions, and long-buried guilt about Alison? Had he imagined the words he thought she had screamed?

Or was he only being allowed to escape because of a deeper and far more fearsome truth?

It had not only happened, but she was right.

He was hers now.

27

Gwen Bricknell stalked into the big house through Julia's studio, avoiding the party still going on out front, and quickly climbed the back stairs to her apartment. She had put her skirt and blouse back on, but she was wet, and pale with cold and rage. When she threw open the door, her trembling gaze landed on a vase of a dozen glorious red roses on her vanity. She had brought them up earlier, from the flowers delivered for the party, to celebrate. But now they mocked her.

She yanked off the garments and stuffed them in the trash, then grabbed a pair of scissors and hacked at the scarf, ripping it into shreds. It had failed her. She had had Monks so close. Everyone had seen him stoned. He would have been found in the spring, tomorrow morning, where he had wandered and fallen in. And that would have been the end of the prying.

Then her hands fell to her sides, dropping the scissors and scarf. The truth was, something in her had not wanted him dead. She had failed herself.

But she could not afford that weakness again.

She put on a fluffy terry robe, kept warm on an electrically heated rack, and started hot water running in the Jacuzzi. Then she laid out a long line of finely powdered cocaine on a china plate. She inhaled it sharply, standing quiet while its sweet energy mushroomed in her brain. When the tub was half full, she added a few drops of Rigaud bath oil and stepped in. She sank back, eyes closing, feeling the steaming warmth recharging her cells. There was nothing for that like hot water, but one had to be careful. Water was not friendly to the skin.

She rose and patted herself dry with deliciously soft towels, like the robe, kept electrically warm. She studied herself at her full-length mirror. Most of the flaws—the tiny crow's-feet developing at the corners of her eyes, the slight slackness in her jaw-line, the softening of flesh where no amount of exercise would tighten it—could be artfully concealed. Her skin was supple with the oil. But it was not what it once had been. It was losing elasticity, that smooth tautness over the muscles. There was even evidence of checking, and traces of cellulite on her buttocks and thighs.

In spite of all the exercising, the vitamins, the skin care, she was losing ground at the age of forty-one. There was no longer any denying it.

The days when men with cameras had adored her, when the phone never stopped ringing and all the good things in the world were hers to pick and choose, were long gone. She had stretched them by going to work for D'Anton—becoming the prime example of his art, a living sculpture that women envied and men were still awed by. But she had nearly lost that, too. She shivered, and dressed quickly in jeans and a sweater.

Then she stepped to the vanity and picked up the vase of roses that no admirer had sent, and threw it, with a *hnnhh* of exploding breath, against the mirror. The vase shattered and the mirror cracked in all directions, like a giant spiderweb with spreading fingers.

28

Coffee Trenette is alone when you find her, curled up on a couch in a darkened side room, watching the poolside party through the windows. She's high from smoking junk.

You knew where she'd be. You've been watching her tonight, getting all this together in your head.

Monks was here, searching for *you*. And Coffee was talking to him.

She doesn't say a word as you walk up—just watches you. She's the queen of cool, with a way of looking at you that puts you right down under her shoes. Like the others, she thinks she knows what you are.

You kneel on the floor beside her, like you're nervous about approaching her.

"What you want?" she says, but her tone isn't too tough. She senses that you're here to offer something.

You keep your voice very quiet. "Here it is, straight. I've got a bottle of pharmaceutical Demerol. Hundred-milligram, the strong stuff."

She stays cool, watching you with that heavy-lidded look. But she's already made up her mind. Smoke is fine, but the needle is the real thing, and there are twenty or thirty shots in a bottle.

"You going to just give it to me?" she says.

You smile timidly. "I've always had a thing for you."

Her lips twist, just a little. She nods and rises unsteadily.

"It's out in my car," you say. "Come on."

You lead her out the back way, to where you've parked, in the shadows. She stands beside the car, rubbing her upper arms like she's cold. You reach across and pop open the passenger door.

She hesitates a moment longer, then slides in beside you.

29

In the hours between midnight and dawn, the world was still and without distractions, even of daylight itself. D'Anton sat in the darkened waiting room of his clinic, surrounded by the images of his women. It was something he did frequently. It soothed him—softened the hard sharp edge he lived on. His mind was usually a clear pool at these times, and his thinking was pure and undisturbed. He had trained himself since childhood not to need more than four or five hours of sleep per night. He had used this predawn time to form himself into a master surgeon—first, for study, then for practice, and ultimately, to envision the creations he would render.

To see the potential beauty of a woman, and then

to be able to render it—to wield the scalpel as it delicately parted the skin, to reshape precisely her living flesh, to take her down to the bone and bring her back transformed—this was a power to which nothing else compared.

But there was no soothing in it tonight. He had made an appearance at the party, put on a good face. He did not want the world to know what Eden's loss meant to him.

Even worse than that—the grotesque fear that he had managed to bury deep in his mind was coming to the surface.

And he was not alone. Monks had spoken the name, Roberta Massey. How in the hell had he found out about *her*?

A glow appeared on the room's far wall. It brightened, swung in an arc, then disappeared. He realized that it came from headlights shining through the curtains—a vehicle pulling into the clinic's parking lot. D'Anton looked at his watch. It was 12:43. No one had any business here. He got to his feet and went to a window.

Gwen Bricknell was hurrying up the clinic's steps.

D'Anton strode to the door and jerked it open, anger overcoming his surprise.

"What has gotten into you?" he snapped. "First you invite Monks to our house. Then you show up here, in the middle of the night."

"I'm trying to save you, darling," she said, stalking haughtily past him.

"Save me? What are you talking about?"

"From death row," she said kindly.

"Death *row*? Gwen, what is this—mad cow disease?" But he felt the unseen blow to his gut, close to where that fear lived.

"You want to play games, Welles?" she said. "All right. Let me tell you a story."

She sat on the desk, crosslegged, hands folded in her lap. It was a little girl's pose—but she was at the station where she controlled the clinic. D'Anton stood before her, powerless, like a patient.

"Once upon a time, there was a beautiful model, who made a plastic surgeon famous," she said. Her tone was childish, too, an eerie high-pitched whisper. "Let's call her Gwen. She spent her career as a living advertisement for him, and then went to work for him. Right here at this desk." She slapped her hand down on it.

"Then one day she noticed that he was doing thousands of dollars' worth of free surgery on some little slut. Let's call *her* Eden. It didn't take Gwen long to figure out what was going on. Gwen knew the surgeon had affairs. He'd had one with Gwen, when *she* was young. She could forgive all that. But this was different. The surgeon was making Eden into his new advertisement. Then he was going to throw Gwen away, like an old rug."

"Oh, no," D'Anton said softly, enlisting that confident voice that women found hypnotic. "Dear, dear Gwen, you misunderstand completely."

She ignored him.

"Gwen started listening to the surgeon when he was on the phone, and one day she heard him tell Eden he'd meet her that night," she said. "But he didn't say where. Gwen drove to all the places she thought they might go, and finally, it must have been one o'clock in the morning by then, she came here.

"There weren't any cars, but there was a light on inside that shouldn't have been. She thought maybe the surgeon had parked in the loading dock, so no one would know he was here. So she let herself in the back door and looked. Sure enough, the surgeon's car was there, and she could hear somebody, farther in."

D'Anton stared at her silently, with his dread rising to the point of nausea.

"Gwen was just about to go in there and let the surgeon and his girlfriend have it," she whispered. "Then she saw that the car's trunk was open, and there was a big plastic garbage bag in it. Now, the surgeon would never have carried something like that in his beautiful car. What in the world was going on?"

Her eyes were wide, with a child's playacting earnestness. But the fear in them was real.

"She walked over to the bag and touched it. Something inside was soft and warm. Her hand knew what it was. She took her shoes off and tiptoed out of there as fast as she could, and ran to her car. She never believed she *could* be so scared."

D'Anton was stepping back, shaking his head, palms held out in denial.

"Don't worry," she whispered, leaning forward as if to follow him. "Gwen didn't breathe a word to anybody. It's their secret—hers and the famous surgeon's."

"No!" D'Anton almost shouted. "It wasn't *me*."

Her eyes narrowed in disbelief.

"You never saw me, did you?" he demanded.

"I didn't need to," she said, in her normal voice now. "Who else could have been here, driving your car?"

D'Anton exhaled slowly. "There's only one other person who drives that car."

"*Julia*? You can't be serious."

He turned away, clasping his head as if he was trying to keep it from exploding.

"You know how vicious she can be," he said. "I suspected it first when that girl, Katie, disappeared. I think there've been others. She's trying to compete with me in some insane way. Taking out her rage. It's been absolute hell to live with, but I didn't know what to do. Just hoped to God I was wrong."

His body sagged, hands falling to his sides.

"I think she murdered Eden," he said.

Abruptly, Gwen laughed, a sound that rang wildly out of place in the stillness.

"Tell the world that if you want, Welles," she said. "Gwen knows the truth." She slid off the desk and moved toward him, slowly and seductively, all full-grown woman again.

"You don't have to hide anything from her anymore," she said softly. "She knows you're the master sculptor. You're driven to push beyond the limits. To see how far you can take the living flesh, toward perfection."

"I'm not *hiding* anything. Haven't you heard what I've said?"

"But you have to remember, you owe everything to Gwen," she said. "It was her face, her body, that the world saw, with your name hooked to them. And you are going to *keep* her the way she was. She's done aging."

D'Anton's forehead furrowed in bewilderment. "What are you talking about? No one stops—"

She slapped his face, a hard stinging blow.

"She's going to make the Monks problem go away," she said. "And then, things are going to be like they used to be. You're going to make her perfect again, an inch at a time. From now on, she is what you *do*."

D'Anton looked into her impassioned eyes, his skin prickling with the realization that he might have thought the wrong woman was insane.

He said, with a quaver in his voice, "Was it *you* who killed Eden?"

"Eden's gone. Now there's just Gwen." She

leaned close, all softness again, breasts against him, lips at his ear. "She'll take care of you, much better than Eden ever would have. And she'll keep faith, to the death."

D'Anton was starting to understand that the beauty he had created was making him a prisoner.

Then he thought he heard a stealthy sound coming from the hallway that led to the procedure rooms.

30

Outside the windows of Larrabee's office, the sky was starting to lighten into dawn. Guido Franchi, Larrabee's detective friend from the SFPD, was sitting at the kitchen table across from Monks. Franchi was a big black-haired man with a drooping mustache, a heavily lined face, and skeptical eyes that were bleary from his being called out at five o'clock on a Saturday morning. They watched Monks steadily.

"So, let me make sure I got this right," Franchi said. "You left there naked, after having sex with this lady? Your clothes are still there?"

Monks had his hands pressed against his face, forefingers massaging his temples.

"I know how it sounds," he said.

"You admit you could have imagined the part about her trying to drown you? What with the drug, and all?"

"I don't think so. But it's possible."

Franchi leaned back in his chair, turning his mug of coffee in both hands, as if trying to warm it through friction.

"That doesn't give me much to work with," he said. "Right off, there's a jurisdiction problem. If she's still up in Marin, it's their case. If she came back to the city, I could pick her up for attempted murder. But how the fuck am I supposed to do that, when my only witness admits he was stoned out of his skull?"

Monks was still shaky, and he felt like there was grit floating around in his brain, but the drug seemed to be gone from his system now.

"I don't have any measure of how far gone I was," he said. "Either of you ever tried it? Ecstasy?"

Franchi shook his head. "Too New Age for me."

"Iris brought some home a couple times," Larrabee said. "It's great for in the sack, but it does twist your head around. What I'm wondering about, Carroll, how could she have known about the scarf? Or Martine?"

Monks had been wondering that, too. More and more, he was fearing that he *had* hallucinated the whole thing.

"Sorry," he said. "I feel like an asshole, believe me."

"I'm not worried about *you* feeling like an asshole," Franchi said. "I'm worried about *me* fucking around with a guy like D'Anton, and coming up empty." He stood and poured more coffee. "You got anything to eat?" he asked Larrabee. "Sweet roll, something like that?"

"Bagels."

"Terrific. My stomach starts acting up if I don't get something in it. Any advice, Doc?"

"Go easy on the coffee. Try Tagamet."

"Yeah, that's pretty much what my doctor said. But I keep forgetting." Franchi stepped to a window and stared out, scowling.

"If it's true, that Katie Bensen was killed, and Roberta Massey almost was," Franchi said, "was Ms. Bricknell the one who did that, too?"

Monks shook his head. "I can believe she slipped something in my drink," he said. "Tried to drown me. Maybe even poisoned Eden. But not that she cut the skin off a woman's face."

But he knew he could be wrong.

"What about that nurse she pointed out? Who's so jealous of D'Anton?" Larrabee asked.

"She'd have the skills," Monks said. "So would D'Anton, or other clinic people."

"All right, we'll run NCIC checks on all those employees," Franchi said, turning back to the room.

"Eden's boyfriend, too. Somebody might have a sheet. Let's locate D'Anton, and let's pick up Gwen. You said she's got an apartment here?"

"That's what she told me," Monks said. "I don't know the address. She might have stayed in Marin, too."

"You call her there," Franchi said. "Don't say the cops are in this yet; that might spook her. If she's gone, try and find out where she is. If she's there, play it like she was right, you lost your head, you want to come talk to her, some bullshit like that."

"Tell her you want your clothes back," Larrabee said. Both detectives looked amused. Monks was not.

The directions Gwen had given him to the party, with the house's phone number, were still in the Bronco. He went down to get them, hobbling on his scratched and bruised feet.

When he came back, Larrabee had popped bagels out of a toaster oven and put them on a plate.

"There's cream cheese," he said. "Sorry, no lox."

"I'll make the call first," Monks said.

Larrabee turned the telephone's speaker on. The two detectives stood listening, chewing quietly, while Monks punched the number.

It rang several times before a woman's voice answered. She was very irritable, and she was not Gwen.

"Do you have any idea what time it is?" she snapped. "Who *is* this?"

"It's Dr. Monks. Mrs. D'Anton? Julia?"

"Yes?" Her tone made it clear that identifying himself had not gained him any points.

Franchi made a cutting motion across his throat with his forefinger. They did not want Julia D'Anton to know that she was on the suspect list, too.

Monks nodded. "I need to find Gwen," he said.

"Then I suggest you call someplace she is, instead of someplace she's not."

"Where's that?" Monks said quickly, worried that she would hang up.

"How should I know? You were her date."

"Her apartment in San Francisco?"

"I'd say that's likely," Julia said. "Although maybe with somebody else. Did you disappoint her?"

"How about your husband? Do you know where he is?"

"Probably in the city, too, at our house there. That's where he stays most of the time."

"I need both those addresses and phones. Cells, too."

"Dr. Monks, what exactly is your interest in us?" Julia said scathingly. "First, Gwen tells me you suspect that Eden was murdered. Next thing I know, you're socializing at our house, staggering around like a drunk teenager. Now you're tracking us. Are we under suspicion? Or are you just trying to screw my cousin?"

Monks looked for help to Franchi, and got none. The cop's big, weary face stayed impassive.

"I wasn't drunk, Julia," Monks said. "Somebody drugged me. This has taken a very serious turn."

Long seconds of silence passed. Monks felt himself being weighed. When she spoke again, her tone was still haughty, but a note of uncertainty had crept in.

"I'll have to get my address book. I don't remember the cell numbers."

She returned to the phone a few moments later. Monks wrote down the information and gave her Larrabee's office number.

"If anybody comes back there, don't say anything about this," he said. "Get someplace private and call me."

He clicked the phone off and looked at his judges, wondering if he had given too much away. But Franchi did not seem displeased.

"Okay," Franchi said. "Let's get after it."

Monks picked at a bagel and listened while Franchi dispatched unmarked cars to Gwen Bricknell's apartment building, a Nob Hill high-rise, and to D'Anton's Pacific Heights home. While they waited, Franchi called downtown to start National Crime Information Center checks on the suspects.

It only took a few minutes to find out that nobody answered the phones, or the doors, at either Gwen's apartment or D'Anton's house. Both their vehicles were gone.

"You could try the clinic," Monks said. "Sometimes she goes there on weekends to catch up on work."

"The morning after she tried to off you?" Franchi said sourly.

Monks winced.

"Well, what the hell," Franchi said. "Can't hurt to look."

He called the cars in the field again. The three men waited.

This time, when Franchi's phone rang back, he started to look animated.

"Get some backup, make sure nobody gets out of there," he said into the phone. "Then see if she'll come to the door. If she does, hold her till I get there. Again, that name's Gwen Bricknell. Very good-looking babe, dark hair, about forty." He glanced at Monks, eyebrows raised, for corroboration. Monks nodded.

"And keep this off the radio," Franchi ordered. "I don't want every fucking unit in the Taraval coming in spikes high."

"Her car's there," he told Monks and Larrabee. "Let's hope she lets them in. We can't just go kicking the door down."

More minutes passed, with Franchi talking tersely to the officers on the scene. Monks could not understand all of the clipped, coded copspeak, but it did not sound promising.

Finally, Franchi confirmed that. "Nobody

answers the phone inside. They've banged on the doors and windows. Nothing. I'll have to go downtown, try to get a warrant to break in. This is *really* hanging my ass out." He was looking bleary again, but now pissed off, too. Monks was aware that police tended not to like it when technicalities got in the way, especially in the way of taking down someone genuinely dangerous.

"You want to ride along?" Franchi asked Larrabee. "Catch up on what you've been missing all these years?" Larrabee nodded. To Monks, Franchi said, "I think you ought to stay here, Doctor. If she is in there, it might not be a good idea for her to see you. You could probably use some sleep. Just keep that phone close by, in case the doctor's wife calls."

Monks was a little hurt, like a child who had been ditched by older boys going off on an adventure too rough for him.

He finished the bagel he had been working on, then went into Larrabee's living room and stretched out on the couch. Sleep was out of the question. But it started to come home to him that he was in a warm, safe place.

That was something he had not appreciated nearly enough in his life.

31

It was just after seven A.M. when Larrabee and Franchi arrived at D'Anton's clinic, carrying a warrant empowering the police to enter it, by force if necessary. An unmarked car with two plainclothes detectives was waiting in front, and two black-and-white squad cars were parked to triangulate the building, watching the other exits. They had tried repeatedly to rouse anyone who might be inside, but there had been no response.

The break-in was not going to require finesse. Ordinary locks could be picked or opened with a lock gun, but the clinic was protected by high-security deadbolts. All narcotics were locked in a safe, but any place that kept them was still a prime target for burglary. The simplest way in, and easiest to repair, was to break a window. That would set off a silent alarm system connected to the Taraval District police station, but they had been alerted and would not respond.

One of the detectives was in his thirties, comparatively young and agile. At Franchi's okay, wearing gloves and goggles, he smashed a ground-floor window with a gorilla bar. They waited, listening. It was just possible that someone was inside, armed, and that the intrusion would make him—or her—desperate.

The detective cleared the shards of glass from the frame, then went in, boosted by the others, pistol in hand. A minute later, he opened the rear door. Franchi, Larrabee, and the second detective went in next, leaving the uniformed cops outside to guard.

They stepped into a utility area, with stainless-steel counters, sinks, and refrigerators. Larrabee was immediately aware of the crisp smell he associated with medical facilities. It was silent except for the faint humming of physical plant machinery.

Franchi led, his pistol also drawn. He opened a door into a hallway, with four more opposing doors opening off of it. All but one were open. They were procedure rooms, fitted with operating tables and equipment, empty of people.

Franchi stepped quietly past the closed door and pressed himself against the wall. The young detective threw the door open, jumping back and leveling his gun.

Nothing moved inside the room, but there was something on the table.

Larrabee's gut understood before his mind did that it was not just something, but someone.

Franchi turned his head and yelled back down the hallway to the cops waiting outside, *"One dead!"*

The body was female, with coppery skin and long, jet black hair spilling from her head off the table's end. Her face had been largely peeled away, leaving rough, dark red crusted patches of raw tissue. The table and the floor underneath were slick with blood. There was a thick smell, not decay yet, but its precursor.

Franchi crossed himself, muttering in Italian. The young detective let his gun hand fall, his other forearm rising to cover his mouth. Larrabee had to fight the urge to hyperventilate. He had seen his share of bodies, but never one like this.

"Don't nobody touch nothing," Franchi said roughly. "Is this Gwen?"

Larrabee shook his head. "I saw her photos on the Net. She's pure white-bread. But—that hair. Coffee Trenette has hair like that. Monks said she was at the party last night."

Franchi took two steps into the room, his gaze moving swiftly. It was chaotic, with objects looking like they had been thrown down in haste. Surgical instruments lay in a jumble on a tray. A wastebasket was stuffed with bloody towels. The fingers of a latex glove showed among them.

Then he pointed at something with his pistol, a little flash of gold beside the sink, almost covered by another towel. He moved closer and lifted the towel away with the gun's barrel. The gold was the flex band of a wristwatch, a man's Rolex with a face of striking deep blue.

"You'd remember a watch like that," he said. "Call Dr. Monks. Ask him if he noticed D'Anton wearing it. We'll keep looking."

Larrabee made the call on his cell phone, while the detectives moved along the hall toward the front area of the clinic. Monks picked up immediately.

"Did you get a look at D'Anton's wristwatch?" Larrabee asked.

"A blue Rolex. You could see it from across the room."

"We just found it. There's a dead woman on an operating table. I think it's Coffee Trenette."

Monks closed his eyes. "Bad?"

"Yeah. It looks like he started cutting on her, and went crazy."

Monks remembered what Roberta Massey had said, about the gloved hands in front of her face.

"D'Anton has big hands," he said. "If there are gloves, they'll be at least a size eight."

"I can see one, in the wastebasket. I better not touch it. Wait a minute, there's a packet of them over

here." Larrabee stepped cautiously to a paper enve-
lope containing surgical gloves, lying on the counter
close to the watch.

"Eight and a half," Larrabee said. "Okay, I'll
keep you posted."

He clicked off the phone and was starting down
the hall to follow the detectives when he heard
Guido Franchi's bellow:

"Two dead."

The second body, also a woman's, lay facedown
on the reception room floor, just inside the front
door. Larrabee's immediate impression was that she
had been running for it, and was caught from behind.
There was no butchery here. The right side of her
throat had been slashed with surgical neatness.

Except for that, she was still beautiful. Franchi
and the two other detectives were standing over her,
looking almost reverent.

Larrabee nodded curtly to Franchi. "This is
Gwen Bricknell," he said.

Outside in the parking lot, Franchi got on the phone
and called more backup—a SWAT team to sweep
the building for anyone who might be hiding, a CSI
unit, uniforms to cordon off the area. Larrabee
could hear the distant sirens, already starting.

Then Franchi walked over to him and said,
"D'Anton's probably trying to get out of the country
right now. Call Dr. Monks again. Tell him what happened. Then let me talk to him."

When Monks answered, Larrabee said, "We found Gwen, Carroll. She's dead, too. It looks like she surprised D'Anton while he was working on Coffee. She tried to get away, but he caught her."

Monks did not say anything. Larrabee handed Franchi the phone.

"I'd like for you to go up and talk to D'Anton's wife," Franchi said to Monks. "Before a bunch of ham-fisted sheriffs come stomping in, and she calls F. Lee Bailey. Don't tell her anything about this, just say you came by to pick up your stuff. See if you can get an idea where D'Anton might be headed, another ID he might use, anything like that."

Monks said, "I'll try. She doesn't like me much."

"She likes you better than she'll like us."

The police units were starting to arrive, squad cars parking to surround the building, and a van spilling out husky young SWAT team members carrying assault rifles. A KPIX television news van came in right behind them.

"You people stay the fuck out of the crime scene," Franchi yelled at the van. He shoved the phone back at Larrabee and strode toward it.

Larrabee faded to the outskirts of the area, staying out of the way. The SWAT team started moving into the clinic, agile crouching men slipping inside like ballet dancers. Snipers were braced across squad car roofs, rifles trained on the exits. Flashing lights and the crackling of radio static filled the air like smoke.

It was a hell of an exciting show. Except that there were two dead women at the center of it.

An hour later, the SWAT team had cleared the building and it was crawling with technicians. Police higher-ups were starting to arrive, and it was rumored that the city's medical examiner himself was on his way. The newspeople were all over it, too. Franchi had long since lost his battle to keep them out.

He and Larrabee were standing together in the parking lot, when he got a call from the office that was running the NCIC checks.

"One of the names just came up," the cop in the office said. "Todd Peploe. Looks like he's the maintenance man at D'Anton's clinic."

"What's the pop?"

"He was working at a hospital down in San Diego, back in the early nineties. Apparently, he was impersonating a doctor, molesting women. He got seven years and did two."

"Find out where he lives and get after his ass, right *now*," Franchi said. He turned to Larrabee, looking very unhappy. "We might be after the wrong guy. The maintenance man's got a record of playing doctor. Christ, could he be that smart, to plant that watch and gloves?"

"Just because they're crazy, it doesn't mean they're stupid," Larrabee said. "I'd better call Carroll and let him know."

Monks did not answer his cell phone. Larrabee's watch said 8:22 A.M. Monks was probably with Julia D'Anton by now.

When Monks's voice mail came on, Larrabee said, "Carroll, it's Stover. Give me a call ASAP." He left it at that, in case Julia might overhear.

Whoever the killer was, he was most likely traveling away from this area as fast as he could. There was no reason for him to go to the house where the party had been.

But Larrabee was seriously annoyed at himself for assuming too quickly that D'Anton had to be the murderer. And a little queasy about the new level of unpredictability.

"All these years we've been doing this, and we act like a couple of fucking amateurs," Franchi said morosely.

"I was just thinking the same thing," Larrabee said.

32

Monks drove somberly along the last stretch of narrow deserted road to the D'Antons' house. He was starting to realize how much he had wanted to find out that all his suspicions about Gwen Bricknell were empty—that this nightmare would end, and maybe, just maybe, the good parts of what he had felt with her would touch him again.

He passed the eucalyptus grove where he had spent the night, and saw the Bronco's tire tracks across the field, outlined in the morning dew.

That part, at least, had been real.

He stopped at the rise that overlooked the property, as he had last night. The vista was the same— the picturesque Victorian house in its secluded valley, surrounded by wooded ravines and ridges that led down to the pale blue Pacific—but now it was quiet, with only one vehicle parked there, Julia D'Anton's white SUV. Monks had called from Larrabee's office to tell her he was coming; she had not answered, and he had left a message on the machine. But it looked like she was still here.

He reached under the seat and unlocked the metal box that held the Beretta. There was still an outside possibility that Julia D'Anton was dangerous, and he had promised himself that he would never again walk into a situation like that alone and unarmed. He made sure that the clip was full, jacked a round into the chamber, and slipped the pistol into his back pocket. Then he drove on down the hill.

As he was parking, the door of the sculpture studio opened and Julia leaned out. Monks recognized her long red-brown hair. She waved to him, beckoning him to come in, then disappeared back inside. A friendly enough reception, he thought, as he crossed the gravel drive. Apparently she'd gotten his phone message and was expecting him. Maybe she'd be willing to talk.

The studio's door was slightly ajar. Now he could hear the sound of a small engine coming from inside, a steady, low rumble like an idling motorcycle. He knocked and peered in.

"Julia?" he called.

He pushed the door open and stepped into the high-ceilinged room. It was just as he had seen it last night, with Gwen, except filled now by the ambient sunlight filtering through the old windows. The rumbling sound was coming from a small air compressor in a corner of the room, its coiled hose lying beside it on the floor. He had never thought of a compressor being used for sculpture; he supposed that she used it to operate an air hammer or blow away dust as she worked.

Monks raised his voice over the engine's noise. "*Julia.* Listen, I need—"

The compressor shut off abruptly, startling him with the sudden stillness. A few seconds later, he let out his breath, realizing that he had frozen along with it. The assemblage of unfinished sculptures—some bare, others draped with tarps—seemed eerily caught in mid-pose, and brought a sharp twinge of the fear he had felt last night. The phrase *still as a statue* flitted through his mind.

"Is anybody here?" he said. Now his voice was too loud. There was no answer, no movement or sound.

He stepped farther into the room. A door at the far end was also slightly open. Perhaps she had gone into the main house, expecting him to follow. He started toward it.

Then he saw a light, a bright cone from a lamp, illuminating a workbench littered with tools and chips of stone. It was partly blocked from his vision by the canvas-draped statue of Eden Hale. He took another two steps, and Julia's figure came into view.

She was sitting with her back to him. Her hands were at rest on the workbench. She was upright, stiff, and Monks's apprehension came back. She might have waved him in a moment ago, but his strong sense now was that she had taken up a hostile posture, and she was not going to cooperate after all—had called him in only to vent anger on him.

"Julia, I need help finding your husband." Monks tried to keep the tension out of his voice, to sound nonthreatening, even placating. It was not easy. "You *have* to talk to me."

She did not move. Monks exhaled impatiently and stepped to her, his hand rising to touch her shoulder. He imagined suddenly that there was a sweetish smell in the air.

That was when he saw the blood seeping down the side of her face and neck.

Monks registered instantaneous bits of visual information in an insane, impossible collage. Her left eye, the one he could see, was half-closed, filled with congealing blood. Her chin was propped on a stone block. The bleeding was profuse and seemed to be coming from under her disarrayed hair.

His hand went to the hair instead of to her shoulder. He gripped it and tugged. It came away in his hand. He reared back, shaking the bloody scalp from his grip. Her body seemed to lean slightly, sliding away as though avoiding his grasp, but then she kept sliding, unchecked, until she crumbled to the floor.

There was a sudden rustling behind him. He started to turn, and caught a glimpse of something like a giant gray bat unfolding its wings and lunging forward. A rough, blinding weight closed over his face and body. He lurched, batting at it with his arms, realizing that it was a canvas tarp, draped over him like a tent. He stumbled around, tripping on it, trying to shake it off. But it seemed to have no end. He managed to grab a handful of canvas and started pulling it off himself, hand over hand.

A searing slash of pain ripped across the back of his right wrist.

Monks screamed. He let go of the canvas as if it were red-hot and clasped his hand close to his body. He could feel blood welling from the cut, wetting his shirt.

Another slash ripped down his back. Then another.

He took two running steps before his feet caught up in the canvas and he fell, crashing onto the floor. His fingers pulled at the pistol in his pocket, but they were slippery with blood. He managed to get the gun free, lost it in the bloody slick, found it again.

The pain ripped through him again, this time down the left side of his head. Monks lashed out with his legs, swinging them, clinging to the gun with both hands.

He felt his feet connect with something solid but yielding. Flesh.

He pointed the gun at it and pulled the trigger

four times, starting low and moving up, crisscross-
ing from side to side.

He heard a cry, a roaring sound of rage and pain.

One of the slashes had slit the canvas near his
face. He thrust his left hand into it and forced the
blood-soaked edges apart, peering through. His panicked gaze took in a man's upper body lunging forward, a patch of blood above the abdomen—

A large scalpel in the surgically gloved hand,
slashing down at him.

The charging weight closed his canvas window.
Monks shot point-blank, again and again, all the five
rounds that were left in the clip. He felt the body
slam down on top of him, and he cried out as the
scalpel sliced down across his hip. He tried to roll,
but he was hopelessly entangled in the canvas, with
the weight pinning him down.

He closed his eyes and waited for the next stabs
or slashes that would open him and bathe him in his
own blood, wrapped in his canvas shroud.

Then he realized that the visceral groan he was
hearing was not his own. The weight on top of him
shifted slightly, in a sort of writhing. Nothing was
cutting at him anymore.

Monks started working his way free. He was losing blood—could feel the wetness down the side of
his face and neck, seeping from his back, and below
his waist into his pants. He was already weak and
getting weaker fast. The canvas had him wrapped
tight as a cocoon, with no end or opening. It was like

fighting some giant soft thing that patiently absorbed his struggles, flexing but never giving ground.

Finally, his groping hands found an edge. He wormed his head and shoulders under it, forearms pushing the weight away, feet scrabbling wearily on the floor as if he were climbing a hill of loose sand.

When he got his head free, he could see that the attacker was lying on his side facing Monks, motionless, curled into himself. There were more expanding patches of blood on his shirt. His face was contorted with pain and rage, but Monks recognized him instantly:

Todd Peploe, the clinic's maintenance man.

His hair and forehead were smeared with blood, too, but that, Monks knew already, was not Todd's. It had come from Julia D'Anton, when Todd had worn her bloody scalp like a wig, to lure Monks in.

33

The following Monday morning at seven, Mercy Hospital Emergency Room's monthly Quality Assurance committee meeting was starting. The conference room was unusually crowded. In fact, it was packed. All the thirty-some seats were taken, and there were more people in the hall. The air was filled with a low buzz of talk.

Monks had gotten there early and found a chair near the back. He was moving very carefully and stiffly because of his wounds. None of the scalpel slashes had been deep, thanks, in part, to the canvas tarp that had enwrapped him. But they had required a total of 173 stitches. He felt like Frankenstein's monster, his torso a tight sack stuffed full of flesh that the wrong twitch could pop open, ripping a seam like a zipper. The cuts hurt like hell, too, and he was almost salivating with anticipation of an afternoon feast of Percocet and vodka.

But not yet. He was staying clearheaded for this meeting. This was where judgment of his treatment of Eden Hale was going to be rendered by his peers.

He did not know which way it was going to go.

Most of the faces were familiar. Vernon Dickhaut was sitting beside him, and all the other ER docs who were not on duty were also present, along with Jackie Lukas and Mary Helfert, the nurses who had worked with him on Eden. Roman Kasmarek, the pathologist, was sitting on his other side. Baird Necker, the chief administrator, and Paul Winner, the internist who had criticized him, were there, too, along with several nurses and physicians from other departments. Apparently, the word had spread. This case was not just interesting—it was now tinged with notoriety.

Dick Speidel, the committee chairman, stood up at the head of the long conference table. He was a commanding figure, big and bearlike. The room got quiet.

"I'm sure I don't have to remind anybody that these procedings are protected from discovery," Speidel said. "I've approved some non-ER personnel who have asked to sit in. But what happens here, stays here.

"We're going to start right off with Dr. Monks's

case, because I don't think we have three times the usual number of people just for the coffee and doughnuts." A sprinkling of laughter arose. Monks did not join in. "Committee members have had a chance to look over the material, including my own review. I'll recap it.

"In brief, it's been established beyond doubt that the patient, Eden Hale, died of florid DIC. We're quite sure now that it was caused by ricin—a poison that was deliberately administered to her—but there was no hint of that at the time.

"Dr. Monks's diagnosis was correct, and, by my lights, very astute. He also acted correctly in addressing the DIC with utmost urgency. It was far and away the most serious presenting problem.

"The pathway he chose is a thornier issue. Blood products are the major treatment for DIC. But heparin's clinical boundaries aren't established. There's no definite evidence it would have helped with someone that far gone. It *might* have helped, and in the circumstances it certainly wasn't unreasonable. He was fully aware that it was a desperate measure, and it probably wouldn't succeed—but it was either that or stand there and watch her die.

"However, there's a case to be made that administering the heparin was an unnecessary procedure, and even inappropriate."

Speidel paused, with a certain amount of dramatic flair, like a jury foreman about to take the poll.

"My own opinion is that the outcome was predictable—the patient was beyond saving when she came in—and that Dr. Monks acted well within the reasonable standard of care," he said. "I'll open this up by asking the other ER physicians if they agree. Gentlemen and ladies, this is not a feel-good encounter session. If you think Dr. Monks performed unacceptably, let him have it."

Monks waited, his sore gut tensed like a prize-fighter's, waiting for a punch.

There was a nervous rustling, people rearranging themselves in their seats, recrossing legs, shuffling through their notes.

No one spoke.

"Birds of a feather, sticking together, huh?" Paul Winner said sarcastically.

"And now," Speidel said, without looking at him, "I'll invite comment from other departments."

Winner stood up, too. "Dr. Monks, I know you just went through a traumatic experience. But this happened *before* that, and we can't just let it slide out of sympathy for you, or because the ER wants to protect its own. Matters like this reflect on the over-all reputation of this hospital, and everybody associated with it. I'm sure a lot of people in this room feel the same way."

He surveyed the crowd with stern eyes, waiting for support. Mary Helfert, the nurse who had questioned Monks's use of the blood thinner, raised a tentative hand, and a few of the non-ER physicians nodded uncertainly. But still, no one spoke.

Speidel gave the silence plenty of time before he said, "What's your specific objection, Dr. Winner?"

"My specific objection is pumping a potent drug into somebody when you aren't sure of the consequences. You can't go treating patients like guinea pigs!"

"How would you have handled it?"

"I'm not an ER physician, but—"

"But you feel free to correct those of us who are?" Speidel interrupted.

Winner slammed his hand down on the table. "He's not the kind of doctor we need at this hospital—him and all the muck he finds to roll around in." His forefinger stabbed the air toward Monks. "I don't want you seeing my patients anymore."

"Done," Monks said.

"I'm taking this up with the chief of staff," Winner said. He left the room, pushing his way roughly through the crowded chairs.

"You want to take my next shift for me, Paul?" Vernon Dickhaut called after him. "I'd like to see you take on the Saturday Night Knife and Gun Club."

There was laughter again, longer and louder.

This time, Monks smiled, too.

Baird Necker was waiting for Monks outside in the hall.

"All right, I should have backed you up," Baird said. "I feel like shit. That's my apology. I don't expect you to accept it."

"I think Paul Winner's right, Baird. I'm not the kind of doc you need around here."

"Fuck him. He's adequate, and he'll be retiring soon. Those are the two best things I can say about him." He clapped Monks on the shoulder and started walking toward the elevator. "Except for all the publicity you can't seem to help attracting, we've come out of it fine. Come on upstairs, I need a smoke."

"I don't think you heard me," Monks said, not moving. "I'm tendering my resignation. I haven't had time to write the letter yet, but I'll get to it in the next couple of days."

Baird stopped and looked at Monks, puzzled, still not seeming to grasp it. Then he scowled.

"You got a better offer someplace else?" he said suspiciously. "If that's it, we could deal."

"No."

"Why, then? You're pissed at me?"

"I am. But don't flatter yourself. That wouldn't run me off."

"Because you killed somebody who needed killing?"

Monks's head snapped back, as if the words were a punch.

"Spoken like a marine," he said. "*Semper fi,* and all that."

Baird's gaze stayed level. "Okay, it was crude. But I know you better than you think, Carroll. You could take something like that to heart. Decide you're not worthy anymore."

Baird was shrewd. There was some truth to it. But only some.

"I feel like I'm in some kind of spiral that's getting out of control," Monks said. "It happened to me once before, and it almost took me down. I need to back away, take some time off. That's the best reason I can give."

Baird rubbed his bulldog jaw. "What are you going to do?"

"I'll still investigate for ASCLEP. There's plenty of locum tenens work around."

Baird pulled one of the foot-long Tabacaleros out of his inside suit jacket pocket and tore at the wrapper, stripping it off impatiently.

"I'll miss having you around, Carroll. These have been some great times," he said. "Never knowing when I might find a body gutted on a gurney. The psychos lurking in the furnace room, the labs getting smashed up, the TV crews shoving microphones in my face. The sleepless nights trying to figure out how the fuck to keep the board of directors from hemorrhaging, and the board of accreditation from dumping us. Hey, hospital administrators are a dime a dozen, but those were the things that made my job special."

"Jesus, Baird. You're making me go all gooey inside."

"You'll be back," Baird said. "It's in your blood." He did an about-face with marine drill precision and stomped down the hall, on his way to the rooftop and a nicotine fix.

Monks walked the other direction, toward the ER, feeling like he had been carrying a sack of huge rocks on his back for so long he had forgotten about it, and now he had dropped a couple of the biggest ones.

There were no witnesses to the complex series of events, and none was likely to appear. But it seemed clear that Monks had suspected all the wrong people. Initial speculation went that Todd Peploe, the clinic's maintenance man, was the one who had butchered Coffee Trenette and had killed Gwen Bricknell—being careful to make it look like D'Anton's work. He had killed D'Anton, too. The surgeon's body, overdosed with Demerol and carefully enclosed in garbage bags, had been found in the trunk of his own Jaguar.

The police had found jewelry in Todd's apartment that pointed to other victims. There was also a crudely written journal, which indicated that the bodies had been left in a cave on D'Anton's property. Search dogs found them. Apparently, Todd was on his way to hide D'Anton's corpse there, too, trying to make it appear that D'Anton had gone on a final murderous rampage, then fled.

But Todd had learned from Julia D'Anton that

Monks was coming. He had killed her, still using the scalpel with D'Anton's fingerprints, then taken her hair as a disguise, and set the trap for Monks.

Further checking showed that Todd had started impersonating a physician while working at a San Diego hospital. He had approached an unknown number of women and given them pelvic exams. This might have gone on indefinitely—hospitals were reluctant to deal with that sort of thing, even when they knew about it—but then his penchant for sharp instruments had come to the fore. Sedated patients started turning up with mysterious incisions. None was seriously injured—Monks guessed that Todd was practicing, working himself up for what was to come—but it had landed him in prison. Then, like many other parolees, he had disappeared from the system's radar and walked into another job at another hospital.

A faked California medical license, a supply of pharmaceutical drugs, and a hoard of surgical implements and supplies, also found in his apartment, made it clear that he had escalated his doctor persona. And in his garage, there was a Jaguar XJS the same color as D'Anton's—several years older, but almost identical. It was unclear whether this was another way of imitating D'Anton, or Todd had used it somehow for disguise.

A huge amount of work lay ahead for authorities—forensically, to probe the physical evidence, and psychologically, to delve into the psyche of

Todd Peploe. His journal included a jumble of beliefs that he was a superior being, above any law, using medical skills to satisfy the hidden cravings of women.

But Monks had already formed his opinion. Anyone capable of doing what Todd had done was a vicious, sadistic son of a bitch whose true reason for killing was pleasure.

That made the memory of pumping five bullets into him a little easier.

Martine Rostanov had not attended the QA meeting because she was not on Mercy Hospital's staff, but she was waiting for him in the ER lobby. Monks recalled that that was the first place he had ever seen her, walking through the door with the slight limp that instantly had awakened a protective urge in him. He had the eerie sense that their relationship was unraveling literally, a step at a time, like a videotape played backward.

"I already heard the buzz," she said. "Congratulations." She was smiling, summery-looking in a long flowered dress, but her face was dark around the eyes.

"It's a relief," Monks admitted.

"How's your body holding up?"

"I won't be playing rugby for a while."

"I feel like I should be nursing you, in your hour of need."

"I don't think either of us wants that," Monks

said. He was surprised by the bluntness in his own voice, and he saw that she was, too. Then hurt. She lowered her eyes.

"It's terrible, what you've been through," she said. "I know I haven't helped."

"Of course you have."

"Are you all right with what you had to do? Never mind. Dumb question."

Neither of them spoke for another moment. Monks thought about asking her if she was getting involved with someone else, perhaps the owner of the black Saab he had seen in her driveway— thought about confessing his own infidelity, if that was what it had been. Thought about suggesting another try. They had talked a lot about an autumn in Donegal.

But the words were just not in him. The issues that had seemed important between them a few days ago had been swept from his consciousness. He was distant from the rest of the world right now, and she was part of that world.

"I'd better go," he said. "Thanks for coming by."

"Don't lose my phone number, okay?"

He walked her out into the parking lot. They kissed quickly, like friends. She waved from her car as she pulled away—maybe sadly, maybe not.

And that was that.

34

The O'Malley Bros. Mortuary on west Geary was respected as one of the city's finest—a century-old, family-owned establishment that had graciously retired the mortal remains of a host of the rich and famous, from governors to rock stars. Monks guessed that he had sent them clients, from the ER, himself.

It was still before nine A.M.—early for the funeral business—but the imposing old wooden door, at least seven feet tall and arched like a church's, was unlocked. Monks stepped into the foyer. Its dark-paneled walls had several dimly lit niches, also arched, each discreetly displaying pertinent information about one of the deceased who was passing through—name, side chapel where the body could be viewed, time of the service, final resting place. It was as still a room as Monks had ever been inside. He had to resist the urge to tiptoe across the tiled floor.

He went from niche to niche until he found the name Gwendolyn Anne Bricknell. She was in the Dove Chapel. A plan showed its location.

Monks was on his way there when a man wearing formal black tails stepped into the room. He clasped his hands behind his back and leaned forward in a partial bow.

"Can I help you, sir?" he said, in the hollow whisper of one who has learned to speak the language of mourning. He was thin, in his mid-thirties, but looked older from pallor and balding.

"I'd like to see Miss Bricknell."

"Certainly. If you'll come this way." His smooth black shiny shoes made only a whisper on the tiles. Monks felt like a mule, clopping along beside him. They crossed the mortuary's main room, as large as the naves of most churches and similar, with pews and a raised dais in front—although it was equipped with a steel track to slide coffins in and out of view. This was a full-service organization.

"Are you family, might I inquire?" the attendant asked.

"Just an acquaintance."

"The service is scheduled for four P.M."

"I'm afraid I won't be able to make that," Monks said.

"Of course." The attendant's voice dropped confidentially. "It's going to be quite an event."

"Really?"

"Oh, yes. We're expecting a capacity crowd, and a *lot* of celebrities. She was quite famous, in her day. But I'm sure you know that."

"So I've gathered."

"Terrible tragedy, isn't it?" He gave Monks a sidelong glance that showed only one wide-open eye, a look reminiscent of a flounder's. "Whoever would have thought it?"

"Very sad," Monks agreed.

"I mean, can you imagine?" the attendant went on, warming to his subject. "A monster, posing as a surgeon? Suppose he'd had *you* under the knife. How would you feel?"

Monks resisted the urge to say, *He did.*

"I'll leave you to pay your respects, sir," the attendant murmured. He stepped aside and gestured Monks into the Dove Chapel, opening off the main room. It was a tasteful space, lush with flowers and candles. The coffin was on a bier at the far end, burnished wood that looked like mahogany, chased with brass or perhaps gold. The upper half of the lid was open.

Her still form brought to Monks's mind an image from childhood, a somber Doré engraving of the

Lady of Astolat—spurned by her lover, Lancelot, floating pale and lovely down a stream, holding a lily to her breast—finally at peace from her torments. Except that Gwen was dressed in black.

And with frightening irony, a black silk scarf had been arranged carefully around her neck, to conceal her wounded throat. It brought back with force the eerie intimacy that he had shared with her.

That Gwen had murdered Eden Hale was almost certain. Among her cache of health care and beauty products, several ounces of castor beans had been found, along with instructions on how to compound them into ricin—a poison that was deadly and would not show up on an ordinary tox screen. Making ricin was not difficult, and her work at the clinic had exposed her to chemical procedures.

The black scarf she had worn that night had been found, too—in her trash, still damp, hacked to pieces.

As with the other events, it was mostly speculation from there. Monks guessed that Gwen had arranged the tryst between Eden's boyfriend and Coffee Trenette, so that Eden would be alone, and then had called Eden and arranged to stop by, on the pretext of bringing comfort. She probably had disguised the ricin in something like chicken soup, which she had deliberately let go bad, so that salmonella would cloak the poison's effects. She probably had also taken Eden's answering machine, although that had not been found.

The whys of it were murkier. Jealousy figured in, no doubt—the fear that Eden would replace her as the queen of D'Anton's world. Then there was her fierce insistence on seeming young. It suggested that in a way, she had been like Eden—convinced, with childish naïveté, that youth and appearance were everything. And he suspected that with her brittle temperament, drug use, and real or imagined pressures, she had gone a little insane.

Monks felt no anger toward her—mostly sadness and pity. Even her attempt to kill him had been self-preservation. There was a dark irony, too, in that her poisoning Eden was what had exposed Todd Peploe. Otherwise, he would certainly have gone on killing.

But there was more, Monks admitted. Those few minutes with her in the night had brought love and death together with an intensity beyond anything he had ever experienced. He was not a believer in the supernatural, but if ever he had been touched by magic, it was then.

Had making love to him been a gift from her, to sweeten his passage? Or an attempt to control him, in some otherworldly way, cut short by her death?

How *had* she known about that scarf?

Monks walked back out of the Dove chapel, footsteps echoing through the halls of the dead, to the world of light and movement. He was eager to embrace the relief he had felt, leaving the hospital.

But he knew that there would be a price, too. He was not a good sleeper. He still woke up sometimes in a childlike panic, croaking hoarsely, after long, helpless seconds of trying to shout at something that menaced him.

He knew that his dreams featured images that came from his actual experiences. The images were distorted, and the dreams themselves were wild collages that melted from one insane scenario to the next—like most people's, he supposed—but when he remembered flashes, he would realize that many specific details stemmed from things he had recently seen or done.

These past days were going to mix themselves into the brew, and on those nights when he came thrashing fearfully into wakefulness, he would be alone.

No need to wait
To get your next injection of suspense
From Neil McMahon . . .

Coming January 2005,

REVOLUTION No. 9

Neil McMahon's next Carroll Monks thriller
Is available NOW IN HARDCOVER for $15.95!

The man who called himself Freeboot crouched in the darkness outside the main security station at Sapphire Mountain Estates, a gated community forty miles north of Atlanta, Georgia. It was 2:11 A.M. He had been hiding for almost twelve hours—coming in in the back of a delivery truck, then after dark, when the groundskeepers and golfers chasing stray balls were gone, sneaking through the shrubbery to here.

Getting into and around a place like this was not hard. Getting back out again was a different thing.

The sky was blue-black and starry, on the chilly side. His mission partner, Taxman, had warned him about the November cold, even in the deep South.

Taxman had done a lot of training in the Georgia woods, during jump school at Fort Benning. *Travel light, freeze at night,* went the riff. But Freeboot hardly felt the cold. In the California mountain hideaway where he spent most of his time, he went barefoot except when it got so bad that frostbite might slow him down. Tonight, he only wore boots to keep from leaving footprints.

At 2:17 A.M., the Estates' security patrol car returned from a routine cruise through the streets. The car, like the rest of security here, was not a Mickey Mouse setup. Freeboot could see the barrel of an assault shotgun protruding above the dashboard.

The driver, a uniformed guard armed with a large caliber semi-automatic pistol, parked under the sodium lights and walked to the station, a concrete building that looked like an above-ground bunker. Like the barrier fence, and anything else that might remind Sapphire Mountain Estate residents that there was a hostile world out there, it was placed out of view of the luxury houses.

The guard was young, Hispanic-looking, and buffed, with a tight-fitting tailored uniform. He seemed alert if not wary, on the cocky side. Like a pimp, Freeboot thought. No—more like a whore, peddling his ass to the kind of people who lived in places like this.

Necks, Freeboot called them. They owned it all now, but the heads were going to start rolling big-time.

When the guard got to the building's heavy steel door, he passed his magnetic badge through a scanner, then pressed his palm against a glass plate. A few seconds later, the door's electronic bolt opened with a solid *thunk*.

He stepped inside. The door closed behind him.

Getting into that building, for Freeboot, was Phase One of this operation.

Security guards were usually untrained and sloppy—even easy to bribe. But these guards were a cut above. The residents of Sapphire Mountain Estates paid for the best, and they got it. A low-end house here cost two-point-five million dollars. The compound was surrounded by an inertia sensor fence that would literally pick up a mouse crawling through. The only entry point was manned by another armed guard and backed up by a video camera that scanned each incoming vehicle's make and license plate, not allowing it to pass unless it compared by computer to an authorized list. A third guard kept watch inside the main station, where individual perimeter and trap alarms from every house were wired in on dedicated phone lines. The system was as secure as anything outside of top secret military installations. There had never been a whisper of trouble here.

In just five minutes, that was going to change.

Freeboot checked his watch, then pressed the beeper on his two-way belt radio—once, for alert, then five times slowly. Immediately, it beeped in return—the signal that Taxman was in place, just outside the barrier fence.

Freeboot flexed his surgically gloved hands to limber his fingers, and screwed a stainless steel sound suppressor onto the barrel of his HK MP5/10 submachine gun. It was set to fire a 30-round clip of 10 mm ammunition on full auto. It was also equipped with a high-intensity Tac light, to illuminate and temporarily blind anyone who got in the way. Along with the gas mask and PVS-14 night vision goggles in his pack, the Tac light would come into action during Phase Two.

With three minutes left to go, Freeboot reached into a pocket of his black fatigues and took out a can of Copenhagen. Instead of chew, it was filled with finely ground white powder. He dipped in the tip of his survival knife and raised a good-sized mound to each nostril, inhaling sharply. The harsh wild rush of methamphetamine burned up behind his eyes and swelled through his brain. The stars took on a crystalline glitter, and the chilly breeze cut into his flesh with a delicious edge.

He was ready. He pulled his ski mask down over his face, slipped the HK's sling over his shoulder, and eased his wiry body into final position—in the building's shadows, five meters from the door. A backlit man stepping through would be a perfect target, standing in what was known as a vertical coffin.

Two minutes and 24 seconds later, his radio beeped twice, fast. He picked up the baseball-sized

rock at his feet and sidearmed it into the security
fence. It hit with a whispering rattle, the same kind
of disturbance as a raccoon or deer brushing against
it, and that was what the guards would think it was.
But they were required to go out and check.

A minute passed, then another. The guards were
in no hurry about this kind of thing. False alarms
caused by animals happened all the time.

He flexed his fingers again, waiting.

There: the thunk of the iron bolt. The guard
appeared a second later, saying something laugh-
ingly over his shoulder to his partner inside the
room. Freeboot kept waiting, so that he would block
the door open as he fell.

When the guard turned and took another step forward, Freeboot opened fire, starting at the knees and
sweeping up, left hand flat over the HK's muzzle to
keep it from jumping. The staccato silenced rounds
were hardly louder than a kid would make sputter-
ing through its lips. The guard slammed back
against the door and slid to the ground, his dead
eyes still open.

Freeboot sprinted past him into the building. The
other guard swiveled in his office chair, startled. His
eyes just had time to register shock and terror before
a second burst from the HK tore into his chest. He
let out a long sobbing groan and slumped into a
shuddering huddle.

Freeboot gripped the back of his chair and
heaved it forward, dumping him onto the floor. This

man was older, heavy-set, with a clipped brindle mustache. He wore a wedding ring on a thick finger. Freeboot flipped the HK's selector switch to single shot and fired an insurance round into his ear canal, angling it slightly upward. The powerful 10 mm slug exited through the opposite temple with a spray of blood. He stepped to the first guard and dragged him inside, pausing to pull off his cap and unsnap the keyring from his belt. There was no need to fire another round into this one.

For ten more seconds, Freeboot waited, regaining control over his breath, listening for beeps on his radio that might signal trouble. None came. Which meant that Taxman had now killed the guard at the Estates' entry station, and that the local police hadn't been alerted. If that had happened, the third member of their team, monitoring a police scanner in the getaway car, would have picked up the call and sent them a warning.

From here on, there was no need to try the risky task of disabling any alarm systems. No one was watching the watchers, and no one was left alive to respond to the alarms when they went off.

He beeped his belt radio three times—*all clear here, ready to move on.*

The answering three beeps came from Taxman. He was ready, too. Taxman was as good as they got. He collected what was owed.

Freeboot closed the door behind him and trotted to the patrol car, pulling the guard's cap onto his head. Driving deliberately, he headed for the entry station to pick up Taxman. It was 2:25 A.M. Phase One had gone down without a hitch.

The home of Mr. and Mrs. David C. Bodewell was a long, low, hacienda style house that took up most of an acre. An intruder could waste precious time trying to find his way around inside, but Freeboot and Taxman had memorized the layout. The blueprints had been easy to get.

The place bristled with silent perimeter and trap alarms, and there was one more major wrinkle in this operation—a live-in bodyguard with an attack-trained rottweiler. The dog was not much of a worry. The bodyguard would require more care. A quiet annunciator in his attached ground floor apartment would alert him as soon as an alarm was triggered. Like the other guards, he would first think that it was caused by an animal, but very quickly, he would know that this was a break-in. If he was loyal, he would move to protect his employers. Or he might hide, try to ambush the attackers, or get outside and go for help.

Taking on a personally guarded house added considerable risk. Which was precisely why they'd chosen it.

He swiveled to the gaunt figure of Taxman, crouched beside him on the street. Freeboot nodded. Taxman nodded back.

They sprinted toward the house.

Taxman circled it, placing four high powered quad-band cell Phonejammers at strategic corners. Freeboot ran straight to the rear, where the underground phone and power lines rose up through conduits into metal service boxes. These were locked with padlocks. He blasted the phone box lock with freon from a spray can, freezing it instantly and turning the metal as brittle as glass. It snapped with a blow from the HK's stock. He yanked the box open and ripped through the low-voltage phone line with his knife.

No one was going to be calling out now.

The power was next—another quickly snapped lock, the master breaker pushed to OFF, and the few dim lights that showed through the windows went out.

Freeboot ran on around the house's corner to the bodyguard's apartment. Taxman had already lined the door with det cord, stuffed tightly against the stops, then sprayed with sound-deadening foam insulation. Both men stepped to the sides and pulled on their gas masks and goggles. Taxman pressed the detonator.

The door blew into the house with a barely heard *whump*, and hung sagging from the top hinge.

Freeboot lobbed in a grenade of CS gas, throwing it as hard as he could. It exploded with a searing burst that should blind the bodyguard at least for a few seconds.

They went in one at a time, low and fast, leaping

to opposite sides. Nearby, a large dog was barking in deep, ferocious challenge. Freeboot scanned the room swiftly. Furniture and objects showed luminescent green through the goggles.

But there was no human figure.

Then he saw something move, a flicker of yellowish light just on the other side of the room's interior door. In the instant it took him to recognize it as a man's arm, extending toward him, a gunshot blast smashed into the wall behind his head.

He dropped prone to the floor. More shots crashed into the wall. Even blinded by the tear gas, the bodyguard was firing at where he guessed they were.

Freeboot fired a burst in return, but there was no time to tell if he had hit—now the dog was charging, a thick snarling shape that appeared in the goggles to be burning with a ghostly fire. Taxman met it with a swooshing spray of hydrocyanic acid. The dog yelped, a high-pitched sound that turned to a near scream as the acid burned its eyes and throat. It pitched forward, paws flailing at its face, sliding and thrashing on the hardwood floor.

The bodyguard was gone.

"You _fucker_," Freeboot hissed. The man was better than they had figured. Now he was loose in the house, and there was the risk that neighbors had heard his unsilenced gunshots.

Freeboot flipped up his goggles and clamped his hand on the HK's squeeze-activated Tac-light, flooding the far side of the room with an instant of blindingly brilliant light.

There was blood spattered on the wall where the bodyguard had crouched.

"I'll get him," Freeboot told Taxman in a harsh whisper. "You take care of business."

They shoved through the interior door and separated, with Taxman running to the master bedroom suite. Freeboot followed the blood trail, stalking cautiously, weapon ready. The red splashes were almost continuous. The bodyguard was badly hit, but a desperate man was all the more dangerous. He moved through a large laundry room, then into a shotgun hallway. The door at the end was closed. Blood was pooled on the floor in front of it.

Deep inside the house, he heard a muted *puh-puh, puh-puh, puh-puh*—Taxman firing businesslike two round bursts.

He had found Mr. and Mrs. Bodewell.

Freeboot charged down the hall, dropping to the ground at the last second like a baseball player sliding into home and driving both boots into the door below the knob. It burst open. He just had time to see the bodyguard's flaming yellow outline as more gunshots smashed into the wall above him.

Lying on his back, aiming between his own spread feet, Freeboot fired a long burst in return.

He heard a "*yeeehh*," a shriek of rage and pain that could have come from an animal.

As he scrabbled up to his feet, another shot burst

from the man's outline, now slumped on the floor.

The bullet slammed into Freeboot's armored gut like a brick, knocking him spinning back against the hallway wall. His hands flew loose from his weapon, but it was still on its sling, and the barrel swung around to slap him hard across the face.

He growled with fury and dropped to his elbows and knees, clawing for control of his gun. His finger found the trigger. This time, he took an extra second to sight at his target.

The bodyguard was holding his pistol in both hands. It was wavering, like it was too heavy to hold. He fired one more round past Freeboot's head, before Freeboot emptied the clip into him.

The pistol dropped from the bodyguard's jerking hands.

Freeboot stood slowly, shaking. He snapped a fresh clip into the HK, then stepped to the guard and delivered the insurance round to his head. His gut was aching from the bullet that had almost taken him out. He welcomed the pain, letting it fuel the anger that he turned now on himself. That had been a mistake, his mistake, and a bad one. It could have fucked up *everything*. From now on, he was going to take men like this more seriously.

He strode back to the door where they had come in, past the rottweiler lying on its side with tongue hanging out and forelimbs stretched, as if it was running in its death dream. Too bad about that. It was a good dog, dying while doing its job. It couldn't have known what kind of people it was protecting.

Taxman was waiting at the outside door, with a
long skinny duffel bag slung over his shoulder next
to his pack. Inside it were the trophies that were
going to put the cap on this mission:

A set of golf clubs.

It was 2:34 A.M. Phase Two had taken just over
three minutes. Now came the third and final phase—
getting out.

They loped around the house once more, collect-
ing the Phonejammers, then sped in the security car
to the hole that Taxman had cut in the barrier fence.
Several hundred yards outside it, two Yamaha Y2F
dirt bikes were hidden in the woods—quiet, light,
and fast. These would carry them three miles to a
road that did not lead directly to the Sapphire Mountain Estates entrance, where their getaway car was
waiting—a luxury Mercedes sedan driven by their
third partner, Shrinkwrap, dressed as a wealthy
middle-aged woman. If police did happen to be in
the area, they wouldn't dream that there was any
connection with the attack. Freeboot and Taxman
would ride in the trunk to a rented storage unit in
Atlanta. There they would switch vehicles and
clothes, and head separately for home—clean-cut,
respectable business people, invisible among millions of others like them. The stolen Mercedes
would be picked up and chopped for parts. Their
bikes, guns and gear would be safely hidden or

destroyed. The video cameras here would show only two men dressed in black from scalp to toe.

Freeboot kicked his bike to life, toed it up into first gear, and popped the clutch, spinning the rear wheel and raising the front one, surging forward in a long, fierce leap of triumph. They had brought it off, the toughest and wildest operation yet. Within hours, this would be headline news, with its implications plain:

The only way the necks were going to stay safe was to build maximum-security prisons.

And live in them.